P

THE CR

"This spotlessly clean, fun-filled read takes plenty of twists and turns on the way to the satisfying ending."
—*Publishers Weekly*

"Readers who appreciate bookseller sleuths such as Marianne Macdonald's Dido Hoare (*Death's Autograph*) or Joan Hess's Claire Malloy (*Strangled Prose*) will welcome this new cozy series. . . . The feisty Delaney is an appealing protagonist, and the secondary characters are charming as well."
—*Library Journal*

"Shelton kicks off a new series featuring a sleuth who'll delight book lovers."
—*Kirkus Reviews*

"Move over Claire Fraser; American bibliophile Delaney Nichols is about to take Scotland . . . by storm!"
—Ellery Adams

"A perfectly twisty-turny puzzler of a mystery . . . Full of wit and whimsy, with a clever plot and delightful characters, this mystery is a fantastic read!"
—Jenn McKinlay

"A foolproof plot, endearing characters, and prose that immediately transports readers to enchanting Edinburgh . . . and leaves them eager for a return trip."
—Lucy Arlington

"A great read for book lovers, mystery seekers, and anyone who enjoys a determined new heroine. Sure to be a winning series."
—Erika Chase

ALSO BY PAIGE SHELTON

OF
BOOKS
AND
BAGPIPES

Paige Shelton

St. Martin's Paperbacks

This is a work of fiction. All of the characters, organizations, and events portrayed in this novel are either products of the author's imagination or are used fictitiously.

OF BOOKS AND BAGPIPES

For information address St. Martin's Press, 175 Fifth Avenue, New York, NY 10010.

ISBN: 978-1-250-13650-3

Our books may be purchased in bulk for promotional, educational, or business use. Please contact your local bookseller or the Macmillan Corporate and Premium Sales Department at 1-800-221-7945, ext. 5442, or by e-mail at MacmillanSpecialMarkets@macmillan.com.

Printed in the United States of America

Minotaur hardcover edition / April 2017
St. Martin's Paperbacks edition / January 2018

St. Martin's Paperbacks are published by St. Martin's Press, 175 Fifth Avenue, New York, NY 10010.

10 9 8 7 6 5 4 3 2 1

For all the old teams.

Thank you for your stories.

ACKNOWLEDGMENTS

I didn't get to experience in person a few of the places I included in this book, but I did look up pictures. Apologies for my inaccuracies, and though the University of Edinburgh library probably doesn't have a bunch of sub-basements, that would be a pretty cool feature.

Thanks to:

Cathy Cole, Denis Barlow, and Lisa Shafer for not tiring of answering questions about Scotland. You all make me feel like I have my very own personal Google. Your patience is much appreciated.

The lovely folks with the Doune Castle who answered all my questions and gave me some wonderful details. It's a beautiful place. If at all possible, everyone should visit.

My agent, Jessica Faust, and my editor, Hannah Braaten, for their continued and tireless support, input, patience, and brilliance.

Charlie and Tyler, for making me laugh when I most need to but think I can't. I adore you both.

A special thanks to everyone who so willingly read and helped spread the word about this series when *The Cracked Spine* published. I am gobsmacked by your support.

Sláinte!

PROLOGUE

He took a drag on the cigarette as he watched the bookshop. The tip blazed and then sizzled as a drop of rain hit it. He glanced up at the dark clouds, grumbled a quiet complaint, and then dropped the cigarette into a puddle next to the curb.

He pulled his coat collar up tighter just as the redhead got off the bus. He'd heard her American accent, but he still didn't know exactly where she was from. The older woman would be no problem. Edwin MacAlister would be no problem either. But the young guy who looked like an artist and the redhead might both be problems.

He'd worked the angles well on one end, but this end might be troublesome; too many variables. He'd think it all through some more.

He smiled to himself as he silently acknowledged that any other time, any other place, he'd like to get to know the redhead. He watched her hurry out of the rain and into the bookshop. He liked redheads, always had.

He reached for the pack of cigarettes in his jacket but remembered the rain so he stuck his hands in his pockets instead.

A few minutes later, having seen all he needed to for

now, he turned away from the corner and headed up Candlemaker Row.

But then he remembered something. The pub. He stopped and turned around again. That's right. The redhead and the guy from the pub. Delaney's Wee Pub was closed right now, lights off, but it would open later. Yes, he might be able to do something there, something that might make this angle easier.

He'd check it out, he thought as he set off again, with a somewhat satisfied pep in his step.

ONE

"Wow!" I said as I stepped out of the cab and looked over its top toward the castle. "It's beautiful."

"Aye, 'tis," Elias said grudgingly. "We've our fair share of these sorts of places around 'ere, I s'pose."

"We aren't very far out of Edinburgh. I thought we'd have to go farther to see something like this," I said.

"No, not far at all."

"The Edinburgh Castle is stunning, but this one's different. This one is much more . . . primitive." I stepped around the cab and moved next to Elias.

"Aye," he said after a brief pause.

"What's wrong?"

"Just wondering where everyone is. This is usually a popular place for the tourists; I've driven one or two oot here myself. Not raining and not too cold right now either." He looked around the small parking lot, empty except for us and his cab. "More on the weekends, I s'pose." He lifted the cap from his head and then replaced it. His eyes scanned again, this time peering up at the castle and then into the surrounding trees.

I didn't think it was the lack of other visitors that bothered him. He was uncomfortable about the reason we were there. He and his wife, Aggie, had made their concerns perfectly clear. The empty parking lot and the lack of other visitors bothered him more today than they would have under different circumstances.

"Well, it's not as cold as it has been, but it's still pretty cold, and it's bound to rain sometime soon," I said too cheerily as I looked up at the dark, cloudy sky and the old castle.

Elias grumbled.

Elias and Aggie had been the perfect landlords as well as a kind and loving surrogate family, but sometimes they were a wee bit overprotective. They hadn't had children of their own. They'd never gone through the process of watching a child grow and become independent. As a result they sometimes forgot that I was an adult. In fact, I was close to thirty, but to them, I was "their Delaney, their lass from Kansas in America" who'd only come into their lives a few months earlier. Most of the time this was ideal; I welcomed their care and concern, and though I'd made the move across the world to prove to myself that I could be brave and bold, I'd had a few moments when the comfort from parents, even surrogate ones, had been appreciated.

But I still had a job to do. I'd known my boss, Edwin MacAlister, was mysterious and eccentric from the first moment I'd walked into his bookshop, The Cracked Spine, so this newly assigned task hadn't seemed too strange. But this morning when I told Elias and Aggie the bare bones of the assignment—that I was going to meet someone on the top of the Castle Doune, just outside of Edinburgh, to pick up a comic book for Edwin—they'd first been intrigued, then curious, then wide-eyed with worry. They'd already decided that Elias would take me in his cab long before I could ask him for the ride.

Edwin had asked me to meet someone at the castle who would bring with him an item that Edwin had purchased, or at least acquired in some sort of transaction. Edwin, seemingly on purpose, had avoided sharing more specific details about said transaction. However, I would know the person who was to hand over the item by their clothing. We would share some secret words to confirm that we'd been successful in finding each other, and the hand-off would follow. It was all very cloak-and-dagger but Edwin had assured me I would be completely safe. I suspected he thought the whole notion of clandestine meetings was something I enjoyed. He was correct. I liked the secretive nature of his world. I liked that he'd been slowly letting me in on his many secrets. I thought that this assignment was doled out in the manner that was "just his way." Elias and Aggie knew Edwin but not as well as I did, so though I was working very hard to look unconcerned for Elias's sake, I did feel a tiny tug of a smile because Edwin would be pleased with the dark clouds adding to the atmosphere.

My contact atop the roof would be wearing tights and a long tunic with a belt, similar to an outfit I remember wearing when I was in junior high school. He would be dressed as a famous Scottish historical figure who had lived and fought during the thirteenth century, a good three hundred years before kilts became a component of Scottish men's wardrobes. According to Edwin, back then men, particularly fighting men, wore whatever they had. They were poor, didn't even wear military garb as they fought for their independence or to defend their property. They were rarely without their longswords though, their wicked and heavy instruments of battle and bloodshed. Edwin made sure to tell me that my contact was not going to bring his sword.

My contact was an actor, a reenactor actually. He spent much of his time near a castle in Stirling, in a clearing next to a nearby William Wallace monument. He acted a role in a playacted battle that, when it was real back in the thirteenth century, had ultimately taken the Stirling Castle away from England and put it back into Scotland's possession. It had been a big win for the Scottish.

My contact wasn't the only William Wallace reenactor in Stirling, but I got the impression from Edwin that he took his role and his contribution to teaching Scottish history very seriously. I didn't quite understand the depth of what was truly behind Edwin's proud tone of voice, but I knew that the history of William Wallace was particularly meaningful to him and, evidently, the man I was to meet.

Edwin was a man of his country; the history of Scotland was infused into his consciousness and bloodstream.

When I'd once had a conversation with Elias and Aggie about William Wallace, they'd both puffed up a little, their faces becoming stern and serious, their reverence showing, though neither had become quite as emotional as Edwin had.

I moved closer to Elias and hooked his arm with mine as he scowled at the castle. I said, "It's okay. It's just a comic book. It's not worth as much as some of Edwin's treasures."

The comic book *was* a collectors' item, though it wasn't like the thin, flimsy comic books I knew from back home. This one was a much more solid book, an annual, a collection of two years' worth of *Oor Wullie* comics, a popular strip that has been a part of *The Sunday Post* in Scotland since 1937. A new annual had been published every other year except during World War II. The annual I was to gather was from 1948, the first one published after the war. It was, apparently, in mint condition and probably worth a few thousand dollars, which was not much when compared to some of Edwin's other acquisitions and collections.

"Aye, ye're probably correct," Elias said. "It's probably not worth as much as some things. I just dinnae understand why we had tae come oot here tae pick it up. It seems like someone is trying tae hide something. Why not just deliver it tae the bookshop, or mail it, special messenger even?"

"That wouldn't be nearly as much fun."

Though mysterious and eclectic, my boss was also a caring man. He and Elias were a lot alike when it came to what my grandmother called the meat and potatoes of a person, even if they had come from completely different places. Edwin had been born into and raised around money. Elias had come from no money—less than no money according to some stories that Aggie had shared with me. Both of them were good men, all the way to their cores, kind people who cared for and put others first. They were much more alike than different and they both saw that. A friendship had formed.

As caring and kind as they were, though, they both had their fair share of secrets and they knew how to keep things lively and interesting, like with adventures such as this one. My time in Scotland hadn't been boring, and considering the friends I'd made and my vast array of duties at The Cracked Spine, boredom wasn't in my near future.

"Maybe Edwin thought I'd like the adventure of it all," I continued. "I do. It's fun. He probably knew I'd get you to bring me out and thought I'd like to see the castle with you."

"Meebe," Elias said.

I laughed, pulled my arm from his, rubbed my gloved hands together, and gathered my coat collar up around my neck. "Come on. Let's wait inside for the guy in some tights with a comic book. We're early and we'll let him find us."

Surreptitiously, I looked toward the parking lot entrance, but no one else was coming this direction.

"I suppose ye're right," Elias said unconvincingly.

It had been drizzling first thing that morning in Edinburgh. Clear blue skies had followed for about ten minutes, and then the clouds had come back, darker and promising more than just a drizzle. Blue skies and shining suns were rare things in Scotland, even more so in late November. My parents had e-mailed me a picture of their farm's front yard after a recent winter storm. Mom's green sewing yardstick had been stuck into the snow just off the front porch, illustrating that there were already twelve inches of the white stuff over their patch of Kansas farmland. The highlands of Scotland had snow, but those of us around Edinburgh hadn't seen any yet. I was told we might not, that it usually didn't snow much in that part of the country, maybe a couple of inches around December and January. If we didn't, it would be the first snow-free winter of my life, as well as the darkest one. The sun set around midafternoon this time of year in Scotland. For the most part my internal clock had adjusted, but during the rare moments when I wasn't busy, afternoon naps had become more tempting than ever.

Castle Doune was located about an hour away from Edinburgh, off the Glasgow Road motorway, and at the end of a short trip down a curvy two-lane road. From the parking lot and the walking path to the castle, it was impossible to know that we were close to a small town—Dunblane, Elias had said—and still close to the motorway. The traffic noise didn't reach us, and Dunblane was in the other direction, past some rolling hills.

I'd never been on those roads before, and for the first time I had noticed that the road signs were in miles, not kilometers. Elias hadn't had a good explanation as to why; he'd shrugged and said that's just the way it was.

As we walked up the path we still didn't see or hear any other visitors. We were in a hidden pocket of the countryside and I didn't want Elias to sense I was spooked at all, but I was glad he was with me.

Castle Doune wasn't like the Edinburgh Castle. There were no ticket booths outside, no tour guides or docents to move us from one spot to the next, no fancy decorations. It was simply what remained of an old stone castle. It was smaller than the castle in Edinburgh, but almost as well preserved. It was made with simple straight lines and corners, intimidating high walls with only a few spots cut for windows and arrow loops, slits that real arrows had been fired through back in the day.

"'Tis a courtyard castle," Elias said. "Once we're through that doorway, ye'll see the courtyard. Up there," he pointed to the roof, "we'll be able tae see the countryside and the River Teith."

"Are those the battlements?" I looked up at the ragged border along the top. Time had given the castle a worn charm and had taken away a few stones that made up the original and onetime straight and even roofline.

"Aye."

"That's where we're supposed to meet him."

"Aye."

"We'll be careful," I said with a reassuring smile. I cupped my hands around my mouth and yelled upward, "Hello! Anyone there?"

No one answered.

Elias grumbled again.

As he had said it would, the doorway we went through led us directly into a courtyard, an open square-shaped patch of land enclosed by more castle walls. A tall stairway was attached to the courtyard wall to our right and would take us up to the living spaces.

"I'll lead the way. Stick close tae me," Elias said.

I was still prone to moments of awe because of the authenticity of Scotland. We were at the edge of a courtyard of an old castle that had been built a long time ago; a place where real people had lived and fought and died. It wasn't some ride at an amusement park or a place to simulate a bygone experience. I'd spent many a moment in Scotland simply soaking in the atmosphere, letting my crazy imagination move back in time and run amok.

"Lass?" Elias said from the top of the stairway. "*Close* tae me."

"Oh. Sorry."

I hurried up the stairs and followed him inside the living quarters.

"Shall we go directly up tae the battlements?" he said.

"We're early," I said again as I looked at my watch. "I bet it will be even colder on the roof. How do we get up there?"

Elias pointed to a narrow opening where I spotted part of a circular stairway. The walls around the steps were tight and claustrophobic. We'd only want to go up once.

"Give me a quick tour down here and then we'll go," I said.

We still hadn't come upon other visitors, but Elias wasn't in much of a mood to play tour guide. We moved *very* quickly, and I didn't ask the questions I wanted to ask about the Great Hall, the large kitchen, and the other rooms that made up the living spaces. I made mental notes for later.

A long worn wooden table with thick round legs had been placed in the Great Hall, but there was no other furniture on the faded stone floors, no throw rugs, no tapestries on the walls. I sensed the history and was strangely, briefly, and unreasonably saddened that it was no longer anyone's home.

Living inside old castles wouldn't make much sense.

Stone walls and floors, no insulation, no modern heating or cooling systems, no plumbing, at least in the sense we twenty-first-century folks were accustomed to. They were not designed for modern comfort. Still, castles had once been homes, places that were fought fiercely for.

I hadn't yet encountered my first Scottish ghost, at least one that I was sure of. I'd had unusual moments that included breathy tickles on the back of my neck or a flash of something out of the corner of my eye. I'd had similar moments back in Kansas but here, in Scotland, those moments had seemed somehow stretched longer, both more solid and more made of vapor too. Real but fleeting.

As I stood still and let myself just "be" in the kitchen with its gaping wide stone fireplace, as tall as me and still darkened with soot, I wished for a spectral visit.

Unfortunately, Elias wasn't on the same page. My moment of silence wasn't given a full moment.

"Lass, are ye awright?" He stepped next to me and looked at the fireplace like he was missing something.

"Fine. I was hoping to sense a ghost."

"Aye," he said as he looked around with a one-eyed squint. "No doot there are plenty close by, but they dinnae accept invitations. They're on their own clocks. Ye need not work so hard tae see one. They'll find *ye* when they want tae. Some arenae all that friendly either. There's no rush."

"Right." I looked around one more time.

Elias rubbed his finger under his nose. "Meebe we should go up. We can better see who's coming from up there anyway. Ye will let me lead the way."

"Sure."

There must have been a good reason for having a cramped, circular stairway, hidden from the living spaces and behind a wall. It probably had something to do with heating and cooling, or perhaps efficient use of space.

The stairs were just means and modes to get from one floor to the next, but they hadn't been an integral part of the cosmetic design.

"Elias, what's with the tight fit?" I asked as we continued moving spirally upward, on a trek that was taking much longer than I would have predicted.

"Och, dinnae ken, lass. If I think aboot it though, it might have been a way tae keep close track of who's coming in and going oot. Scots are suspicious folks. Back then even more so. If ye didnae have a moat to deter yer enemies, at least ye could watch the stairs and trap someone ye didnae want inside, kill them dead before they caused any harm."

"Of course," I said. "I should have thought of that."

By the time we made it to the roof I was breathing like I'd just done a few hundred-yard wind sprints, and the cold wind was even colder. I would not have made a good fighter—even the stairs would have made me want to surrender.

"Oh, it *is* beautiful though," I said as we stepped next to the edge.

We weren't in the highlands, but the nearby view was made of rolling hills, less green and lush in their winter states, but still appealing. Large estates dotted the countryside here and there. Edwin lived in a country estate—though it was more like a castle than an estate—and his was like these; fairly new, big, and built with modern amenities inside, old-world charm on the outside.

A wide river snaked around the hills, homes, and trees. The highlands, topped with snow, beckoned from far off in the distance. Perhaps my ghost waited for me there. I hadn't yet had time to see and experience that part of Scotland, but I wanted to. As I looked at the faraway mountain range, the desire to visit the highlands deepened. They called to me. I was going to have to make the trip a priority.

"Aye," Elias said, his breathing similar to mine, as he rested his arms on the stone facing. "'Tis beautiful. They could see their enemies coming at them. 'Tis why all the castles are built up on hills."

I'd known that, but I nodded and made an agreeable sound.

My eyes moved to the parking lot. The cab was still the only vehicle there.

"I'm beginning to wonder about the tourists too."

Elias shrugged. "Aye. Weel, ebb and flow, I guess. No guided tours, but I ken that tour vans stop here. We must be in between groups."

I cleared my throat and stepped back from the ledge. I turned in a slow circle so I could take in the entire 360-degree view, but I only got about 100 degrees around.

We were on one end of the roof, but it wasn't all flat. There was a bricked peak that ran down the middle of the space, followed by more open space. I thought I spotted something on the ground on the other end of the peak.

"Is that a sandal? A sandal on a foot?" I said as I pushed past Elias and moved quickly in between the peak and the battlements. It wasn't an overly tight space and there was no concern that I'd go over the edge, but I leaned inward anyway.

The angle at which I saw what I thought was a foot made me think that someone was flat on their back over there.

Unfortunately, my eyes hadn't been playing tricks on me. The foot was attached to a person—a man's body extended backward down a short flight of stairs, his head at the bottom, his sandaled and tights-clad feet at the top. Two things became immediately clear: the man was dead, and he was surely my contact.

"No! It's him! The man I was supposed to meet!" I yelled, and stomped my foot. I threw my hands up to my mouth and looked at Elias with wide, confused eyes. I became frozen in a surreal sense of unreality. Something in me wanted to scream, something else wanted to run. Part of me wanted to faint.

Involuntarily, I doubled over and started to breathe even more loudly, quickly, and noisily than just after the trip up the stairs.

Gently, Elias moved me away from the scene, guiding me to sit down at a spot away from the body and back from the battlement wall. He said things, but I didn't register the words. Oddly, the only things I could focus on were those faraway snowcapped mountains. I'd sensed that I needed to go to them.

Now, I wished I was already there.

TWO

I recovered from the initial shock. I might have hyperventilated if I hadn't, and I knew I needed to get it together to help Elias, or the dead man if there was any help to be had for him. Once I could breathe normally and my ears started to hear again, I stood and walked, with only slightly shaky legs, back to Elias and the body.

He had the police on his mobile, his side of the conversation including things like, "We've come upon a dead body atop the Castle Doune. Aye, I checked for a pulse and listened for breath. Nothing. No, I cannae see right off what might have happened. We've just got a dead man in a . . . weel, I think it's a costume of sorts." I nodded but didn't interrupt. I hadn't told Elias about my contact's acting job at the Wallace monument.

The dead man was the man I was supposed to meet, I was pretty sure. He fit the description Edwin had given me. It was more than the costume. Edwin had said he would be a big man, late forties, shoulder-length auburn hair, somewhat gray at the temples. I'd commented that William Wallace had been tortured and executed when he was thirty-five. Edwin had been impressed by my historical knowledge, but then shrugged and said that if someone wanted to play the part of William Wallace, there's usually a place that would welcome him aboard, no matter his age. The sandals, more like Birkenstocks than something from the thirteenth century, didn't necessarily fit with the rest of the getup, but they were probably close in style.

He was dead, there was no doubt, and Elias had been correct when he'd said that there was no visible cause. There was nothing gruesome about him, no blood, no injuries, though it was certainly a morbid scene and I had to work hard not to fall back into freak-out mode. I wondered who he was besides a reenactor of a famous historical Scottish figure. What was his real name? What was his job? I hadn't asked Edwin, and he hadn't offered. It was supposed to be an adventure. I thought his lack of details was on purpose and meant I wasn't supposed to ask too many questions. Turned out it was an adventure, but surely not in the way Edwin had intended, and definitely not in the way I had expected.

I'd forgotten all about the cold until voices rode up to us on a gust of wind. Happy voices and jovial laughter.

"Uh-oh." I stood and looked over the battlements. A van had parked in the parking lot, and a group of people were making their way up the path toward the castle entrance.

"I'll go talk to them," I said to Elias.

He looked at me, at the body, and then at me again. "Do ye want me tae do that?"

"No, you stay here," I said, giving him the worse of the two tasks. Though staying with the dead man wouldn't help him come back to life, it seemed wrong to leave him alone.

I hurried along the in-between space and tried to formulate what I would say to the group of people that would keep them away but not scare them too much, though if there was a killer in the vicinity maybe we all needed to be a little scared, or at least on guard.

I stopped at the entryway to the spiral staircase and looked back over the roof. There were a couple of juts and corners that the killer could still be hiding behind, but it was unlikely that we wouldn't have noticed someone from the other end.

"Be careful!" I said back to Elias.

"Aye, ye too, lass."

"I will be," I muttered quietly, hoping I didn't come upon a killer in the tight stairway.

If I hadn't stopped and hesitated I might have missed the flutter out of the corner of my eye. My heartbeat picked up again when I saw the movement. I focused my attention on the spot around the wall and on the other side of the staircase entrance. It was a piece of paper, perhaps stuck behind a decorative stone cube that jutted upward.

As I moved toward the flutter I'd all but forgotten about the *Oor Wullie,* but the memory came back full force when I saw that it was a book wedged into the space. I crouched, unwedged it, and inspected the cover closely. Edwin had told me the *Oor Wullie* cover would be an illustration of the lead character, Wullie, with his short spiky hair and dungarees, in sixteen different poses. The book I held matched the description. The book wasn't in mint condition, but the tears on the cover and first few pages could have been from a recent windblown trip across the top of the castle.

I couldn't see Elias or the body from where I crouched. I looked in that direction to confirm he couldn't see me. I shouldn't have picked up the book. It might have been evidence. Elias and I were going to have to explain to the police what we were doing atop the roof of Castle Doune. We'd have to tell them about our meeting, about the handoff that was supposed to have taken place. Maybe the comic book had something to do with the man dying, or being killed. I should have left it where it was.

But even though Edwin was a good man, kind and considerate, some of the secrets he'd been sharing with me sometimes skirted along the edge of legal; sometimes they spilled over a tiny bit.

I'd become fiercely loyal to him and my coworkers, Rosie and Hamlet. Of course I didn't suspect that Edwin had played some part in the death of the man at the other end of the roof, but something was amiss. If there was a murder, how much did Edwin have to do with it, even peripherally?

Ultimately it was pure instinct. At least that was the excuse I would use later when I pondered exactly why I grabbed the comic book and put it under my jacket before going to talk to the approaching tourists.

They didn't believe me at first. They were from Berlin, Germany, and though they spoke English much better than I could have faked German, they thought it was strange that someone who was so distinctly American was instructing them that they couldn't go into the Scottish castle. It was an awkward summit meeting that was ultimately successful because the police were quick to arrive.

I was prepared to hand over the comic book if Elias spilled the beans about our visit to the castle. I would apologize for tainting evidence, and become appropriately humbled about my actions.

But the police didn't ask why we were there. They asked if we knew the dead man, for our names, our phone numbers, and our home and work addresses, but not for the reason behind our trip to the castle. We kept our answers brief and noncommittal, which I'd noticed was always Elias's way when speaking to law enforcement. I was typically more forthcoming but today I followed his lead. He sent me a questioning expression when he noticed I was giving the same sorts of answers he was giving, but he didn't comment further.

It must not have occurred to the police that there would be any reason to visit Castle Doune other than to see it. And they would probably be right most of the time.

We were dismissed and the German tourists were sent away without getting a chance to even step into the courtyard. They were disappointed and sent me angry eyes as Elias and I got into the cab.

Neither he nor I spoke until we reached the busy motorway again, headed back toward Edinburgh.

"Lass, who was that man?" Elias asked.

"I have no idea," I said, but I told him about the connection to William Wallace and the monument in Stirling. I told him I knew he was my contact because of the costume and Edwin's description.

"Och, what a mess. Poor lad," Elias said.

"What do you think happened?"

"I have no idea. He could have had a heart attack, I s'pose. The police will investigate."

"Do you think it's weird that there were no other vehicles there?"

"Aye. Verra much so, but I dinnae ken what tae make of it. Tour caravans and vans make their way tae the castle all the time. He could have taken a ride with one of them."

"That makes sense. I . . ."

"What?"

I opened my jacket and pulled out the comic book.

"Ooh, where did ye get that?" he asked as he smacked his forehead with his hand, knocking his cap backward.

"I found it at the other end of the roof, by the circular stairway, when I was going down to meet the tourists. I should have given it to the police, huh?"

"Aye, ye shouldnae have even sae much as touched the wee thing."

"I know. I really do know, but . . . well, here it is."

"Aye."

"Do you think I should take it back to the police?"

Elias rubbed his finger under his nose and adjusted the rearview mirror. He frowned as he looked in it and then in his side mirror. I got a final disgruntled glance before he said, "No, talk tae Edwin. See what he says."

"Yeah. That's what I was thinking. Good idea."

"Aye," Elias said doubtfully.

THREE

It took us just over an hour to get back to Edinburgh, which was *about* the right amount of time to recover from our time at the castle, and formulate the questions I had for Edwin. I hoped to find him at the shop, but his hours were unpredictable at best. Once in front of The Cracked Spine, I sent Elias on his way, wondering how he would break the news of our travels to Aggie. I was sure we'd have to convene later to discuss the events.

The bell above the door jingled as I went through. Everyone I worked with was there. Edwin, Hamlet, Rosie, and Hector, the tiny terrier with the long bangs (today, a bright pink barrette held the bangs up in a miniature feathered fur fountain), and Rosie's boyfriend, Regg Brandon, who'd recently become a frequent fixture in the shop. They all looked over to greet me. Rosie had witnessed Regg get hit by a bus a couple of months ago, and their romance had sparked when she'd sought him out at the hospital. His bruises and injuries had healed but he still walked with a slight limp. Since he was seventy-something, he'd accepted that he might have the limp forever and was grateful he wasn't in worse condition. He was an architect with an office not far from the bookshop and his almost daily visits, usually with coffees in tow, were always welcomed.

Hector sat up from his stretched position on the corner of the desk in the front of the shop and greeted me with a tail wag. His tail stopped being so happy when he must have sensed something wasn't quite right. He sat and watched me with the cutest questioning brown eyes you've ever seen. I took a deep breath and told my face to normalize.

I also pushed away any bookish voices that might want to talk. I had to focus, and I really needed to have an uninterrupted conversation with Edwin.

Though Rosie had her own office on the other side of the wall, the dark side, she usually sat at the front desk, either looking over her handwritten bookkeeping ledgers, helping customers, or visiting with Regg. Hector went home with Rosie every night, but we were all his people. He was well in tune with each of our moods and dispositions.

Edwin stood on the rolling ladder attached to the side of the shop's ceiling-to-floor, jam-packed shelves.

"How did it go, lass?" he asked with a smile that faded when he looked at me.

"Delaney? Ye awright?" Rosie asked as she peered up over a steaming mug.

"Hi, everybody. I'm fine, thanks."

"You don't look so good. Pale even for you," Regg said.

"I'm okay." I smiled. I liked Regg. He was the most direct person I'd ever known.

Edwin stepped off the ladder. "Lass?"

"Edwin, can we talk privately in the warehouse?" I said.

"Of course," he said as his eyebrows came together.

Hamlet stood at the back of the shop, holding a broom

and dustpan. Even with my hurried steps toward the stairs that would lead us up and over to the dark side, I glanced quickly at the ground next to his feet, noticing shards of glass.

We gave each other curious scrutinizing glances, both of us wondering what was going on with the other one. Our nods and blinks indicated that we'd discuss things later. Though we were a close-knit group and I cared deeply for them all, my bond with Hamlet had been the most surprising and maybe the deepest. It was part friendly, part sibling-like, made up of fun times and laughter but also of serious discussions about the world. Eight years my junior, his wisdom belied his youth, and our deep conversations were moments I looked forward to. I'd come to Scotland almost on a whim, a desire to be bold because I felt like I'd lived my life too safely. I hadn't thought I would ever give a second thought to my motivations to move to the other side of the world, but I had. Hamlet had been forced to live his life with no other choice but to be brave. In my moments of self-doubt he had helped me realize that my impulsive decision had been a good one.

After traveling down a small walkway at the top of the stairs, Edwin and I went through another door to a cooler, darker, and mustier space lit with only an exposed bulb hanging from the ceiling and whatever outside light could make it through the blacked-out and grungy front and back windows. The shop side had once been a bank; this side had sat empty and unused for years until Edwin acquired it to use for office and warehouse space. A small kitchen took up one corner and the water closet another one.

At the bottom of the stairs, we turned left toward the large, ornately carved red wooden door that kept Edwin's treasures hidden from the world. The warehouse used to also be Edwin's office, but now it was mine, with my worktable and a desk that dated back to seventeenth-century Scottish royalty. I'd only recently become accustomed to working at the priceless desk, but I still had to cover it with paper that I tore fresh from a roll every day. Edwin said the setup reminded him of a doctor's office, but I'd told him it was the only way I could keep working on the valuable piece of furniture.

I pulled the large blue key from my pocket, looked all directions in the small hallway—this had become a habit after watching my coworkers do it. I didn't think any one of us had ever come upon an unwelcome visitor, but you could never be too careful when doors hid rooms full of treasures. I placed the key in the lock and turned it three times to the left, releasing the deadbolt with a metallic thud and echo, and pushed the heavy door open. Edwin followed me inside and I closed and locked the door behind us.

Other than one shelf full of old but not particularly valuable books, I hadn't had time to organize much of anything in the warehouse. The task was daunting, to say the least. It was a room with shelves packed with things—the widest variety anyone could imagine. Not only were there books, but I'd recently started cataloguing genuine Egyptian artifacts and some wicked-looking items I'd first thought were turn-of-the-twentieth-century medical instruments but had now concluded were torture devices. Under one of the devices, I'd found a small burlap bag full of arrowheads, things any good Kansas girl would recognize. I didn't know where they were from and neither did Edwin, but they were on my continually growing list of things to research. And I knew it was only the beginning of many discoveries to come.

I flipped the switch for the overhead fluorescent lights, giving the room a dungeon-like glow since the sky outside the small windows at the top of the back wall was thick with clouds. Edwin still liked to spend a lot of time in the warehouse so I'd brought in another comfortable office chair. I rolled it from the corner of the room to the other side of my desk and then moved to my chair.

The warehouse smelled like the best sort of dungeon— old books, ink, wood that had expanded and contracted more than a few times from moisture over the years, cold metal that had become grimy with time, congealed motor oil that had never been cleaned away. The surprisingly pleasant combination of the scents and the old stone building had more than once made me think I could travel through time when I was in the warehouse. I just hadn't figured out all the particulars yet.

I unzipped my jacket and pulled out the copy of the *Oor Wullie* annual, placing it on the desk in between us.

"Ah, you retrieved it! But why was it in your jacket, lass? And was it this damaged when you received it? What happened?" Edwin said.

"Things didn't go quite as planned, and I might have messed up," I said.

I'd formulated questions; I'd tried to think of the best way to tell him what had happened and why I'd taken the comic book instead of just leaving it there. But as I spilled the details, I got as far as "dead on the roof" before I had to stop, thinking I might have to get some help for my boss.

"Dead?" Edwin said as his face drained of color and his knuckles came up to his mouth.

"Yes." I stood and hurried over to crouch next to him. "You okay?"

"I need a moment, Delaney. Please don't tell Rosie and Hamlet. I'll come back here when I've gathered myself."

"All right, but . . ."

"Please."

I stayed close by him as he stood and made his way
to the door. He was sturdy on his feet, but I watched as
he climbed the stairs and as his long legs took him down
the short upper hallway that led to his official office. I
held back from following him. He'd been clear that he
wanted to be alone.

I wanted to kick myself. I hadn't thought that Edwin
might know the dead man. I'd shared the events as if he
had simply been an anonymous messenger. There'd been
something about the way the transaction had been orchestrated that made me think I was meeting a stranger,
someone who sometimes dressed in a costume and had
been hired for the task.

"Stupid, stupid, stupid," I said to myself as I closed the
big red door and leaned against it.

A few moments later I sighed and opened the door
again. I couldn't just wait. I closed and relocked it and
then took the stairs to the upper offices two at a time.

There were only two rooms and a supply closet on this
floor. Rosie's sometimes-used office, and Edwin's rarely
used one.

"Edwin?" I announced from the end of the hallway
when I noticed his door was open. "I couldn't just let you
go."

As I came to the opening, I saw him sitting behind his
desk, slightly bent over to the side as if he was placing
something on the floor. He straightened and sent me a
weary smile.

"I'm sorry, lass," he said. "Come in."

I took a seat in the chair across from his desk but didn't
close the door. The small room was way too claustrophobic when the door was closed.

"What? What happened? Who was he?" I said.

Edwin sighed. The color had mostly come back to his

face, but strain pulled at his glassy eyes. If he'd cried, he'd wiped away the tears before I could see them.

"I didn't know the lad well. Of course, he was a grown man now. But I knew his father." He cleared his throat. "We knew each other when we were young."

"Is that who you bought the book from, his father?"

"No, his father died two years ago, in a fire." He sighed again and his mouth formed a straight, tight line before he continued. "His father and another friend of ours. It was such a tragedy." He swallowed hard.

"Oh, Edwin, I'm so sorry."

"Thank you, lass. The man you were tae meet was William Armstrong—Billy. His father was Gordon. I didn't mean for it all tae be such a mystery tae you, but when Billy called tae tell me about the book that he thought his father wanted me tae have, I asked him not tae come in here. There was a reason, but it's a story from long ago and not important at the moment." Edwin paused again but not for long. "I couldn't meet him, Delaney, I just couldn't, but I said that I would send someone tae him, and I . . . well, I don't know why but I suggested the castle. I guess it was a place I thought you'd like tae see, and it was neutral tae everything and everyone from the past. That was important, but again, now's not the time."

"Why couldn't you meet him?"

"Too painful."

"Because of his father?"

"Aye," Edwin said.

But I sensed there was something else, and I needed more than cryptic answers, or past history excuses. I forged on. "Other reasons?"

"No."

I didn't believe him.

"Did you know anything about Billy's health? Did his father have any sort of problem that might have been passed along to his son?"

"What did . . . how did the lad, how did Billy look?"

"There was no obvious sign of the cause of his death."

"No blood?" Edwin said.

"No. He was in the costume, as you'd told me he would be. That's how I knew . . ."

Edwin nodded. "He loved doing that."

"Being William Wallace?"

"Aye. He took it very seriously."

I inspected Edwin closely. "So, you knew him well enough to know that part of him? Had you watched him reenact?"

A moment later he nodded again. "Aye, I did. A few times. He didn't know."

"Edwin, I don't understand. Why didn't you want to meet him yourself?"

"Gordon and I lost touch many years ago; things ended badly. Somewhere along the way I wanted tae mend our friendship, get tae know his son, but it wasn't tae be. Then fifty years went by."

"That's how long ago your friendship ended?"

"Close tae that."

And yet he'd been interested or curious enough to watch Billy, keep tabs on him maybe.

"Delaney, there are too many layers of memories and too many years have passed. It would be difficult tae make you understand the history, but Billy contacted me tae tell me he thought his father would want me tae have the book, that there was some sort of story written inside it that might explain part of what had caused us so much trouble all those years ago."

"Written inside it? Like something handwritten, or the strips told the story?" I said.

"I don't know. I asked the same question, but Billy didn't give me an answer."

"I didn't see anything handwritten, but I'll look again," I said.

Edwin nodded. "Tell me what happened at the castle. All of it. I'm ready tae listen."

Edwin winced as I told him about Billy's body, but he didn't break down this time. He didn't say anything until I finished.

"The book must have blown across the roof," he said. "Perhaps there were other papers tucked inside it."

"It's a possibility," I said. "Should we go back out there?"

Edwin shook his head. "No, not right now. I'll call my contact at the police and see what they've found, if there's any foul play suspected. I'll tell them I knew the lad and why he was there. Maybe that will help."

"Elias and I didn't tell them why we were there. They just thought we were tourists and we didn't correct them. Our . . . lack of details and me taking the comic book were why I thought I might have messed up."

"I shouldn't have made it all such a mystery," Edwin said. "I don't know what the police will think about you taking the book, but let me do this one step at a time then. First, I'll see what they know and if there is any suspicion of foul play, then we'll go from there. I'm so sorry, Delaney."

"Don't be sorry. I'm sorry about Billy, and the way I told you about his death."

We heard a noise that sounded like someone coming through the door at the top of the stairs.

"We're in Edwin's office," I said so they wouldn't go down to the warehouse first.

"Edwin, there's someone here tae see you," Hamlet peered around the door frame a moment later.

I hadn't registered it at the time, but now I remembered the distant sound of the bell above the door a few minutes earlier.

"Who?" Edwin asked.

"He wouldn't say, but he's in a foul mood and . . . well, he smells like fish," Hamlet said.

"Aye? We'll be right over," Edwin said as he stood with movements as weary as his smiles had been.

Hamlet waited and then led the way over. Edwin seemed to be mostly recovered by the time we were on the other side, but his steps held much less forward purpose. Unfortunately, it seemed that it was meant to be a day of jarring surprises for my boss, because his face drained of color once again after we turned the corner to face the man standing at the front of the shop. He was dripping from the rain and smelled of fish and cigarette smoke.

"Gordon?" Edwin said so weakly that both Hamlet and I hurried to catch him if he fainted. Rosie and Hector both made a small gasping sound, and Regg grumbled a noise that reminded me of Elias.

Hadn't Edwin and I just been talking about someone named Gordon, and hadn't *that* Gordon died in a fire two years earlier?

"Edwin. What have ye done tae my son?" the man said.

"I think I need tae have a seat," Edwin said.

A small commotion followed, but before long we'd turned the sign on the door to "Closed" and were all seated around the shop's back table, waiting less than patiently to hear the dead man's story.

FOUR

"I don't understand, Gordon," Edwin said. "It was confirmed. You and Leith died in the fire."

"No, it was confirmed that Leith died. It was only assumed that I did," Gordon said as he pulled a drag on the cigarette he'd just lit.

Regg had made sure our visitor wasn't there to do harm and then excused himself to go back to his office. Rosie went to gather coffee from the kitchen as the rest of us sat around the table in the corner of the shop. When Rosie came around the stairs she took the cigarette from Gordon's hand.

"There'll be no smoking in here, Gordon Armstrong, or whoever ye are." She placed the pot of coffee on the table and then disappeared around the stairs again, the cigarette pinched in her fingers and held away from her face. I grabbed the coffeepot and started filling the mugs that Hamlet had set on the table.

Gordon blinked and frowned at Rosie and then looked at Edwin. "Weel, I'm not dead, but now my son is and I've come tae find oot what ye did tae him."

Rosie was back a moment later without the cigarette, and Gordon's question, along with heavy anticipation, hung in the air until she was seated on the other side of

Edwin. Nobody was interested in the box of day-old pastries that sat in the middle, but the coffee was popular. I was chilled, probably from both the weather and the strange turn of events, so I held my hands around my mug to warm them.

"I didn't do anything tae your son, Gordon. I would never. You know that," Edwin said.

The fishy-smelling man was, in fact, the same Gordon that Edwin had been telling me about perhaps at the exact moment he'd been walking through the shop's front door. I compared him to the body I'd seen on the castle roof and saw no immediate resemblance. Gordon was a small man with steely gray hair, and no sign that it once might have been auburn—no telltale freckles or fair complexion. The man on the roof had been tall, broad-shouldered, with a filled-out chest and auburn hair that was a few shades darker than my own.

"What happened tae you?" Edwin continued, his eyes still wide with remaining grief, confusion, and perhaps fear. He was disheveled, a state I'd never seen him in. Even when his own sister had been killed I hadn't noticed him run his hand through his short hair once. He'd done it a few times just since we'd sat around the table. His tie was off-kilter and his dress shirt seemed to have suddenly become wrinkled.

"Doesnae matter, does it?" Gordon said as he reached for the pack of cigarettes in his shirt pocket. Rosie shook her head and he reluctantly pulled his hand away. He took a deep breath and in a voice strained with emotion continued, "What's more important is what happened tae Billy. What happened, Edwin?"

"We'll not tell you one other thing until you tell us why you pretended tae be dead these years. The fire? Leith?" Edwin's voice raised in volume and pitch.

It wasn't just Edwin and Gordon; the air was thick

with sadness and confusion, and distrust hung tight and heavy in the room. Hamlet had been silent, but kept his eyes on Gordon. Rosie had seemed the least surprised of everyone, but now her mouth puckered and her eyebrows came together as she waited.

My bookish voices and I had come to an agreement. I'd wanted to keep their interruptions under control, and they'd gone along with the plan, only filling my head when I let them in, when I needed my instincts or intuition to help me through something, maybe help my subconscious move me in the right direction. Since I'd moved to Scotland and wrangled them some, I'd found my odd memory trick sometimes more useful than annoying.

For an instant I let them talk.

I only know that it was and ceased to be; and that I have written and there I leave it.

David Copperfield from Dickens's book of the same name spoke the words, his voice rising above any others that might have contributed. I couldn't understand exactly how the words applied to the moment except that perhaps what these two men had shared ended a long time ago and there should be no reason to bring it up again. But these things weren't always clear at first. I'd keep the words in mind as I returned my full attention to Gordon.

"Awright, I'll tell ye, but ye willnae like it and ye may never forgive me, but ye'll also see how I had no choice."

The rest of us might have blinked in tandem as we still waited silently.

"I thought I'd killed Leith, Edwin. I thought I'd murdered him. I had tae fake my death or I would have been arrested, or so I thought. It was an accident, but the law wouldnae have seen it that way." Gordon sighed and shrugged with one slow shoulder. "Later, when I learnt the truth, I had tae stay away or my wife wouldnae have kept the insurance money, and I would have been arrested anyway." He slumped into himself. "It was one mistake after another, and I couldnae see a way oot of it."

"Why did you think you'd killed Leith?" Edwin asked.

Gordon shook his head slowly as he looked at his old and calloused hands folded on the table, deep with cavernous wrinkles and thick, uneven nails. He was not a young man, and his hands showed his age even more than his deeply wrinkled face. "It's all in that book, Edwin. The *Oor Wullie* that William was tae give tae ye. I wanted tae let ye know that I was alive, but I was afraid tae be caught. But I wanted ye tae know. I wrote it down, thought that would be easier than telling ye in person. I thought Billy would give it tae ye himself and he could be there tae explain. What happened?"

"Hamlet, the book is on Delaney's desk, I believe," Edwin said. I nodded. "Will you retrieve it for me?"

Hamlet hurried away reluctantly. No one wanted to miss the rest of this story.

"I'll look through the book, but you need tae tell me what happened, Gordon. In your own words. Cameron House, Loch Lomond. What happened that night?"

Gordon stopped himself from reaching for the cigarettes again but I saw the twitch of habit in his fingers. He sighed again, a raspy breath, before he told us what happened. Or, as Rosie later called it, his version of what happened.

"We were on holiday, Leith and I, just the two of us. I left my wife at home, and as ye probably ken, Leith's wife had died some years ago. It was just the boys." He looked at Edwin as if for a moment he thought of when Edwin was part of that camaraderie, but though both of their expressions told me they remembered that decades-ago time, neither of them seemed to be melancholy about it. "Leith had almost more money than ye, Edwin, and he wanted tae fish on Loch Lomond. Wanted tae stay in the beautiful house, Cameron House. Aye, and 'twas beautiful. We had a wonderful time. Until that night." He looked up as Hamlet came around and put the book on the table. He thumbed through it. "Is that all?"

"Aye?" Hamlet looked at me.

"Yes," I said. "That was all."

"I dinnae understand," Gordon said. "Who are ye?"

I wasn't quite sure what to say, wasn't sure he deserved an answer, but Edwin jumped in.

"Delaney is the newest member of The Cracked Spine, and I sent her tae gather the book. Delaney and her friend found Billy. They called the police."

I nodded once and looked at Gordon. He wasn't looking at me.

"Ye didnae go?" Gordon said to Edwin.

"No, I sent Delaney. I couldn't, Gordon. I just couldn't."

"Ye're a fool. It's been . . . so long."

"I won't deny that I'm a fool, but you'll just have tae try tae understand. Or not, it's up tae you."

Gordon's eyebrows came together. He thumbed through the book again, slowly this time. His eyes jumped back to mine. "Ye're sure this was it?"

"Yes."

Gordon shook his head. "I dinnae understand."

"What was in there?" I asked.

"The story of what happened," Gordon said.

"If you inserted other pieces of paper inside it, they might have blown away," I said. "The book wasn't exactly with . . . Billy. It had gotten caught under a piece of the castle roof."

Gordon looked at me, his eyes unbelieving at first, but they transformed in less than a blink. It was as if he suddenly registered that I was really there and a part of the tragedy he was going through.

"The police called me," he said when he finally looked back at Edwin.

"I don't understand," Edwin said.

"I was Billy's emergency contact. It's not my name listed on his mobile, of course."

"Who did they think ye were?" Edwin asked.

Gordon shrugged. "I go by the name of Barclay Sheraton."

"What did the police tell you?" Edwin asked Gordon.

"That William Armstrong's body was found on the roof of Castle Doune and foul play was tae be suspected. They were investigating but asked if I was William's next of kin. I told them I wasnae and gave them Fiona's number, which they already had but hadnae called her yet."

"Foul play?" I interjected. "How? What did they say?"

"That he'd been hit over the head with something hard enough tae kill him, a blunt object." Gordon's voice cracked with emotion. He cleared his throat.

"I'm so sorry," I said. "There was no indication of anything like that. There was no . . . blood."

I wondered silently if the police were mistaken about possible foul play. But if he'd hit his head on the corner or edge of a piece of the castle jutting out, there would surely have been blood from a cut. I thought about how the body lay backward down the stairs. Maybe he had tripped. I knew a police officer, but I didn't know if he would give me more information. It couldn't hurt to ask.

"Tell me what ye saw. Tell me everything," Gordon said.

"Delaney, I do think that Gordon has a right tae hear what ye've got tae say," Edwin said, "but I have more questions for him tae answer before you go on." He looked at Gordon. "You were telling us about the trip to Loch Lomond, Gordon. And Fiona, I'm sure she's devastated. What can I do for her?"

"I . . . she doesnae ken I'm alive, Edwin. I thought it was best that way. She'd want tae give back the money. It wasnae a good idea, what I did. I only got in contact with Billy aboot six months ago. I've . . . I've got a cough. I'm not going tae a doctor, but it's only getting worse. I think there's not much time left anyway. I wanted a little more with my son, and I took the chance. Fiona doesnae know."

"I will check on Fiona," Edwin said, no sympathy in his voice. "Tell us what happened with the fire."

"Aye. It was a mistake, all of it, but again, I didnae ken until it was too late. We'd been oot all day on the water, fishing, drinking, we were enjoying ourselves. No harm meant tae anyone. We docked the boat and stayed there. I dinnae remember many of the details, but I ken that we stopped for a rest. The night was strangely warm, the sky bright with stars. There was no need tae leave the boat and go back up tae the room, at least for a wee bit.

"We fell asleep, or at least I did. I was struck awake by the fire that was engulfing the boat. It wasnae a big boat but there was so much smoke. I yelled for Leith, reached for him, but it was all so hot and smoky."

"They found Leith's remains. I thought they found yours too," Edwin said.

"There wasnae much left of Leith. I . . . I guess my shoes were off and they and my wallet went into the water. The fire was so hot that they thought I'd burned like Leith had or the rest of me went into the water. Maybe it was bad police work, but the next day they declared two victims, Leith and me."

"Where did you go? Why did you leave the scene?"

"Two reasons, Edwin. First and most important, I swear tae all that is holy, I left tae look for Leith. I hoped he'd gotten away, and I jumped oot of the boat to search, but I couldnae find him. I went tae his room and searched there too. I was never where the emergency people were. We kept missing, and then I hid."

"Why?"

"I thought I'd caused the fire. At first they said it was suspicious." He patted the pocket with his cigarettes. "The drink and the cigarettes. My lighter. Leith and I had had a lot tae drink. He might have been passed oot. Meebe my cigarette caused the fire and he couldnae wake up. I didn't know. I was scared. I was so scared, and heartbroken of course."

"You were a coward," Edwin said.

"Aye," he conceded quickly. "And then I knew Fiona and Billy could use the money. It was the insurance policy ye bought for them, Edwin. In a strange way I thought ye'd be pleased."

Rosie made a gurgled sound that punctuated the fact that Edwin would never be pleased about the circumstances. Hamlet sat back in his chair and crossed his arms in front of himself. I knew they hadn't met Gordon Armstrong before, but I wondered if they knew much about Edwin's past with him. I made a mental note to ask later.

Edwin just shook his head and closed his eyes as he pinched the bridge of his nose.

"I couldnae get myself oot of the mess," Gordon said. "Not without getting in other trouble, meebe not without getting Fiona in trouble. I weighed the options, all of them."

"Where have you been?"

"Here, weel, close tae Edinburgh. I work at a fish market. I have a small room close tae there. I work and go home. I . . ." his voice cracked again. "I was enjoying my time with my son."

"Oh," Rosie said as tears suddenly started to fall down her cheeks. "I didnae ken yer son, and ye're an unlikeable man, Gordon Armstrong, but I'm sad for yer loss. So sad."

Hamlet grabbed a box of tissues from a shelf and handed them to Rosie.

Edwin swallowed hard and then continued, "I'll help Fiona get through this."

"Thank ye," Gordon said.

"Who would have wanted Billy dead, Gordon? Who would have killed him?"

"I dinnae ken. He didnae do much but play William Wallace and keep his mother company. There are others who play the Wallace character and I wonder if he angered one of them. Recently, there was a lass. . . ."

"Och, there's always a lass in the way," Rosie said.

"Aye," Gordon said. "He said recently that he was going tae break things off with her."

"What's her name?" Edwin said.

"He wouldnae tell me her name."

"You need tae tell the police about Billy's William Wallace friends and about the lass. Fiona might not know," Edwin continued.

"Aye. I s'pose I do." He didn't commit to sharing the information with the police, but sniffed and then looked at me. "Now, please, tell me the details of what ye saw."

I nodded, but before I spoke I looked at the *Oor Wullie* on the table. Edwin had glanced at it like it was much more than a book of two years' worth of comic strips. The fact that Gordon had used it as a means to communicate with Edwin must have meant something too. I noticed Edwin's brief but real longing toward it and filed that to the back of my mind with all the other questions that were accumulating. There was nothing sentimental about the main character, Wullie. It seemed he always got the short end of the stick, but he was cute and lovable with a good attitude. Or that's what I thought. I'd only researched enough so I'd recognize the book when it was given to me.

Curiosity is not a sin. . . . But we should exercise caution with our curiosity, yes indeed.

It was just yesterday that someone had come into the shop and dropped their worn copies of the Harry Potter series on the front desk. The young woman and her husband were moving to France and had to leave many things behind. Even though The Cracked Spine was packed with books that might be considered more difficult to find than the recent classics, Rosie had looked at the books, seen the wear along the dust jackets where hands had spent many loving hours, and agreed to give the woman a small amount for them. Though I'd adored the books I hadn't thought much about the characters since they'd come into the shop with the recent acquisitions, and though I couldn't totally understand his cautionary warning, I would take Dumbledore's advice—guided by my intuition—seriously.

I nodded again, this time toward the stack of books still on the front desk. I'd tell Gordon the story, and I'd eventually ask all the questions I wanted answers to, but I'd be careful with everything I shared and everything I asked. I was sure the old wizard nodded back his approval.

FIVE

Tom blinked and placed the chip—which I'd call a French fry—back into the paper boat, next to a large piece of fried fish. "You found a body?"

"I did." I nodded and then put my piece of fish down. It seemed like the polite thing to do.

"And his father was supposed tae be dead, but isn't? I don't understand, Delaney. Tell me again what happened, but from the beginning." Tom wiped his fingers on his napkin, pushed his food back on the narrow counter, and then turned a little on the stool to give me his full attention.

His cobalt eyes reeled me right in. They always did. I'd tried desperately to think of them as normal eyes. We'd been together for a few months now and it was high time to find his eyes much less fetching, maybe take them for granted a little, and not let them speed up my heart rate. But I hadn't gotten there yet. I still blushed when he looked at me the way he sometimes did. To his credit, he'd pretended not to notice, most of the time. Every now and then I caught an amused smile pull at his lips when I blushed, but he'd look away quickly.

And don't get me started on his lips.

We were having dinner at one of our favorite spots, a

place close to the bookshop and Tom's pub; a small take-away restaurant where I'd had my first proper fish and chips, and many more orders since. Though most customers ordered their food and took it with them, there were a few stools and a counter—well, a ledge-like counter along the front window—for those who wanted to stay and eat. Tom and I frequently ordered our dinners from Mica, the owner and an immigrant from Russia who was there whenever the shop was open. We enjoyed our usual meal of fish and chips as we sat on the stools or, if the weather was agreeable, on one of the benches in the Grassmarket Square, the shared common space for both our places of work. It was too cold to sit outside this evening and the stools inside had been vacant.

As customers moved in and out, ordering everything from fish and chips to fried haggis and fried hamburger, I quietly told Tom what had happened earlier that afternoon, slower and with more details this time. If there was anyone I would tell the whole story about almost anything to it was Tom. Our relationship had come out of the blue for both of us, and it had been a surprisingly easy transition into "couple," so far at least. He'd known my coworkers for years, so he knew how wonderful they were but he'd also sensed Edwin's secrecy. He never asked me much about that part of my boss's life, and there were parts of it I wouldn't be willing to share even with him, but Edwin had given me full permission to show Tom the warehouse, just as long as he agreed not to tell anyone else about it. He had.

"Gordon's been living and working in Edinburgh, at a fish market?" he asked.

"That's what he said."

"It's a big city, but that's a pretty risky move for someone who was pretending tae be dead."

"I thought so too, everyone did, but his family was close by. I get that. He'd been watching them and said he only recently made contact with his son. He says he's sick with a bad cough that he won't see a doctor about so he wanted another chance to see his son before it was too late. Sad story all the way around."

"Aye, but . . ."

"I know. It's risky."

"Did Edwin want tae tell the police about Gordon?"

I shook my head. "I don't think so. I think Gordon's secret is safe with him, even if he didn't like what Gordon had done. I don't know, maybe the story needs to soak in. Edwin was pretty shaken up."

"I can imagine. Did Edwin call his police contact tae confirm if Billy had been murdered?"

"I don't know. Shortly after Gordon left, Edwin did too. I didn't have a chance to talk to him again."

Tom looked out the window and rubbed his chin as he thought a moment. "What's their history?"

"I'm not sure. Hamlet had never heard of him, but Rosie had, though she wouldn't tell us anything today. I do know that whatever happened between Edwin and Gordon, it happened a long time ago. There were bad things, bad memories, but it's been about fifty years. I think Rosie wants to be extra cautious about what she shares. That's not necessarily like her, so I get the impression that it was all pretty serious."

"An *Oor Wullie* comic strip book? The story was in the book?"

"That's what he said." I shrugged. "An annual. In good condition, the book itself was one of the more valuable annuals, but not worth a fortune."

Tom rubbed his stubbled cheek. "Lots of Williams in this."

I blinked.

"William Armstrong—Billy—William Wallace, and Wullie—Willie, William."

"I didn't even think about Wullie being William. I haven't spent much time reading the strip. I should have put that together. It must mean something."

"It's a good name. Maybe that's all." He glanced out the window again toward a boisterous group of teenagers passing by. "There's no similarity between Edwin and the comic character, the lad Wullie, but maybe there's something similar with Gordon or their other friend, Leith. I don't know. Just a guess. There must be a good reason for that specific book tae have been used."

"Probably. I don't know what Gordon did before he went into hiding, but is Wullie a fisherman?"

"No," Tom said. "School lad who sits on a bucket and often seems down on his luck. If he's fished in any of his stories, he's never caught anything, or it got away. Cute, lovable, but probably a challenge to his parents."

He looked at me with a half-smile and one raised eyebrow.

I half smiled and raised one eyebrow back. I was sure I also blushed, but that couldn't be helped. "Oh. Well, Gordon's none of those—cute or lovable—might have been a challenge to his parents though."

"It doesn't sound like something Edwin would find himself caught up in. Old news, men pretending tae be dead."

"I don't think he wants to be caught up in anything that has to do with Gordon. It was forced on him today. There are many secrets there," I said.

"I bet you'd like tae know what those secrets are, some of them at least."

"Of course."

He wiped his fingers on his napkin again. "Shall we drive out there tonight?"

"Drive out where?"

"The castle. I suspect you'll want tae go on your own tae see if you can find that paper with the story written on it. I'd rather we went together, and our days are always so busy. The weather's not too terrible. Now's a good time."

"Tonight? It's so dark," I said.

"And a wee bit cold but not too late. It's only six. It'll be fun. It's not too far away. I'll keep you safe and warm, I promise. Maybe we'll find you a ghost."

"Well, the idea of a ghost *is* irresistible."

"I bet."

"And, I'm sure I'll be pretty cold. You'll have to work hard to keep me warm."

"I'm counting on it."

"Let's go," I said.

We threw away our paper boats and bid Mica good night. As he always did he sent us an enthusiastic *"do svidaniya"* as we went through the doors.

Tom helped me with my coat and then glanced up at the partly cloudy, dark sky as he swung his jacket on. "Let me make a quick run into the pub. I'll let Rodger know I won't be coming back this evening."

We crossed the street and covered the short distance over Grassmarket Square. I waited outside as Tom made his way inside. I wondered if our trip out to the castle would be canceled because of the large crowd, but Tom weaved his way back out again only a few minutes later. As he came out through the doorway, he and a patron going inside bumped shoulders. It looked to me like the man ran into Tom on purpose, leaned and veered that way, but maybe he'd just already had too much to drink.

"Excuse me," Tom said. He turned toward the man he'd run into. But the man kept his cap-covered head down and his coat collar up high as he mumbled something before melting into the noisy crowd inside.

"Weird," I said as Tom looked in after him.

"A wee bit, but it happens. Let's go."

———

The drive in the dark along the motorway didn't seem all that different from the ride with Elias, but once we'd exited onto the narrow road that seemed to hide itself and its travelers from civilization, all we could see clearly was the light from the car's headlights, broken by the shadows of the trees that lined the road.

"Just like any good horror movie," I said.

Tom laughed.

"There wasn't a fence around the grounds, but will we be locked out?" I said.

"It's a possibility, but we'll see."

I looked at his profile again.

"What?" I said, in response to his mysterious tone

"Nothing," he said far too innocently.

He had something planned. If it didn't include killing me and leaving my body at the castle or dumping me into the nearby River Teith, it would probably be something fun. He was good that way.

"Do you know about the castle, who used tae live there?" he asked.

"No. I meant to research it, but things went sideways."

"Aye. It was the home of Robert Stewart, the first Duke of Albany, who was for all practical purposes the ruler of Scotland from the late thirteen hundreds to the early fourteen hundreds. It was a bloody time in our history, and he and his son, I believe, spent much of their time fighting and acquiring land. He was ruthless, but it was probably a necessary trait tae have. He was also the great-grandson of Robert the Bruce. You've heard of him?"

"Of course. He and Mel Gibson did something together once. In fact William Wallace was involved in that story. Maybe that's why this castle was chosen as the meeting place, even if Edwin said he'd picked a neutral location."

"Neutral?"

"I still don't understand completely, but a place neutral to what went on in the past."

"I see. Maybe, but Stirling is just about the same distance from Edinburgh. Edwin's historical knowledge would extend to Robert Stewart, but maybe he didn't think about it."

"Maybe it was just a place that popped into his head."

"Aye. We Scots love the films but your Hollywood isn't much for the facts," Tom added.

"I know. I heard about the kilt issue. William Wallace would never have worn a kilt."

"Other things too. Movies might be required tae stretch the truth, but Mel Gibson, a fine actor, isn't a big man. William Wallace was huge, according to what we think we know at least. It's difficult tae find many specifics. Then there's Liam Neeson, who took on the role of Rob Roy. Roy was a smaller man of stature than Neeson, but thick and muscled. Also, there's little evidence that William Wallace was ever married. It's thought he became such a warrior because his father was killed, not his wife."

"That's a pretty big difference from the movie," I said.

"Aye, but it's still a great film."

"I agree. And I've just been given an item to research from Rob Roy's time. It's a letter he wrote. Well, allegedly. That's what I'm going to try to find out."

"Aye? That's fascinating."

"Wanna see it?"

"Definitely."

"Deal. It's in the warehouse. I'll show it to you tomorrow."

"I look forward tae it." Tom slowed the car. "What was Billy Armstrong's job?"

"Other than reenactor I don't know."

"That wouldn't have provided him with any income."

"I'll ask Edwin if he knows."

As Tom steered the car around the curve next to the parking lot and at the bottom of the walkway that led up to the courtyard door, he said, "There's some evidence that Castle Doune might be built on the remains of another castle."

"Who did that castle belong to?"

"It's a mystery, but here comes someone who's trying tae solve it, or who is at least assisting those who are trying tae solve it." Tom turned the key, making the night silent, extra dark, and the approaching disembodied flashlight's glow really eerie.

"Come on, let's get out," he said.

I hesitated, but only briefly. I hadn't seen the other car just past the lot and next to the walkway, but I noticed a glimmer off its chrome as a voice that seemed to be with the flashlight spoke.

"Delaney, dear lass who has straightened oot my boy for only the guid." The flashlight moved closer.

"Artair!" I said. "What a nice surprise."

"Weel, how could I resist?" he said. "Tom calls me aboot a dead man on the top o' the castle. I grabbed my torch and came right oot."

"I don't understand, but I'm glad you're here." I hugged him.

Artair Fletcher, pronounced AR-ter, Tom's father and a librarian at the University of Edinburgh, had been another welcome surprise in my Scotland adventure. I'd become so woozy with book love when Tom had taken me on campus to visit his father that I frequently teased that I continued to date the dashing Scot with the cobalt eyes only for the fact that his redheaded father worked inside a library as magical as any I'd ever seen. The building stretched both long and tall, and was replete with packed but organized shelves, curved cornices, and domed ceilings. I could get lost inside, forget to eat or drink ever again, my body someday to be found under a stack of books. However, there would be a smile on my lifeless face.

"Da is working with some of the researchers at the university regarding the remains of the earlier castle. They don't lock the castle up at night, but I thought he should let the appropriate people know about our visit. Technically it's past closing. He wanted tae come along."

"That's perfect. Thank you, Artair," I said.

"Och, 'tis a pleasure. Come along. It will be dark, but I've got the torch," Artair said as he turned and started back up the walkway.

"Thank you," I said quietly to Tom.

"It's too dark tae see your expression, but you sound like you're smiling. That's thanks enough," Tom said.

"Are you for real?" I said.

"I keep telling you I am," he said. "Come on."

When Tom and I began dating, directly before our very first date in fact, I'd been warned about his habit of short-lived relationships and his issues with commitment. As a result, for a while I'd spent precious time wondering if he was being sincere or playing some sort of game with my emotions. One day, not long into our quickly lit romance, I decided I'd have to take him at face value and quit worrying so much. If it worked out, great. If not, I'd be sad, devastated maybe, but going into any sort of relationship with an underlying thread of waiting for it to be over might end up being the reason it failed. If it was going to fail I was pretty sure I wanted it to be his fault, not mine.

We followed Artair up the path as he walked with his ever-present quick steps. He and Tom looked nothing alike, Tom having gotten his dark looks from his mother, who'd died when he was a child. Artair's short stature and wiry frame seemed healthy until you noticed that his clothes were all slightly too big. Tom told me that his father had always dressed that way, not baggy or slovenly, but with shoulder seams that fell slightly too far down his arms, and belts that seemed to bunch about an inch of his pants' waistlines. He was just comfortable that way.

Tom's taller and wider frame was always dressed with clothes that fit perfectly. He didn't wear much other than jeans and dress shirts and the occasional kilt, but I'd discovered that he was meticulous about keeping his clothes clean and pressed. He was much better about it than I was.

Though continuing to date Tom was, of course, more about him than his father and that stunning library, Artair and the giant building full of books were good perks. The kilts were nice too.

"Stick close tae me," Artair said at the doorway.

We stepped into the courtyard. I kept close to Tom, and felt his fingers entwine mine. To say the dark, torchlit courtyard was spooky was an understatement. I didn't see any ghosts, but there had to be some within the ancient stone walls, didn't there? I imagined them and their murky, milky glow.

"Awright. Here we are," Artair said as he scanned the space with the light.

"You scared?" Tom asked me.

"No, not really. It's just so dark," I said.

"I understand," Artair said. He cleared his throat less confidently than he probably hoped. "Nothing tae fear though. The ghosties are long unable tae inflict the harm they did when they were living. Come along."

Artair took off for the stairs that led up to the great hall. I'd all but forgotten that it was cold outside, but a small wind nipped at my nose and I shivered.

"You sure you're okay?" Tom asked.

"Fine, I promise."

I squeezed his hand and then let go of it before I followed Artair up the stairs. I made sure Tom was close behind.

There was no handrail on the exposed side of the stairs so I stayed extra close to the wall on the other side, my fingertips and shoulder tapping along until we reached the top of the steep climb.

"A wee bit different under the moonlight," Artair said. "I like it."

Light from a half-moon shone through a window at just the right spot to illuminate most of the table in the grand hall.

"Weel," Artair said. "The ghosts are kind tonight. Nice effect."

"It's so real," I said. "I mean, it's like it must have been."

"Aye. This was probably what it leuked like in here back in the days of Robert Stewart. People dinnae live this primitively anymore, but we like tae keep it authentic when we can," Artair said.

I took a cold breath and let out a foggy cloud. "I can't believe I get to be here."

"Aye. We're happy tae have ye," Artair said. "Now, should we go on up tae the battlements? That's where Tom said ye found the body."

"Sure," I said.

If I'd thought the narrow, enclosed, circular stairway was endless, disturbing, and claustrophobic during the daytime, I experienced a few moments of real terror as we climbed it at night. I didn't even know I was *that* claustrophobic before that dark, winding, and impossibly long climb.

Once up to the battlements, Tom grabbed my hand again.

"There's not much of a chance of accidentally going over the side, but I'd like tae keep hold," he said.

"Works for me," I said, still trying to catch my breath. I took a quick look over the top at the lights from the smattering of estates and the motorway. The moonlight glimmered off the river and I wondered if there could be a better castle-top view in all of Scotland.

Despite the sights, however, the wind was definitely colder and stronger up here. We'd be fine but shouldn't linger.

"Where was the body?" Artair asked as he shone the light down the long part next to the battlement wall.

"Over on the far side, past the middle peak that juts up, on the stairs, but I found the comic book over here. May I borrow the flashlight . . . the torch?" I asked.

Artair handed it to me. I shone the light in the space where I'd found the book. I was fairly certain I hadn't seen any other pieces of paper, but I'd been in some shock at the time. I moved the light slowly, up and down and around the space, moving a little farther with each pass. There were no other pieces of paper anywhere.

"I guess he might have had that paper on him still. Maybe. We didn't check his pockets or anything," I said. "Let's check the spot where we found the body."

Carefully, I led us to the other side of the roof.

"He didn't look like he was hurt," I said as I shone the

light down the now vacant stairs. "There was no blood." There was still no sign that something tragic had occurred.

"Let's just take a leuk around. Use your mobiles and we'll see what we can see," Artair said. "If there's any paper up here, we should be able tae find it."

I couldn't believe we hadn't thought of using our phones for light, but I welcomed the additional brightness. Though the roof was good-sized, much of it was taken up by the peaked part, so ultimately there weren't many places to explore. We shone our lights everywhere we could, up and down the stones beneath our feet, over the peak and down the jagged walls, still sturdy but broken down here and there.

There was no paper.

"It was a long shot, I suppose," I said after we'd explored the entire rooftop more than a few times.

"It could have blown off the roof too. Let me shine the torch and we'll see what we can see," Artair said as he swung the light out to the grounds around the castle.

We couldn't see much or very far away, but a copse of trees started back a good distance from the castle. The open ground we saw didn't have any obvious pieces of paper fluttering over or around it.

"Yeah, definitely a long shot," I said.

"Aye, maybe, or maybe it's too far away tae see now," Tom said. "Or, there's the other possibility. If Billy was killed, then perhaps his killer took the story with him."

I'd thought about that. If a killer grabbed the *Oor Wullie* after doing the evil deed and then took the story but not the book, maybe the story was the reason Billy was killed in the first place. If the written version was at least some of the same version that Gordon had told us at the bookshop, there might have been reason to take it. Perhaps someone thought it might make for some profitable blackmail. However, I didn't think Gordon had told us the whole story. Maybe the parts he left out had more to do with Edwin. Edwin was well known in Scotland, and his fortune was well known. His warehouse had become the stuff of legend. When so much was unknown, the possibilities seemed endless.

Artair turned away from the wall, the light from his torch skimming over the back stairway again.

Briefly I again saw the glimmer of the river in the light, but then realized what I saw couldn't have been the river. The river wasn't on the roof.

"Could I see the torch again?" I said.

"Certainly."

I moved it the same way and with the same speed Artair had. I caught the glimmer again, but it was brief and difficult to zone in on. I slowed down and did it again, finally homing in on the spot.

The glimmer was located on the side of one of the steps and seemed to be under the outer wall more than next to it.

I hurried down the few steps and crouched, aiming the light into a small open space that had been worn away over the hundreds of years.

"What do you see?" Tom said as he moved to the step behind me.

"I think . . ." I reached my fingers underneath and carefully unwedged the item and extracted it from its close space. "I found a knife. A dirk, I believe they're called."

"'Tis a lovely one," Artair said from the landing above us.

I looked at it a long moment and then up at Tom and Artair. "Do you suppose it has anything to do with Billy? Maybe I shouldn't have touched it. Maybe we should have called the police."

"I dinnae ken, lass," Artair said.

The dirk's dark wooden handle had been carved with overlapping shapes that I thought were Celtic but I couldn't be sure, and one single symbol in the middle hilt that had either been painted or stained a lighter whitish color. It wasn't a small weapon, not the five or six inches I used to think dirks would be. My experience in Edwin's warehouse taught me that most dirks were closer to a foot long. This one looked old. There was no sign of blood, or anything else gory for that matter, on it.

"Not certain how we could know," Tom said. "It could have been hidden under there for years, for whatever reason. Might be old and valuable, but maybe not."

"Wouldn't a dirk be part of an old Scottish getup?" I said.

"Aye, possibly," Tom said. "But William Wallace used a longsword. Dirks didn't come about until later, though I'm not sure when."

"I can research that," Artair said.

"I've probably ruined any fingerprints that might be on it, but we should take it to the police," I said.

"There's something else under there," Tom said as he angled his phone light under the wall. He moved to the step below me. "It's a piece of paper, but it's not in the exact same spot as the dirk was. It's small."

"Grab it, but try not to touch too much of it," I said.

Using his fingers and the edge of his phone, he had the piece of paper out a few seconds later.

"Is it the story or part of it?" I asked.

"No, it's a business card. 'Grizel Sheehy, Bagpipes,' and then an address in Edinburgh," Tom recited.

"That could have been dropped at any time. A coincidence," I said.

Holding on to just the edges of the card, Tom turned

it over. "There's something handwritten on the back. Armstrong." He looked up at me, a moon shadow over half his face. "Billy's last name, right?"

"Yes," I said. "We'll take that too."

"Aye," Artair said, his voice slightly shaky.

Tom and I looked up at him.

"There's not only a geal tae the air up here, it's becoming bluid gealing with the wee dirk and the last breaths of the dead man. Perhaps we should take our leave," Artair said.

I had no idea what Artair had said. I looked at Tom.

"Da thinks there's a chill to the air up here, blood-chilling. Spooky. You ready tae go?" Tom said.

"If there's nothing else under there," I said.

"Nothing else," Tom confirmed with another inspection.

Tom carried the dirk down the tight stairway and out to his car. He hadn't offered to carry it, but demanded it—in a sweet but insistent way. A part of me wanted to protest and tell him I could handle it. But a bigger part of me was okay with him carrying the weapon, particularly down that awful circular stairway.

"Do you want tae find some local police?" he asked after we were in the car and following Artair onto the motorway.

"No, actually I'd like to take it to Inspector Winters," I said. "Or at least an officer at that station tonight. I'll want to take pictures of the dirk and the business card before I turn them over though."

"Makes sense."

"I have a feeling they're important to Billy's murder. Maybe very important."

"I'll wager that you'll figure it out."

"I hope so," I said.

SIX

"Delaney, we've just received a pauchie of books," Rosie said from behind the front desk. She placed her hand on a canvas bag, making me interpret "pauchie" to mean bag, or perhaps pouch. Hector stood on all fours on the desk and panted excitedly in my direction. His love for books was almost equal to his love for the humans he hung out with, so I couldn't tell if his delight was because of me or what was in the pauchie.

I looked over at Hamlet, who'd stuck his head out from behind the back corner wall to greet me.

"A bundle," he said.

I nodded and smiled. "Am I late?"

Rosie was usually the first one into the shop. Lately and because of school obligations, Hamlet rarely arrived before I did, and on those infrequent occasions that he did he never seemed to have already delved into a project, which looked to be the case today.

"Not at all," Rosie said. "We were both wanting tae get tae work since yesterday was interrupted by that foul-smelling man." She shook off her irritation at Gordon. "Such a tragedy, that poor lad." She cleared her throat and sniffed once.

"Yes, it was. You okay?"

"Och, I'm fine. Just back and forth, upset and angry all night long."

I nodded and stepped to the desk, where I scratched behind Hector's ears. "You really had never met him before?"

"Gordon Armstrong? No, never met him, but I've heard many a story. He, Edwin, and Leith were a trio of troublemakers, I believe, back at university."

"I can't imagine Edwin as a . . . actually, I *can* imagine him as a troublemaker. Not in any sort of cruel way, but silly pranks maybe."

"Aye," Rosie said with a doubtful huff.

I shared a look with Hamlet. He lifted his eyebrows, shrugged, and then joined us at the desk. He looked much less Shakespearean today in jeans with no holes, and a dress shirt. He either had an appointment with a customer or a class presentation.

"I've never even heard any stories," he added. "I didn't like Gordon Armstrong, though, and I don't trust that he was honest about much of anything yesterday."

"Me either," I said.

"Och, no, I imagine Edwin didnae believe some of what he said either. I didnae believe him," Rosie said. She looked at me. "I'm sorry ye had tae find that poor lad's body. I'm certain that Edwin feels badly aboot that too."

"I'm okay, but I question Gordon's claim that the police told him that Billy had been murdered. I can't imagine why he'd lie about something like that, but I'd like to be sure. I might call the police on my own and ask. What do you two think of me doing that?" I said.

"Whatever ye want tae do," Rosie said.

"Let me know if I can help," Hamlet said. "And I'm sorry too. That had tae be terrible."

"I'm just sorry for . . . them all, I guess," I said.

"Aye," Rosie said.

Actually, I'd already been in touch with the police. After we found the dirk and the business card, Tom drove me directly to the station at the bottom of the Royal Mile where Inspector Winters worked. We took a bunch of pictures of both the weapon and the card, though we tried to be careful about additional fingerprints, before we took them inside. The night officer on duty took a brief statement from us and said he would take care of the items. He said he'd call Inspector Winters and that someone would be in touch soon. I thought maybe I'd get a call last night, but I still hadn't heard from anyone.

And, I *was* okay, but I was becoming attached to Billy Armstrong, albeit in a weird posthumous way. Or, probably more appropriately, I was speculating things about him, which was giving me a sense of knowing him.

"What books do we have?" I asked.

"Och, they're delightsome, for certain. Two different authors," Rosie said as she opened the bag and reached inside. She retrieved two hardback-bound green books that seemed identical until you read their titles.

"*Penny Wheep* and *Sangshaw*," I said. "Hugh M'Diarmid."

"*Mac*Diarmid," Rosie corrected my pronunciation.

"Of course. That's the Mac sound," I said.

"Aye."

"I've heard of him. Poetry. First editions?" I said.

Of great meaning in slight symbols, the heavily accented voice said in my head. I focused on it, hoping it would give me more; maybe where the words had come from or when they'd been written, or what words followed.

"Delaney?" Rosie said a moment later. She'd said other things too, but I'd missed them.

I blinked. "A poem titled 'Scotland.' He wrote a poem about Scotland that included the line 'Of great meaning in slight symbols.' Right?" I said.

"I dinnae ken," Rosie said. "I wouldnae be surprised."

"That's correct, Delaney," Hamlet said with a smile. "It's an extraordinary poem. He wrote a number of extraordinary poems. How did you know 'Scotland'?"

I shrugged. "Not sure. Must have read it somewhere along the way."

"Lovely," Rosie said.

Hector sat and looked up at me with suspicious eyes under today's blue-barretted fountain of bangs. I smiled at him and scratched his ears some more. The small dog seemed to question my bookish-voice moments more than anyone else.

"I don't know if that poem is in one of these books. I don't remember. We'll check. If not, I'll find the complete version. You'll love it," Hamlet said.

"Aye, weel, these are two first editions and they'll be sought after the moment Hamlet lets the world know they exist. Mr. MacDiarmid was a much-loved Scottish writer," Rosie said.

"They're in great shape," I said.

They were in great condition but faded with age. The simple, dark covers weren't badly worn, and each was emblazoned only with the book titles and an imprinted design.

I lifted the cover of *Penny Wheep* and my heart gave a tiny happy jolt. The title page was there and intact; in wonderful condition. It read: *William Blackwood and Sons Ltd. Edinburgh and London. 1926.* A further quick inspection uncovered a small smudge of something on the front board, but nothing else seemed to mar the book, other than a corner of the paper having been worn from the passing years. *Sangshaw* was in equally good condition.

"Extraordinary. Who's the other author?" I asked.

"Ah. Ian Hamilton Finlay," Rosie said.

"Never heard of him," I said.

"A bit of a rebel, I believe," Rosie said.

"Well, I guess he could be looked at that way. He was an intellectual, considered controversial at times," Hamlet said. "A voice of the 1960s in Scotland. You should read him."

"I will," I said. "Is it a valuable book?" I lifted the cover of *Midway: Letters from Ian Hamilton Finlay to Stephen Bann*. This title page was also intact, but I didn't know who Stephen Bann was either.

"I don't think so," Hamlet said. "Not much. We can research though."

Rosie's excitement regarding new acquisitions always showed in the pink of her cheeks. I'd become familiar with each of my coworkers' expressions of excitement when something new and wonderful came into the shop. Rosie's cheeks matched her name; Hamlet grew wide-eyed, quiet, and pale; and Edwin's eyebrows came together skeptically as he made a couple of harrumph noises while lifting covers and turning pages.

I looked at Hamlet. "You'll have a buyer quickly, you think?"

"Aye, for MacDiarmid, certainly. Don't know about the other one though. I'll put the word out today and let you know what I hear."

"I dinnae think ye'll have much tae do tae get them ready," Rosie said to me.

"I'll give them both a good look," I said with a forced enthusiastic rise to my voice. I loved my job, but today the ideas of researching the bagpipe shop and the pictures of the dirk on my phone were my real reasons for wanting to lock myself in the warehouse. Hamlet blinked at me.

"What broke yesterday? What were you sweeping up when I walked in?" I changed the subject.

"Oh," Hamlet said. "It was a small glass, left on the ground outside the front door. I suspected it was from Tom's pub or another one close by, but I wasn't sure. I brought it in tae either return it tae Tom or just throw it away, but I dropped it."

"Someone just left it outside the door?"

"Aye. Someone had too much to drink, I suppose. They probably walked out with it, got this far, and didn't want tae go back."

It wasn't an unlikely scenario, and it pinged something in my memory. I couldn't get to the specifics, but I filed it away for later contemplation. I had more important things on my mind, or so I thought.

Rosie reloaded the bag with the books and handed everything to me. I hesitated; I should have told Rosie and Hamlet about what we'd found on the roof of the castle. I should have called Edwin last night after finding them. I hadn't done either of those things, and I didn't want to quite yet, even if I didn't completely understand why.

"Thank you," I said.

"Aye. Lass . . . Hamlet, wait," Rosie said before I could turn around.

Hamlet and I waited as she took almost half a minute to gather her resolve.

"Do ye think that when Delaney calls the police, she should tell them that Gordon is alive? I ken ye've befriended an inspector, Delaney. Do ye think ye should tell him?"

I had considered it, but only briefly.

"I'm sairy," she continued before I could speak. "It's that I'm worried about Edwin and his decision not tae let the police ken about Gordon. I dinnae think it's a good idea. 'Tall."

I looked at Hamlet, who lifted his eyebrows.

"Are you sure he won't?" I asked. "In fact, maybe he has."

"No, he willnae," Rosie said. "He'd never do anything tae put Gordon Armstrong in jeopardy. Because he'd never do something tae jeopardize Gordon's wife—Fiona, I believe. It's just a guess though. I didnae ken Gordon or Fiona, but those stories." She shook her head.

"Were they stories about bad things, maybe illegal?" Hamlet asked, as he and I shared a look again.

"Just of their wild youth. Confusing at best at this point," Rosie said. "But I think the police should know aboot Gordon, that we ken he's alive."

"Confusing how?" I asked. If I was reading her correctly, there was more than wild youth or confusion to Edwin's stories.

"This is serious business. None of us want tae be involved," she said.

"Rosie, tell us some of the stories," I said.

"I cannae tell ye. I cannae. Not now."

It was the innocent victim, Fiona Armstrong, who I hadn't even met, that also kept me from wanting to tell the police about Gordon, but a trail of goose bumps had ridden up my arms when Rosie said we were dealing with serious business, particularly in the grave manner she'd spoken the words.

"Tell you what," I said, "let me see what I can figure out about Fiona first. I don't think the three of us are at risk of being in trouble with the law, Rosie, if that's your concern. Not yet at least." That wasn't the complete truth, but we were still at a point we could fudge the truth enough to get away with it. "Give me a day or so."

Rosie's mouth pinched as her eyes moved back and forth between Hamlet and me. She gathered Hector into her arms.

"Weel, awright," she said a moment later. "And I have tae add that I hope Gordon will not come back into Edwin's life ever again. I dinnae like that man, and I dinnae want him in our lives either."

"Edwin can't be influenced by Gordon, by anyone, Rosie," Hamlet said.

Rosie shook her head. "No, not influenced by. Hurt maybe."

"Rosie, please, what happened? What aren't you telling us?" I asked.

She pinched her mouth and shook her head. "No, I cannae, but I remember the fire that kil't Leith and supposedly Gordon. Edwin told me that he wondered if the fire had been Gordon's fault, meebe that he set it on purpose tae kill Leith, and Gordon accidentally died too."

On cue, some dark clouds moved over the sun and the light in the shop diffused, casting shadows in corners. The hair on my arms stood up.

"Why would Gordon have wanted Leith dead?" Hamlet asked.

Rosie shrugged. "I cannae be sure."

"Let me find out more about Fiona. Maybe we should tell the police that Gordon is alive, eventually, but I really wouldn't want to do that without telling Edwin first," I said.

"Aye," Rosie said, trying to hide her disappointment.

Rosie might tell the police herself, but I could see her struggle. She'd probably hoped for support from us. I felt a tiny bit bad that I couldn't agree with her yet, but I just couldn't.

Hector whined and looked around at the three of us. We all responded with appropriate pats or ear scratches, glad for something to break the tension.

Interrupting the moment, the front door opened with a noisy gust of wind. We all jumped and Hector barked

once. A cold pocket of air that smelled like home came
in with the well-wrapped woman, and I looked out the
front window to see if it was snowing. It wasn't even
raining, but the crisp scent had unmistakably reminded
me of a Kansas winter.

"Hello, can we help ye?" Rosie said as she sat Hector
back on the desk and then stepped around it.

The woman unwrapped a scarf from around her head,
exposing her short gray hair and strained green eyes. Her
wrinkled but regal face held high cheekbones, a short but
impossibly straight nose, and thin lips.

"I'm not here for a book," she said, her accent slight
and peppered with something other than Scottish but I
couldn't tell what. "I'm here to see Edwin MacAlister. Is
he available?"

I noticed that her green eyes were rimmed in red, and
her straight nose was raw. She'd been crying.

"Not at the moment. Can we help ye?" Rosie repeated.

"My name is Fiona Armstrong. I would be ever so
grateful if you would ring Edwin and ask him tae come
in and talk tae me immediately. He'll do as you ask if
you tell him my name. I . . . lost his number years ago."

I have no idea how we kept our cool, but we did, giving Fiona Armstrong no indication that we'd just been
talking about her, just like when Gordon came to see us
at the same time Edwin had been talking about him. It
seemed we'd conjured them. We did not immediately
mention that we knew that her son was tragically gone.

And that her husband wasn't.

SEVEN

"Why would she want to talk to Edwin?" I whispered loudly to Hamlet.

We were in the kitchen on the dark side, by ourselves, so there was no need to whisper, but it seemed like the right thing to do.

Hamlet shrugged.

"Wow," I said. "Rosie didn't miss a beat."

"She was very good." Hamlet frowned as he handed me the coffeepot. He grabbed some mugs.

"What are you thinking?" I said.

Hamlet hesitated. "At the risk of sounding unsympathetic, I don't trust any of them, Delaney. Fiona Armstrong included. They removed themselves from Edwin's life and now they seem to be trickling back in, and Billy Armstrong is dead."

"I can't imagine a mother . . . I can't even go there," I said.

"Aye, and though I'm suspicious, I don't want tae cause her any more pain either."

"We'll tread carefully."

"Aye. I hope Rosie does the same."

Hamlet had a sensitive, artistic soul. His empathy was one of his best qualities, though I had a feeling this might conflict with his intuitive suspicion and cause him some inner turmoil.

"Let's have a signal; if we think someone's getting too close to spilling some unwanted beans or Fiona says something we think needs extra attention, we can pull on an earlobe or something," I said.

Hamlet smiled and his concern dissipated a bit. "That works."

Rosie had been gracious to our visitor, guiding her to the back table and then sending Hamlet and me to gather coffee and whatever snacks we could find. We hadn't come upon even a stale container of biscuits but the coffee had been easy enough.

"I hope Rosie got ahold of Edwin," I said.

"We'll find out soon enough. Come on." Hamlet led the way out of the small kitchen.

———

"I got the news late yesterday," Fiona Armstrong said after another long and elegant sip of coffee. Without any prompting, she'd already given us a brief history of how she knew Edwin.

Fiona and Gordon Armstrong had gotten married even before they'd gone to university. They'd moved to Glasgow when Gordon graduated. Fiona hadn't finished school, but had devoted herself to being a mother to Billy, who had been born that last year at university. At one time, during those younger years in particular, Gordon, Edwin, and Leith had been "the closest of friends." Fiona and Gordon had moved back to Edinburgh about ten years ago, but she said she hadn't seen Edwin since their college years, not even at Gordon's or Leith's funerals.

I got the impression that *she* hadn't been as close to Edwin and Leith as Gordon had been, and from all indications after graduation the friendships between the three men lost steam. Obviously, something big had happened, but no matter how many times I interrupted and asked for further clarification, like Rosie, Fiona kept the secrets to herself. Hamlet pulled on his earlobe a couple of times when I asked the same question more than a few times in a row.

I was sure he was as relieved as I was when Rosie didn't tell Fiona about Gordon. If she truly didn't know about her husband being alive, the ramifications of that reality were huge and the delivery of the news would, in itself, be earth-shattering, and not something we were prepared to deal with. I wondered if Edwin would tell her.

No matter how often I looked toward the door, Edwin didn't come through it.

"My son was a grown man with a life of his own, but he was still my son," Fiona said. "I'm not sure how I'm supposed to survive this." There was no question in her voice. She wasn't looking for answers, just stating facts. Her voice hadn't cracked with emotion, but was heavy and deep as if she couldn't pull in the full amount of breath needed to speak. I didn't know if I'd be able to even speak in the face of such a tragedy, let alone pull myself together and seek out someone I'd known long ago. She must have thought it was very important to talk to Edwin.

None of us told her that Elias and I had been the ones to find her son's body. I was relieved; she might have other questions that I didn't feel adequate to answer at the moment.

Rosie patted Fiona's hand and nodded sympathetically. "I wish I could say something that would help."

"Fiona," I said, "I'm sorry to even ask, but have the police told you if there was foul play involved?"

She nodded. "Yes, he was murdered. Their words

were 'cause of death was a blunt instrument to the head.'
They're investigating. But that's why I'm here. I mean,
well, I guess I mean what I already said. I just need to talk
to Edwin. I wonder about Gordon and Leith too. Were
their deaths really an accident or is there something the
police missed? I just need to talk to Edwin."

"What information would he have that might help
you?" I asked.

"It's too difficult to explain, so much history, but
Edwin will understand."

"Did you tell that to the police?" I asked.

She blinked. "No."

"Why?"

"I wanted to talk to Edwin first." She lifted a tissue to
her nose and dotted its corners.

Fiona fell into her thoughts for a moment, but then her
eyes locked onto the books on the shelf across the room.
Her sad, somewhat bewildered expression hardened.

"Books," Fiona said with a huff. "They were such a
big part of our lives. Oh, I suppose that's a stupid thing
to say. There's not a life that isn't somehow touched by
books, is there?" She stood.

Rosie, Hamlet, and I looked at each other before we
stood too. The space wasn't big, so even if we hadn't
wanted to we all stayed close to her as she faced the books
and ran her finger across a middle row.

She turned and faced us. "They were all writers back
then. Did you know that?"

We shook our heads.

"No, Edwin never mentioned that he held any interest
in writing," Rosie said, her tone full of genuine surprise.

"What did they write?" I asked.

"Everything. They met when they were part of the
university newspaper."

"Edwin, a reporter?" I said. More perplexing was that

Gordon had been a reporter, but that was unfair and judg-mental.

"Aye," she said with a smile. "They wrote news stories, short fiction stories, other silly things too. I believe they tried a novel once. They were very talented." Her smile faded. "When they worked together. They weren't as talented when they worked apart. It was sad actually, how they couldn't function as well as individuals as in a group."

"Was it . . . fun?" I said.

"It was . . . perfection. Until it wasn't."

"What do you mean?"

"Nothing. Not really," she said. She smiled sadly at me. "We all knew Edwin had money, and we all knew he'd open a bookshop someday. It was a good day for him when this became real. This is my first time in the shop. It's lovely."

She was a contradiction. She spoke kindly of Edwin, but she hadn't seen him for years. She wanted to see him for reasons she wouldn't tell us. Whatever fallout had oc-curred, she'd either forgiven him or now needed some answers and was willing to overlook any remaining bad feelings. Or Hamlet's intuition was correct and there was reason to be suspicious of this elegant woman who'd just lost her son.

I listened for the bookish voices.

I heard something, but the words I heard were garbled, as if more than one voice was speaking at a time. Con-fusion. Even my subconscious was getting mixed signals.

"What did Edwin do before he had the shop?" I asked before anyone had a chance to notice I'd checked out for an instant. "What did your husband do? Their friend, Leith?"

"Edwin traveled the world for a while. Gordon became an accountant, and Leith opened a pub."

"Aye, Edwin traveled," Rosie added.

"And then opened the shop?" I asked.

"I believe so," Rosie said.

Hector had been following close at my heel. He whined and I picked him up.

The front door opened and we all turned toward it.

"Goodness, it's cold out there," Edwin said after he made sure the door had shut behind him.

He stood a moment and gave a cautious glance to the back corner of the shop. If he'd worn a hat, he'd have held it in front of himself, like an unsure suitor. This was the first time I'd witnessed a look of youthful uncertainty on his face.

A moment later, though, his air of confidence and caring returned and he said, "Fiona, I'm so sorry about Billy, so very sorry."

They closed the space between them and Edwin pulled her close as she began to cry quietly into his shoulder.

I listened for my bookish voices again, and got only silence this time. I looked at Hamlet but couldn't read what he was thinking.

"Come along. Please come with me tae my office. We'll talk there," Edwin said.

The rest of us watched Edwin guide Fiona up the stairs and over to the dark side.

"I don't suppose there's any way to eavesdrop?" I said when the far door clicked shut behind them.

Hamlet smiled. "I don't think so."

"I wish," Rosie said. "I'm sairy for the lass, but I'd like tae hear what she has tae say tae Edwin. I dinnae trust her as far as I could throw her, and I really do think we need tae talk tae Edwin aboot letting the police know about Gordon."

"I agree," Hamlet said.

"Let's talk to Edwin later," I said.

"Aye," they said together.

I retrieved my bag from behind the front desk. It seemed heavier, but that was probably my imagination. I also grabbed the pauchie with the newly acquired books.

"Let us know if you hear anything," Hamlet said as he stepped toward the back table and his current project.

"Aye," Rosie added.

"I will," I said. "What are you thinking, Rosie?"

"I dinnae ken, so many things, I suppose," Rosie said. "But something's agley."

"Awry." Hamlet added the translation from the back corner.

I nodded before I made my way up the stairs. After I went through the door, I stopped briefly on the landing to see if I could hear anything from Edwin's office. I didn't even hear muffled sounds. His door was shut tight.

I knew I wouldn't hear anything from the warehouse as I went through its red door and locked it behind me, but I'd sure make an effort to listen extra hard.

EIGHT

Once I was locked behind my own red door and had confirmed that I wouldn't be able to hear anything from Edwin's office, I lost myself in my own world. It was easy to do, and the way I worked best.

I knew I needed to give attention to real work tasks first so I placed the books on the desk. It didn't take long to confirm they were all in extraordinary condition, and unquestionably first editions. I also confirmed that they were all fairly valuable, but that the MacDiarmids were the most valuable, and would probably garner a few thousand dollars each. I was curious about both of the authors, their lives and adventures, but I decided to research them at a later time.

Before I told Hamlet to spread the word that they were available, I would check with Edwin about whether he wanted to put them for sale in the shop, sell them in a Fleshmarket Batch auction, or perhaps donate them to a library. He donated more books than he sold, but that was one of the secrets he'd asked me to keep. One of the good secrets.

The Fleshmarket auctions were gatherings with a secret group that Edwin had been a part of for years, and the items put up for auction were usually extremely valuable. Some books were bought and sold by the group, but I doubted the ones currently on my desk would go that way; they weren't worth quite enough. Edwin had told me I could make the decisions as to whether to donate or sell, but I still wanted to consult with him first, particularly if he was in the shop.

After I made sure the books were safely stored in a bottom drawer of the desk, I pulled out my phone, scrolled to the pictures of the dirk, woke up my computer, and Googled.

Dirks became the weapon of choice for Scottish High-landers sometime in the 1600s. William Wallace had definitely used a broadsword, but I couldn't let go of the idea that the dirk had something to do with Billy Arm-strong.

Dirks wouldn't have been used in Wallace's time in the late thirteenth and early fourteenth centuries, and Billy's clothes, the leggings, and the tunic-like shirt were authentic representations of the time period, at least from what I knew and what Edwin had told me. Billy wouldn't have been allowed to carry a broadsword to Castle Doune. Had he thought he needed a weapon, something less conspicuous? He might have dropped the dirk before he could use it, or the killer had snuck up on him.

I knew of tests that could be done on both the wooden handle and the metal blade to determine its age, but I didn't have the equipment. I didn't know what the police could do to determine its history but I had taken many close-up pictures of the handle and the blade.

Maybe there was another way.

Another few keystrokes later, I found "The National Museum of Scotland." It wasn't far from Grassmarket and I'd already made a friend there who worked Satur-days. I clicked through to confirm the museum hours and made a plan for tomorrow.

I didn't work Saturdays, unless I wanted to. I usually wanted to, but maybe it would be okay to take at least part of this Saturday off. Maybe Elias's cab would be available.

I remembered that he was dropping by late this afternoon, and I promised I'd have a book ready for him to give to Aggie for her birthday. I wondered briefly if he'd be available today too as I returned to Google.

I started with "Fiona Armstrong, Scotland." I found two immediately; one a teacher in a local primary school academy, the other a member of a punk rock band that had a gig tonight in Glasgow. I found a few others as I went through the first available pages, but I didn't find anyone matching the Fiona Armstrong I'd met earlier today.

Per the business card that we'd found with the dirk, I then searched for "Grizel Sheehy, Bagpipes, Scotland" and got a hit immediately. A link to her shop came up first thing and I clicked through.

A picture of the front of the small shop with Grizel next to the window filled the home page. Probably in her late thirties, she wore her hair big and bleached and her lipstick bright red.

"Not the look I think of when bagpipes come to mind," I said to myself. "But Grizel does it well."

As I read quickly through the site, I learned that bagpipes had been a part of Grizel's family's life for a long time. Since the late eighteenth century, her ancestors had made, sold, and/or played bagpipes. I decided she was particularly talented when, after clicking on a video of her playing "The Bonnie Banks of Loch Lomond," I teared up.

I concluded that she seemed fun, like someone who would be the life of the party but mature enough to make sure everyone got home okay. If he had the time I was sure Elias would drive me by the shop.

I glanced at my watch. It was already after four. As usual, while inside the warehouse I'd lost track of the passing hours. I powered down the computer and gave the big room my habitual all-over inspection as I stood at the door. I switched off the light and made sure the door was locked before I headed back over to the other side to talk to Rosie and Hamlet, and hopefully Edwin.

I climbed the stairs and hesitated on the top landing. I still couldn't hear anything from Edwin's office. Though I doubted they were still there, I tiptoed down the hallway just to see.

The office door was wide open, and there was no one inside. The light had been switched off, but I couldn't resist switching it back on.

I stood in the doorway and peered into the small room. Edwin had often commented that his office was always open to us.

To be fair, he didn't keep much inside it. The warehouse used to be his office. When he gave me the space, he took only a container full of pencils and a couple notebooks with him, and still spent plenty of time with me and all his things inside the secret room.

I would never rummage around in the drawers of someone else's desk, but as I glanced inside I hoped to see some remnant of the conversation he'd had with Fiona. There was nothing of course, but I couldn't help a quick, closer check for some clues. I stepped inside.

The ever-present container of pencils was on the corner of the desk, but there was also something I hadn't noticed before: a diploma on the floor against the wall. Hadn't he been leaning in that direction when I'd followed him to his office the day before? Had he been looking at it? Where had it been before then?

Half of the frame was hidden behind a low file cabinet. I stepped closer and crouched.

I pulled out the dusty frame and held it so I could read the details. It looked as if Edwin had earned a bachelor of science in biology. I smiled as I thumbed off a dusty corner of the glass. I should have known he'd chosen to become educated in something he wouldn't need in order to own and run a bookshop. Maybe he'd planned on doing something scientific, but I didn't think so. He probably just wanted to get the degree.

If I'd just looked over the diploma as it sat on the floor I might never have noticed the small sticker at the bottom right corner on the glass. I had to angle the glass and hold it closer to read the raised embroidered letters on the sticker. "SP" on one line, "EC" below it. That was all there was. Red letters over a gold background. It was off-kilter, giving me the impression that it was unofficial and didn't have anything to do with the diploma itself. It struck me as something he'd put there because he had the sticker and just wanted to stick it onto something.

But the letters must have some meaning.

"Hmm." I pulled out my phone and snapped some pictures of the diploma and sticker. I knew a few people I could ask, including Edwin if he were still around. He wouldn't care that I'd looked at the diploma. I didn't think so, at least.

I replaced the frame just as my phone buzzed.

"Elias," I answered. "I'm on my way back around."

"Aye. 'Tis cauld oot here."

I didn't disconnect as I hurried toward and down the shop side's stairs. Was the front door locked? Most of the lights in the shop were off, but a lamp had been left on at the back table. The sun had only recently set.

"Hamlet? Rosie? Edwin?" I said as I held the phone away from my mouth. No response. It wouldn't be the first time they'd closed up the shop and gone home while I was working in the warehouse, and they *had* gotten there early today.

As I passed by the front desk, I grabbed a piece of folded paper that had my name written on it.

"Come in," I said as I opened the door. The wind had stopped but it was definitely still "cauld."

I kept the sign turned to "Closed" as I relocked the door and opened the note.

"Ta, lass. Where's everybody?" Elias asked.

"Uh, they closed the shop," I said as I skimmed the note. "Didn't want to bother me in the back. Hamlet might be back later, but they decided the weather would keep most customers away this evening."

The note also said that Edwin left before Hamlet or Rosie could talk to him. He mentioned that he'd be in tomorrow. In Rosie's scribbled handwriting, she ended with *Talk to the police about Gordon?*

I still wouldn't do that until I talked to Edwin. I didn't think either of them would either.

"Aye? Weel, makes sense to me." Elias rubbed his arms.

"Let's find that book for Aggie," I said, warding off the chills that crept up my arms. Was I cold or had the empty shop put me out of sorts? Most likely both.

Aggie and Elias owned and rented out two guesthouses. They lived in one of their small cottages behind the guesthouses and I rented the other one from them. I hadn't seen the insides of the guesthouses until about a month after I'd been in Edinburgh. I'd been surprised by their fancy, elegant furnishings, and shocked by how spotless they were. Aggie was a fine housekeeper in her own home, but she was tireless when it came to the guesthouses. There wasn't a speck of dust or a wrinkled piece of fabric in them. The weekly rent they charged visitors was three times what I paid monthly, but it was well worth it. Aggie would clean every day if visitors requested it—on the guests' schedule. When the houses were unoccupied, she still cleaned them.

She would also cook for guests on occasion. I'd helped with a few meals, and Aggie's attention to detail and Scottish authenticity were unrivaled. Cooking in a kitchen with Aggie as head chef was a stressful but exhilarating experience. Perfection was required.

But when it came to books, she would fall quickly in love with almost anything. I'd watched her take a book, hold it in both hands, and then cradle it over one arm. She always traced an outline around the edge of the cover with her finger before lifting it to look inside. I never saw her open a book without awe overtaking her features. I'd told Edwin about the ritual and he'd asked to be included sometime when she was given a book.

"I've been thinking," I said to Elias.

"Guid. I need some ideas."

I walked to the desk and opened the top drawer. I'd put a book aside a few days earlier.

"It's not expensive. It's an old copy, but certainly not a first edition. It's in good shape." I handed it to Elias.

Edwin had told me to give the book to Elias if he wanted it, but I knew there would have to be some money exchanged for Elias to feel like it was a proper birthday gift for his wife.

Elias grabbed a pair of reading glasses from the inside pocket of his jacket. "*The History of David Grieve* by Mrs. Humphry Ward," he read aloud. "Mrs. with her husband's name?"

"I know. It might set Aggie off a bit but she loves seeing progression and where things once were. Mrs. Ward is Mary Ward, and I think Aggie would find the novel interesting. Well, in a dated way of course, but I think it would introduce her to an author she might not have read yet. I'm pretty sure this would be new to her."

"Mary Ward?"

"Yes, she was a British writer who died around 1920. She was born in Tasmania to a literary family, her father a professor, her uncle a poet, and her husband, Humphry, was also a professor, I believe. Her father became part of the Catholic Church when she was five, which caused some trouble. The family had to leave Tasmania for Ireland. She was educated throughout Britain and wrote a number of books and articles. Despite the use of her husband's name, I think she was a strong woman."

"Aye. The novel is aboot?"

"A bookseller who ends up falling in love in Paris, though it's not necessarily a happily-ever-after book. There's some struggle, regarding both marriage and religion, which probably very well reflected the time and almost certainly the author's family's situation." I'd prepared the quick synopsis.

Elias gave the book some good, long, chin-rubbing contemplation, but I knew he'd be happy with the choice.

"Sounds perfect, lass. Thank ye," he said a moment later. "How much?"

I quoted a price I thought would be acceptable to everyone. In the end we both felt good about the transaction, and Edwin would be thrilled too.

After we finished, I debated taking Elias over to Edwin's office to show him the sticker, but that didn't seem like the right way to handle it. I pulled out my phone.

"Elias, do you know what this is?" I scrolled to a picture of the diploma and held it toward him.

"Looks like part of a diploma or a government document maybe."

"It's a diploma, but I mean this little part here. Do you know what the sticker is? It's on the glass."

"SPEC? No, I have no idea. Meebe Aggie will."

"Good point. I'll ask her." I put the phone back into my pocket.

"Anything more about the lad we found on the roof?" he asked.

"Oh, yes, lots more. Let's go, though. I'll tell you on the way."

"Awright. Dinnae tell Aggie aboot the book, lass. It's tae be a surprise. Dinnae tell her aboot the party either. She might not like being surprised, but she'll be happy when she sees who's there tae celebrate with her."

"Mum's the word," I said. Elias had told me every day since he'd been thinking about the party to keep quiet about it. It wasn't until next Friday evening, but I didn't mind a week's more of reminders.

"And yer coworkers will be there too?"

"I think so." Who knew what the passing of another week might bring though?

"Guid."

"Hey, any chance your cab is available for a few extra minutes right now, and then tomorrow morning?"

"Aye, ye've got some investigating tae do?"

I smiled. "I guess I do."

"Are we meetin' anyone atop a castle?"

"Not this time. Feet flat on the ground. Just a little research. I can take the bus tomorrow but it's more fun in the cab. And with you."

He smiled. "Aye. Weel, the cab and I are both at yer service, lass. I'm glad tae help, and glad tae watch yer back."

"Thank you."

I hurried back over to the warehouse for my bag, and then turned off all the lights and locked the doors again. I sent Tom's pub a farewell glance before I jumped into the cab. Friday was one of his busier nights, even with bad weather. I wouldn't get a chance to see him until Saturday afternoon, or maybe even Sunday, and I suddenly missed him.

The pang of longing I felt didn't pass unnoticed. It was unsettling, this romantic stuff, particularly when more than just a wee bit of emotion got attached to it. Or to him, as the case may be.

Och, I thought to myself. *Och.*

NINE

The bagpipe shop sat on a corner, toward the bottom of and around another corner from the Royal Mile. The simple sign above the front window, "Bagpipes," said it all. Elias parked the cab across the street from the shop, and he and I got out.

"What now?" he asked as we stood on the busy sidewalk.

"I don't know. It looks like the shop is still open." I lifted myself up to my toes. "I can see Grizel inside. She's talking to someone but I can't see them."

"Let's just go in. We can pretend tae be in the market for some bagpipes," he said as we moved out of the way of a passing couple.

"Can you play?" I asked.

"No, but Aggie can."

It was cold and we were in the way of too much pedestrian traffic.

"Okay, let's go in," I said.

We crossed the street, dodging traffic there too, and then stopped outside the front window.

"I've never seen so many bagpipes and so much plaid in one place in my entire life," I said as we looked in.

"I need tae take ye tae a parade one of these days," Elias said.

I smiled and then watched Grizel. She spoke, using her hands a lot, to a man whose back I could barely see.

"She doesnae look happy," Elias said.

She looked adamant, forceful, maybe a little angry.

"I'd like to just ask her some questions about if she knew Billy," I said. "But I might lie first and tell her we're there to look at some bagpipes for Aggie. How does that sound?"

"I'll play along with whatever ye say." Elias shrugged.

I had told Elias that we'd confirmed that Billy had been murdered. I shared with him that I'd gone back to the castle with Tom and Artair because they were curious, and Artair was working on something regarding the castle for the university so we'd let the appropriate people know about our after-hours excursion.

We'd been lucky to find the dirk and the business card. Elias was so proud of me for taking the items to the police so quickly that he didn't seem to catch on that I might have left something out. I did not tell him about Gordon and the circumstances behind his false death and Leith's real one, nor about the alleged handwritten story. I still might, but not yet.

"Let's go," I said as I took a step toward the door.

"Hang on," Elias said. "The customer is coming oot."

Elias was gifted at looking like he belonged anywhere or behaving casually without garnering suspicion. I wasn't such a natural and even with the cold air I felt warmth from my cheeks as I blushed from my efforts at being covert.

However, this time even Elias couldn't keep us camouflaged.

"Delaney?" Inspector Winters said after he came through the door. Grizel came out behind him.

He put on his uniform hat, something I would have recognized if he'd been wearing it inside.

"Inspector Winters, hi!" I said.

"Hello."

Even if he hadn't been a good police officer, he would have had a good idea why Elias and I were there. He sent me a brief impatient look before he said, "You here tae shop for some bagpipes?"

"Aye," Elias said. "My wife Aggie loves to play."

Grizel smiled. "That's fabulous! Come in, come in."

"Aye," Elias said before he smiled at Inspector Winters and then followed Grizel inside. He stood in the open doorway and looked at me. "Ye coming in?"

"I'll be right there," I said.

"Aye, take yer time," Elias said before he shut the door.

"You got the things I brought by. I'm glad," I said to Inspector Winters.

"I did. Thank you. I was just on my way tae find you," he said. He nodded toward the shop. "You were curious?"

"Yes, very," I said. "What did she say? Did she know Billy Armstrong?"

"See, and I thought you'd probably already beat me here," he said with a half-smile.

"I've been busy." I wanted to add that he must have been busy too if it took him this long to talk to Grizel.

"Aye," he said. "Me too, and unfortunately the officer on duty last night didn't think that your visit was something urgent. I'm sorry tae have tae say this, but next time you find things that might turn out tae be evidence in a murder, maybe you should just call me, or not drop things off with one of our less competent officers."

"I'm sorry, Inspector Winters, I didn't think . . ."

"No, you did the right thing. I'm bothered by our poor protocol, but I'm trying tae catch up quickly. Do you have some time we could discuss what you know?"

"Of course, let me get Elias and we can come to the station if that would help."

"It would be best if you didn't ask Grizel any questions. I know you sometimes don't believe me that the police are on the case, and after the . . . lack of professionalism I witnessed in our department today, I wonder a wee bit myself, but we are on the case. I am. I'll share with you what I think is appropriate, but let me do the hard parts. All right?"

"Of course."

"I'll wait right here. We can take a table in there," he nodded toward a small café a couple doors down, "and I'll send you on your way quickly."

"I'll be right back," I said before I disappeared into the shop.

Elias was already charming Grizel into a good mood. The two of them were laughing and speaking so quickly with interspersed Scots that I would need an interpreter if we stayed too long.

"Lass, we were just discussing Ms. Sheehy's contribution tae the Stirling William Wallace monument activities. She was telling me how one time a piper fell doun a hill and rolled head over bare arse all the way tae the bottom. The bag saved the lad's harn, but the cords nearly took off an ear." Elias shared a smile with Grizel.

"'Twas a sight tae behold," she said as she patted what I thought was a happy tear at the corner of her eye.

"I bet." I smiled. "I'm Delaney, a friend of Elias's. We did come in to shop for some bagpipes for his wife, Aggie, but I'm afraid we need to go now. May we come back later?"

"Certainly! Come back any time. I'm here all the time, when I'm not in Stirling. . . ." Her smile retreated. "No, I'm here all the time now."

"Is everything okay?" I asked.

"Och, all is weel. Sairy." She forced a smile and then looked out toward Inspector Winters. "The police yer friend?"

"He is. Kind of. I reported a stolen computer a few weeks ago," I fibbed. "Since we all ran into each other he was hoping to give me an update on the case."

"Oh, I hope they found it!"

"Me too," I added with too much enthusiasm. I cleared my throat, hoping she didn't really think about how weak my story was.

"Weel, I hope tae see the two of you again," she said.

"You will," I said.

"Thank ye, Grizel. 'Twas a pleasure," Elias said.

"Nice tae meet ye, Elias," she said as they shook hands.

I'd seen this before. Elias was one of the best at finding things he had (or things he made up) in common with just about anyone, but it seemed he and Grizel were most definitely cut from the same cloth. Or tartan.

As we left the store, we met Inspector Winters outside, and then traveled to the café. There was not one moment when I could have asked Elias about whatever he and Grizel discussed, but he did manage to send me one secret wink that told me that he had a little something.

After we were seated in a corner and coffees and biscuits had been ordered, Inspector Winters began the conversation that felt much more official than it probably was. I didn't think he knew how to ask questions without trying to get you to confess to something.

"You and Elias found the body?" he began. We nodded. "Tell me the details. Why were you two at the castle?"

He was the first one to ask why, but I still didn't give him the real reason.

"I had some time off. Elias had told me about the castle and he was available." I shrugged.

Elias nodded.

"And there was no sign of violence? No blood?" Inspector Winters said.

"None," I said.

"No," Elias said.

"It was horrible, but my first thought wasn't murder. Was he murdered?" I said.

"Aye. Blunt force trauma to the head. He didn't bleed, wasn't even cut, but . . . yes, he was killed," Inspector Winters said. "You didn't see anyone else there until the police got there? Is that correct?"

"Yes," Elias and I confirmed, and I told him about stopping the German tourists.

"And you didn't find the dirk and business card until that night?"

"I found it," I said. "I was with Tom and his father, Artair. Artair works at the University of Edinburgh library and he's helping some other folks research if there's a castle buried under Castle Doune. Officially the castle was closed, though it wasn't locked up, so Artair called the appropriate people to give them a heads-up, I guess. I can give you his and Tom's contact information."

"Aye. I don't think I'll need tae call them, but it wouldn't hurt to have the information. Was Artair curious?"

"No, it was more about me being curious. I knew the police had been there, but my visit with Elias had become a blur and I . . . just wanted to see it again."

"In the dark?"

I shrugged. "Schedules and all."

Inspector Winters rubbed a finger under his nose and looked down at his notepad a moment. He looked up again and said, "Delaney, does this have anything tae do with Edwin, with the bookshop?"

And then I really lied. I didn't like lying, and lying to

a police officer was not only illegal, but pretty stupid too. But I couldn't think of a way to tell him the truth without it ultimately leading the police to Fiona Armstrong and her illegally obtained insurance money. I made a silent deal with myself, that even though I lied now, I would talk to Edwin as soon as possible, maybe even talk him into talking to Inspector Winters himself.

"No," I said.

He believed me. Mostly. I think he was always slightly doubtful of anything to do with Edwin.

"Other than the body and then later the dirk and card, you saw nothing suspicious, either time? No other people, no items?" he said.

"No," I said. "Just the Germans, later."

He seemed to have no interest in his coffee or the biscuits the waitress had put on the table.

"Inspector Winters, what do the police think?"

"I don't really know," he said as he closed his notebook and glanced at his watch. "This isn't my case, but since you brought by the dirk and the business card, you put me into the middle of it a wee bit—that's not a bad thing. I'm sorry if it sounded like it. I just want tae help the other officers as much as I can, as accurately as I can."

I swallowed a gulp of coffee and nodded. "Did you check the dirk, the card, for fingerprints?"

"We did, and there's nothing on them that tells us anything. I don't even need to fingerprint you—there's nothing that could help at all."

"Do you know anything about the dirk?" I asked.

"I know that when the case is solved and if it isn't used in solving the case, it will be yours. You found it."

"Can you tell anything about it? Where it's from?"

"My crime people are testing it. Do you think it's valuable?" Inspector Winters asked.

"I have no idea, but I know someone who might be

able to help. He works at the National Museum of Scotland."

"I'll keep that in mind. For now, I'll let my people look at it."

"And Grizel? Did she know the victim?"

"She did, very well, it seems." Inspector Winters lifted his coffee cup and took a sip.

"Mind if I ask how?" I said.

"They dated. The victim recently broke off the relationship," he said. His eyes shadowed briefly as if he'd said too much.

"Do ye think she kil't the lad?" Elias asked.

"I don't know. She has no real alibi for the time of the murder, but I've got nothing that I could use tae bring her in for further questioning. Do either of you?"

"No," we both said.

"Aye," Inspector Winters said. "And you need tae keep in mind that it's better that way. A murder's been committed. It's good tae be wary."

"We will," I said as Elias and I nodded together.

"I hope so."

"Well, thank you both. I'm sorry I didn't call you sooner." Inspector Winters stood and put his hat on again. "I've got tae go. Call me if either of you think of something important tae the case."

"We will."

He stepped away from the table, but then turned around again.

"You haven't asked for the victim's name," he said.

I suddenly realized this whole coffee-and-chat time had been orchestrated so Inspector Winters could see if I would say the victim's name. I didn't think anything had been released on the news and I had already thought to be careful. If I knew who he was I would have much more explaining to do. Keeping a lie going is exhausting.

"I didn't think it was my business, but what was his name?" I asked.

"William Armstrong," Inspector Winters said. "His father was killed a couple of years ago in a fire."

"That's terrible," I said.

"Aye," he said. "Coincidences are funny sometimes though. As I was looking through the file for Gordon Armstrong, the victim's father, I came upon Edwin's name. The police had talked tae your boss back then. Do you know anything about that?"

"Nothing at all, but I'll ask Edwin," I said.

"Aye," Inspector Winters said before he turned.

"Inspector Winters," I said, causing him to stop and pause a second before he faced us again.

I continued, "Is there any chance the blunt instrument that killed William Armstrong was a bagpipe drone? That's what they're called, right? The wooden parts of a bagpipe."

"If there is a chance, it's ever so slight, but I'll be looking into everything," he said.

"Thanks. And, I have no doubt. I mean, that you'll be looking into everything."

I smiled and Elias tipped his cap before Inspector Winters left. He and I might get along so much better if our relationship hadn't been built around murders.

I breathed a heavy sigh. "I'm not very good at this."

Elias laughed. "On the contrary, lass, I think ye're verra guid at it. Come along, let's get home tae Aggie. I'll tell ye what the bagpipe lass said that I thought was interesting."

I couldn't wait to hear.

TEN

We started the morning with a hearty Aggie breakfast. She cooked for the guesthouse visitors and had made sure to whip up a couple extra helpings of beans and eggs, the parts of a Scottish breakfast I liked the best.

I'd learned that it's safest to stay away from anything in the UK that includes the word "pudding." It's not the same sort Americans are used to. I once tried black pudding, and it was only after I said I didn't like it that someone mentioned it is made with pork blood.

As we helped Aggie in the kitchen, we discussed Grizel Sheehy and the thing she said that made her seem suspicious to Elias.

"Aye," Elias said, "Ms. Sheehy said that she was oot of sorts because the police officer came tae visit her 'so soon.' I asked, trying tae sound casual, if meebe she thought the police officer would stop by *later*. The look she gave me was as if she ken she'd been caught almost saying something she didnae want tae say, and then she started tae be delightsome and funny."

I didn't find this brief conversation enlightening but Elias was good at reading people. Aggie was even more dubious than me.

"I dinnae think that means much of anything, Elias,"

she said. "Ye might have been looking for something tae find suspicious."

Elias shrugged. "It's guid tae notice everything."

"That is true," I said.

I also asked Aggie about the sticker on the diploma, SPEC, and her answer only made me more curious to understand it fully.

"I cannae be sure, lass, but ye ken what a secret society is?"

"Yes. Well, they're never something I've studied or been a part of, but yes I've heard of them, particularly in a university setting."

"Aye, SPEC sounds like something I remember from a long time ago, something aboot a university secret society. I cannae remember the details, but if I remember it at all, there must have been some news about it at one time. I'll try tae think on it."

"I'll try to do more research too," I said.

———

The weather had surprised us all. It was still cold, but the sky was surprisingly clear, bright blue with no sign of rain. I was sure it was in the forecast, though; it was always in the forecast.

The National Museum of Scotland wasn't far from The Cracked Spine, less than a mile, on Chambers Street right off Candlemaker Row. I'd walked to it a number of times from the bookshop.

The museum was actually two museums. The older part was built back in the 1800s and a newer part had been completed in 1998.

The older part was a half-block-long wide brownstone building with a wide and inviting stairway to the front doors and two rows of arched windows. The newer part was made of lighter brown stones as well as a few pastel-toned additions. The two sections somehow worked well together. It was my opinion that everything worked well together in Scotland; modern sat comfortably beside old and weathered. I was one of the few people who even liked the Parliament building; this was not a popular Scottish opinion. I kept those thoughts to myself most of the time.

Both of the buildings were modern on the inside, vast and full of thousands of items that would take me years to discover. I'd learned that it was best to visit these sorts of places on my own when I was planning to see the exhibits. Not everyone liked to linger as long as I did.

It was on one of my first visits that I met Joshua, a young university student from Paris who was intelligent beyond his years. He couldn't have been more than eighteen, but he was well on his way to his PhD. He'd seen me peering at some old railroad pictures and had spotted a soul mate of sorts. He was a lingerer too.

"This is a tame adventure," Elias said as he pulled the cab to a stop in front of the museum. He'd managed to snag an available parking space, which I took as a sign that our parking Karma was already working hard this morning.

"Not one for museums?" I asked.

Elias scratched under his nose. "Weel, ye like them."

I laughed.

"I've been in this one a number of times," he said. "Probably more than I ever thought I would."

"Aggie likes them?"

"Aye."

"We're just going to talk to a friend, but he has a secret office."

"Ah. That sounds guid."

Joshua's office was away from the other administrative offices in the museum, hidden by the secret door.

He'd explained that it was all that was available when he started working there. At first he was bothered to be separated from everyone else, but now he enjoyed the privacy, and the oasis he'd created inside what used to be a storage closet. He was afraid of being discovered by visitors who seemed to immediately tune into the fact that he could answer almost any questions they might have, thus he required a secret three-knock code to enter.

I led Elias through the first floor and then looked around furtively before I knocked three times on the camouflaged door. Elias took the hint, turned, and made himself a little wider as he sniffed once authoritatively and then kept an eye on our sixes.

The door cracked open a few seconds later.

"Delaney! Wonderful! Always good to see you," Joshua said with a wide smile and a welcome pull of the door.

"Hi, Joshua. Sorry for just dropping by. Do you have a minute?"

"Always a minute for you."

Joshua had a tiny crush on me. He didn't hide the fact, and I'd already made it clear that I was too old for him, even if he and I could probably fill every moment together with long museum visits that would never bore either of us. He'd taken it well.

"Thank you. This is Elias," I said.

"Any friend of Delaney's . . . come in."

Joshua's French accent was almost nonexistent when he spoke English. He was fluent in six languages, seven if you included his self-education in some Scottish Gaelic, a language that fewer than one hundred thousand Scottish folks still spoke, most of them in the Highlands. He had also mastered the accents that went with each language. One of his coworkers told me he could also play any musical instrument, but I hadn't witnessed that talent yet.

"Thank you," Elias said as he removed his cap once we were ensconced in the small office space.

The utilitarian furnishings—a steel gray desk, matching chair, two sparse visitors' chairs, and one long file cabinet—were overwhelmed by a giant computer screen that always seemed to display something with more numbers than anything else. I'd inquired about the numbers once. Joshua had said that spreadsheets were important to his research but he never explained the details of that research, even when I asked him to.

One yellow notebook and an array of different-colored ink pens were always in the general vicinity too, but the notebook was always turned facedown when I was in the room.

Elias and I wedged our knees into the sliver of space between two chairs and the desk as we sat down and Joshua sat on his side. He slid the notebook and pens to the far edge and leaned forward on his elbows.

"How can I help today?" He smiled his boyish smile, his brown eyes lighting up. His long arms and legs would probably fill out someday and he'd become better proportioned and transition from cute to handsome. He pushed up his modern black-framed glasses.

"I have this," I said. I pulled out my phone, turned it toward Joshua, and scrolled through the pictures.

Joshua whistled. "A dirk! Beauty."

"Aye, 'tis a nice one," Elias said, his voice lined with a hint of admiration for the nerdy guy who knew a good weapon when he saw it.

"What's your question?" Joshua asked.

"Can you tell me about this one specifically just from the pictures? Is it old or new? Anything," I said.

"May I?" he asked as he reached for the phone.

"Of course," I said.

"There are ways to date things like this," he said. "If I had it, not just pictures of it, I think I could get access to the machines in the basement, but . . . ah, yes, this is what I was looking for." He held the phone closer to his squinting eyes and enlarged the picture on the small screen.

A second later he placed the phone on the desk and his fingers moved to his keyboard, where they clicked away at warp speed.

"As I suspected," he said, sounding very pleased with himself. "Here, look at this."

Elias and I leaned forward as Joshua picked up the phone again. He scrolled and then enlarged a picture.

"It's some sort of insignia," I said. "I think."

"It is." He swung the giant screen around, and we saw the same insignia, in a much larger version. "It's the mark of the manufacturer, Scotland Exports. A maker's mark."

"Something tells me Scotland Exports wasn't around a couple hundred years ago," I said.

"No. In fact they began their business," he turned the screen so he could see it again, "back in 1963, here in Edinburgh. They're still in business, though they moved up to Inverness."

"I see. So, it's not old, or historical."

"No, but it's a nice treasure. If they're still making them, I imagine the quality has gone down since 1963. This is probably a good dirk. I'd like to see it in person."

Joshua's instincts were probably another reason he and I had forged such a quick friendship. My bookish voices were to me what old things' vibrations were to him, inanimate objects that spoke to things deep inside us. I hadn't told him about my bookish voices, but I hadn't doubted him when he'd told me about his own acumen.

"It wouldn't have been used by a William Wallace

reenactor?" I said, not meaning to test his knowledge of the time period, but just to confirm mine.

"Oh, no, probably not. Those folks used swords, big ones." Joshua leaned back in his chair and tented his fingers authoritatively. "Best guess is that dirks came along around the mid-1500s. A couple of its precursors were swords, of course, daggers, and things called ballocks. You can find a few on the Web and see what I mean. Nevertheless, there was a time when Highlanders were always prepared for a fight, either with England or other Scots who wanted to take their land. They were always dressed for battle, which basically meant they always had a weapon on them. Dirks were much handier than swords. It's a bloody but spectacularly beautiful history."

"Aye," Elias said.

"Where is this one? How did you get access to it?" Joshua asked me.

"We found it on top of Castle Doune. It was wedged into a space at the bottom of a stone wall up on the battlements."

"I can't think of any reason there should be a dirk at that particular castle. That's a great place to make such a find though. I'm a tad bit jealous. What were you doing up there?"

"Just visiting," I said.

Joshua nodded.

"Elias and I went. Next time, we'll let you know. Maybe you'd like to go with us," I said.

"I'd love that." His eyes brightened. "Anyway, this could still mean something interesting. I mean, why would it be there? Even if it had been put or lost there recently, or fifty years ago, why? Could it be something as simple as someone dropped it? I don't know. It's curious, to say the least."

I couldn't muster much interest in anything other than

Billy Armstrong's possible attachment to the dirk, but I nodded agreeably.

"Not something the museum would want?" I said.

"Only if we were preparing some sort of exhibit regarding the weapons specifically as a sample of a slice—pardon the pun—of history. Your boss might like it though. What did he say?"

I sensed he was fishing for some information. I tried not to miss a beat. "I haven't had a chance to show it to him yet."

"I bet he'd like it. I'm sorry it's not one that might have actually been used in battle," Joshua said.

I smiled. "Not your fault. And thanks for taking the time with us."

"Always a pleasure." He drummed his fingers on his desk and bit his bottom lip.

"What?" I said.

"I have a question, Delaney."

"Sure."

"I've heard talk about your boss and a room full of treasures."

He had been fishing. Though I didn't like lying to the sweet young man who'd just helped me, I was well practiced in this particular lie. I laughed. "I've found that there are lots of rumors about Edwin. He's much better known than I would have ever guessed before I moved here. Don't believe everything you hear."

"And not a thing aboot what ye read," Elias added.

"That's certainly true. All right then. You'd tell me if you came upon such a room, wouldn't you, Delaney?"

"You'd be the first," I said.

Elias and Aggie and Tom knew about the warehouse, but as far as I knew they were the only ones outside The Cracked Spine who had been invited in. The Fleshmarket Batch group had some ideas about it, but I knew Edwin hadn't invited even his closest confidants from that group inside. Many of them had asked me about its possible existence more than once.

Aggie had told me that the room, jam-packed as it was, had made Elias nervous and claustrophobic, but had been magical for her. I got the impression she'd like to spend more time there. Edwin told her she was welcome whenever, but she'd been too shy to take him up on the invitation. And probably too busy too.

Tom had visited it just once, feeling like he'd gone somewhere he shouldn't. I thought he'd become more comfortable with it over time, but he hadn't.

"Excellent. Lunch sometime soon?" Joshua said as Elias and I stood, filling the small space way too full.

"Of course," I said. "Next week looks good."

"I'll call you."

As Elias and I descended the outside stairs and were far out of Joshua's range of hearing, Elias said, "He kens ye have a lad in yer life?"

"He knows. Tom has even gone to lunch with Joshua and me before. I think it's a harmless crush that will abate the second he meets someone his own age who's as interested in the things he's interested in."

"A lass his age interested in that sort of stuff?" Elias whistled. "That might take a miracle. A rare thing that a lass his age is impressed by things such as dirks and auld museum pieces."

"They're out there, and I like to think they're worth the wait."

Elias laughed. "Aye. Tae be sure. Where tae now?"

I looked at the time on my phone. We hadn't been inside the museum for very long and it was only midmorning. The details about the dirk hadn't been totally disappointing. At least I knew it wasn't an overly valuable item, which was something to file away, but I still sensed it was tied to Billy Armstrong. I had a number of ideas on how to explore that possibility, but with a clear blue sky and a full open day ahead, one thought overrode the others.

"How about a big trip?"

"Where tae?"

"Stirling Castle, and the William Wallace monument."

"Aye?" He rubbed his chin. "Certainly, I s'pose. Aggie doesnae need my help around the hooses. In fact, I think she's pleased tae get me out from underfoot today. Let's go."

We climbed into the cab and Elias drove us out of town. I hadn't noticed when I'd become so used to riding on the left side of the road, but as he steered us out of Edinburgh, I realized that I didn't have one moment of wrong-side-of-the-road panic.

ELEVEN

"There, it looks like they're going to start a skit. Or, I mean a reenactment," I said as I pointed down toward the clearing and pulled my scarf up over my mouth against the cold wind.

"Ye want tae ask if any of them knew the lad who was killed?" Elias said.

"I do. We can watch their skit, and talk to them afterwards."

"Awright."

We moved down the short slope and into a narrow but long natural clearing. The wind was much less biting here. Elias and I blended in with the eager audience. Other than my trips to the Castle Doune, every time I'd visited a place for tourists, I'd seen plenty of them. Today was no exception.

A man who was dressed the way Billy Armstrong had been dressed stepped into the middle of the performance space. It was more than his clothes that reminded me of the dead man. His wide shoulders, big frame, and longish hair were similar too, though his hair was more brown than auburn. He held a longsword, but I didn't think it was real. There were no dirks in sight.

I didn't want to take the time to climb the 246 steps

up to the top of the Wallace monument today, but it was certainly impressive; a tall stone tower. The views from it were spectacular—all Scottish rolling hills—but from the top they must be even more stunning. I'd probably want to linger inside it too; best not to have Elias, or maybe anyone, with me for that.

Along with us and the other onlookers, a group of actors stood to the edge of the skit, observing the ones who were performing. It was almost like looking at a group of old-time clones. Except for slight variances in their ages, body sizes, hair color and length, they looked similar; they all wore the costume.

The actor who introduced himself as William Wallace and the others who joined him proceeded to dispel almost every idea the movie *Braveheart* had presented.

Wallace had fought valiantly for Scotland's freedom from England, that was true. But as I'd already learned from Tom, the event that spurred his rebellion was likely the murder of his father, not of a wife. When the actor said this, a rumble spread through the audience and he gave us a moment to let the fact soak in.

As the skit continued, other actors joined in to reenact a battle that had taken place beside a bridge. I heard Elias sniff once. When I glanced at him he quickly ran his finger under his eye and then gave me a brief smile.

I put my hand on his arm and told myself not to choke up too. Scottish pride had been slowly seeping into my own bloodstream.

Finally the main actor told us about Wallace's death, and it was as gruesome as the movie had said. Wallace had been hanged, drawn and quartered, eviscerated, and beheaded. The manner in which the well-rehearsed actor spoke about Wallace's unfair trial and death struck my already tender emotional chord, and I sniffed and wiped a tear too.

"He's a fine lad," Elias said. I couldn't tell if he was talking about the actor or Wallace, or both.

As the reenactment came to an end, the main actor pulled back from the others, who stepped forward to answer questions.

"I don't know where he's going." I nodded toward the main Wallace.

"Aye. He might be done for the day," Elias said.

"Come on, I'd like to talk to him," I said. I *needed* to talk to him specifically. His performance had roped me in maybe, but I knew I had to try to catch him.

We hurried around everyone else and caught up with the actor in the parking lot just as he was about to open a car door.

"Excuse me," I said.

He looked around and then said, "Yes?"

Even with that one word, I noticed the absence of the Scottish accent he performed with.

"Hi," I said as we stopped next to him. "My name's Delaney and this is Elias."

"Okay," he said. "Can I help you?" He looked behind us. "The others usually stick around for questions."

"Right. I . . . thanks," I said. "I have a question for you specifically if that's okay."

"Sure," he said, but didn't really mean it.

"William—Billy—Armstrong. He was . . . I mean, did you know him? Do you know what happened to him?"

"I did know him, and I know he's dead." He reached for the car door again. "Who are you?"

"Aye," Elias jumped in. "Could we buy ye a cup of coffee? I believe there's a coffee shop up in the monument."

"I don't think so. I really do need to get going."

"Just a moment of yer time," Elias said. "The coffee will be my treat. We willna keep ye long."

I had no idea how Elias's words convinced the man to come with us, but they did, and a few minutes later my landlord was walking up to the counter to get the coffees as the reenactor and I sat at a table in the corner.

"I'm Delaney Nichols. I work at a bookshop in Edinburgh, but I'm from the U.S.," I said.

"I'm Carl Hooper. I'm from California." He sent me a conceding smile and extended his hand over the table. "I thought you might be from home."

"Small world," I said as we shook.

"Scotland's home now, but it's always nice to talk to another American."

"I get that." I'd been homesick for Kansas and my family a time or two, but nothing that had lasted more than a few minutes. I felt a little guilty about that. I cleared my throat. "How'd you get the job of portraying William Wallace in Scotland?"

Elias joined us, doled out the coffees, and sat on Carl's other side.

"My wife. She's from Inverness," Carl said. "We moved here a couple years ago so she could be closer to her family. I'm a schoolteacher in Edinburgh."

"The acting gig doesn't pay, does it?" I interrupted.

"No, it's volunteer, not a full-time thing. Well, we get lunch and coffee and a drink or two sometimes but that's it. We don't really know what Wallace looked like except that we're pretty sure he was big and powerful. I love history; I found this group, or really, this group found me. One of the old guys that runs it, Oliver, approached me one night at a restaurant, said I was the right size and asked if I would be interested. It's been fun." He shrugged. "Normally, I'm only out here a couple evenings a week, but after Billy's death—may he rest in peace—I was called in to cover this performance and a few others. He's . . . he was the main one, the main Wallace. He loved it." Carl cleared his throat, but I wasn't sure if it was because of emotion or for a pause of respect. "We have others to cover, but most of the others you saw today are just here to answer questions. The old guys are scrambling for actors. You knew him, Billy? Do you know what happened to him?"

"We didn't know him." I looked at Elias. "My boss knew his family, was friends with his father years ago."

"Your boss? Did he ask you to come out here?"

"Kind of," I said before taking a gulp of the coffee. "Carl, do you guys ever have any occasion to use dirks?"

"The weapons? No, not at all. We have some dulled longswords, just props, that we use, but nothing smaller than that. Why?"

"Just curious," I said.

"We heard that Billy was probably murdered. Was he stabbed?" Carl said.

"No," I said. "I did hear he was murdered, but not stabbed. The question about the dirk was just my curiosity."

"I feel terrible for his family," Carl said. "His father didn't seem all that friendly, but I'm sure he's devastated."

"I thought his father died a couple of years ago," I said.

"Oh." Carl's eyebrows came together. "I might have the wrong person. Maybe. Or maybe I'm confused. As a group, the actors get together socially sometimes and I thought that his father was there one night a few months ago. Maybe not. Billy didn't want him to stick around. I remember Billy asking him to leave. I must be mistaken, though, if his father died a while ago." Carl scratched the side of his head and then took a sip of coffee.

"What did the older man look like? Where? What pub?" I asked.

Carl shrugged. "I don't remember the pub exactly. Somewhere in Old Town, but the guy I thought was Billy's dad just looked like an old weathered guy, wrinkled face, gray-white hair. Small; yeah, I remember thinking that Billy didn't get his size from his dad. I don't remember much more than that."

"Billy wanted him to leave?" I said.

"Yeah, it was weird. He was embarrassed maybe, or . . . I don't know. Billy seemed to not want anyone to notice him, maybe that was it. I didn't ask him about it. He was bothered enough."

"Did you know any more about Billy, like what he did with his free time?" I said. "He must have had a job somewhere?"

"I thought he must have had one too, or enough money that he didn't need one. But I never learned what he did. I think I asked a couple of times, but he never answered. We weren't close though."

"Did Billy get along with everyone around here?" Elias interjected.

"I don't know. He was the king of the reenactors. There are a couple other really good ones, but he was by far the best. There's no real jealousy, though, because it's all for fun."

"Did he have any issues with anyone?" Elias asked.

Carl took a sip of his coffee. "Yeah. Well, there was an issue recently."

"What happened?" I said.

"I told Oliver what I saw and he called me last night to tell me I'd be able to talk to the police this evening at a meeting we're having. I don't feel like I should say too much until after that. I had a feeling it had been murder, with the police and everything."

Elias and I shared a look.

"We're not the police, Carl, but it wouldn't hurt to tell us what you observed. We're here for a friend, someone who cares very much about Billy's family. It must not be a huge deal or you would have called them instead of waiting until tonight. You can trust us. What happened?" I said.

Elias and I were quiet and still as Carl thought a moment.

"I think it's a stretch to think that she had anything to do with murder, but there was that bagpipe lady that he dated. She had an odd name . . . that's right, Grizel. He broke off the relationship, I guess—it's hard to know what really happened because, like I said, I didn't know Billy well—but last week, he and Grizel—she has a bagpipe shop in Edinburgh—anyway, they were arguing. All I heard was her saying something like he didn't deserve her anyway. It was uncomfortable and I tried to mind my own business. But . . . oh, man, this is tough to say now, but she was hysterical and . . . Billy slapped her. It wasn't a hard slap, but that doesn't matter. She ran off and I don't know what happened after that, but I told Oliver when I saw him about an hour later and he seemed pretty upset."

"I see," I said. "Do you suppose Oliver was going to ask Billy not to be a part of the reenactments anymore?"

"I do. Oliver didn't tell me that, but Billy's behavior wouldn't be something the old guys would tolerate."

"When did this happen?" I asked.

"Tuesday."

"And Billy hadn't been back since?"

"No."

"This happened here?" Elias said, and Carl nodded. "Why was the lass here?"

"For a few weeks, we had a bunch of bagpipes adding to the atmosphere. It was amazing, truly. She was in charge of the bagpipers, I guess. I don't know if she and Billy met here, but I'm assuming so. They were together a bunch when she was around and he wasn't acting. She'd watch his performances. Actually, it was kind of cute. Until it wasn't."

"You didn't talk to Billy afterwards?"

"No, and Grizel packed up her bagpipes, told the pipers to go home, and then left. Like I said, it was uncomfortable."

"Is Oliver here?" I asked.

"I didn't see him today."

"Can I get his number?"

Carl thought, and scratched the side of his head again. "I don't think so. That feels weird." He paused. "We do have meetings every couple of weeks, and they're always held in a pub. That's what I was talking about earlier. There's a meeting tonight. It's a public place I suppose, and apparently the police are going to be there."

"Where?"

"Tonight, it's King's Wark. The meeting starts at eight." Carl glanced at his watch. "I really do need to go."

"Sure," I said. "Thanks for your time."

"Thanks for the coffee."

"Ye're welcome," Elias said as we all stood. "And, lad, it might not hurt tae give the police a call about what ye saw. They might need the information before tonight even."

"Right. You're right. I should have done that. I will do that today," Carl said.

Elias and I nodded. As Carl turned to go, a pack of cigarettes fell from what must have been a hidden pocket under his belt.

He picked them up and quickly hid them with his hand. "Talk about bad behavior. The old guys know I smoke, but I'm not supposed to let anyone see me with these. Bad for tourists to think William Wallace had such a vile habit. Sorry about that."

"Your secret's safe with us," I said.

He moved quickly now as if the cigarette patrol were close on his heels, but when he reached the door, he paused, turned around, and came back again.

"This just came back to me. Billy had a tattoo on the inside of his wrist." Carl looked at Elias. "SPEC. Is that a Scottish thing? I wondered."

"Not that I'm aware of," Elias said.

"All capital letters?" I asked.

"Yeah. My wife didn't know what it was either. When I asked Billy about it, he turned his hand over quickly and wouldn't say a word. In fact, he wouldn't even tell me that it was none of my business or anything. He just went silent."

I gave Carl my mobile number. I didn't think he wanted to give me his, but he did anyway. I promised I wouldn't bother him. He said it was good to meet us both and that he'd enjoyed talking to someone from America before he left for good this time.

I watched him through the window as the wind lightly blew his long tunic. I thought about bagpipe sellers, dirks, and tattoos, and how, if in any way at all, they were connected.

Every man dies, but not every man really lives, William Wallace said in my mind.

I didn't know if I'd read the words in a book, heard them in a movie, or perhaps seen them here at the monument sometime today. They might have been written on something in the coffee shop. I smiled at the voice that had sounded nothing like Carl's. Perhaps I was really hearing the man himself. No better place to find my ghost, I thought.

"Delaney?" Elias said.

"Yeah?"

"Ye're getting better at this. Asking questions, getting answers."

"That was the American connection."

"Meebe," Elias said. "Why did ye need tae talk tae him specifically, not one of the others?"

"He was the main guy today. I figured the main guy knew the most, I guess. Just a feeling I had. What did you think of what he said?"

"I'm not certain. Do ye think the lass, Grizel, had anything tae do with Billy's murder?"

"I have no idea. Did you notice any dirks, souvenir or otherwise, in her shop?"

"No. And I leuked."

"Want to see if Aggie wants to go out to a pub tonight?"

"We'll ask her. Come along. The clouds are finally coming over. I think the rain's on its way. Let's get back tae Edinburgh."

TWELVE

It turned out that neither Elias nor Aggie could join me at The King's Wark, but Tom could. I got the impression that my landlords bowed out when they realized Tom was available, on a Saturday night of all things. They frequently extricated themselves from the room when Tom showed up at my house. We were used to their less than subtle ways of encouraging our relationship.

Tom and I could see right through them but we agreed that it was all working out just fine.

However, we had run into a few moments of discomfort of another sort—for Tom, not for me—over the last few months. And those moments had nothing to do with Elias or Aggie.

Edinburgh was a large city, but not quite large enough to keep all of Tom's previous dates and girlfriends hidden from us. When I first mentioned The King's Wark as the place I'd like to go and why, he quickly tried to hide a cringe.

"What?" I'd said.

"Well, it will be fine, but I'd rather we went almost anywhere but there."

"A girl?"

He nodded. "Aye. More long term than anyone but you."

I'd asked for honesty. He'd been good about it.

I smiled. "I'm the longest term?"

"Aye, you and I have been together longer than I've been with any other woman. That's a ridiculous thing tae discuss, but there it is. And I have no plans tae put the record tae the test."

"Not ridiculous at all. So what's keeping us together, I wonder?" I said.

"Your smile. Among other things," he said seriously, not playing into the banter I thought we might be about to engage in.

I nodded and smiled, staying silent so I wouldn't risk ruining the moment.

Now, though, as we made our way through the pub, I began to wonder if this might be more than just slightly uncomfortable for Tom. I watched a really pretty woman behind the bar give us the stink eye.

"I'm sorry, Tom, we don't have to do this," I said.

"It's okay, lass." He winked at me and led us to a small table on the perimeter of what I'd thought looked like the group of William Wallaces. There must not be many secrets in the group if they were so willing to meet in such a public place as a pub, or maybe their meetings were strictly social.

I didn't spot Carl or any police officers, but the group that had taken over the few tables and the rest of the space in the corner was made up of broad-shouldered men, most of them with longish hair. They didn't look so much like clones in their street clothes, but there were more of them in the pub than had been at the monument, and the sight of them together was still unusual. The other pub customers sent frequent curious glances over in their direction.

Tom and I sat at a table close to the group with the hope of blending into the beautifully carved woodwork and the river view out through the pub's front windows. We thought our hope was thwarted when the woman who'd been behind the bar approached the table, a fiery march in her steps.

"Tom?" the woman said much more quietly than the melodrama in her expression would dictate.

"Kate, hello," Tom said. "I know this is a bit unorthodox, but my friend heard about your pub and really wanted tae see the inside of it. She's from America and I wanted tae be the one tae show it tae her."

Kate blinked at him and then at me. Her long, straight, almost-black hair was pulled back into a neat ponytail. The lack of frizz, even with the rainy weather, made me want to smooth my own hair but I resisted. Her blue eyes almost matched Tom's. Given a few moments, she finally seemed more perplexed than angry.

"I see. I'm Kate." She extended her hand.

"Delaney."

"Aye? Like the name of his pub?"

"Yes."

She smirked. "Weel, welcome to Scotland. It's been some time since I've seen Tom. Forgive my surprise." She paused, took a deep breath. "I'll warn ye now, though, he's not one for settlin' doon. Be prepared tae have yer heart broken if ye've any idea for something long term."

I nodded.

She held up her left hand. "I married a few months ago."

"Congratulations," I said.

"Congratulations," Tom said.

I thought he might add something like "lucky guy," but he knew better. The trait about Tom that I'd come to cherish the most was his sincerity. He didn't say things he didn't mean one hundred percent. He wasn't sarcastic. He might have dated more than his fair share of women, but he'd never lied to them, according to the information I'd been given. His honesty was sometimes too brutal, I guess, but never left anyone in the dark as to where they stood in his life. I realized it was a trait I cherished because it hadn't been used against me yet. If that day came, I might rethink how much I admired it.

"Aye. He's a wonderful man." She blinked at Tom again. "Can I get ye both some whisky?"

"Delaney?" Tom said.

"I'll just have a pint," I said.

"I'll have the same," Tom said.

"Aye. It will be right over. I willnae be yer waitress, so I'll bid ye a good evening. I suppose."

"Thank you," Tom and I said together.

After she made it back to her spot behind the bar and my tensed shoulders relaxed, I said, "That wasn't terrible."

"I knew she'd gotten married or I'm not sure I could have come in tonight. It was an ugly breakup. I'm sorry tae rehash it even in that wee way in front of you."

"That wasn't much rehashing. I can't decide if I want to know about all your breakups or if it's just better to stay in the dark about them."

Tom smiled and then looked down at the tabletop a moment before he looked back up at me, his eyes prompting the butterflies in my stomach to flap their wings.

"They're not all as bad as that, Delaney. I have dated a few women. I can only wish I would have met you sooner, then the list wouldn't be quite so long."

I smiled, and blushed.

"Now," he said as he nodded toward the group of big men that seemed to have convened their meeting, "let's see what we can hear."

One of the older gentlemen in a thick white sweater began. "We have serious matters tae discuss this evening, lads, and I'm pleased with the turnout. Thank you all."

He glanced at the men, at Tom and me, and then out to the rest of the pub before angling his body as if to cut off everyone but the reenactors from hearing what he had to say next.

"This was the best we could do for privacy, considering the request from the police came just yesterday. Some officers will be here soon and there are rooms in the back that can accommodate private interviews. I'm sorry, but it was either this or the police station, and we chose this."

Tom leaned over and said quietly to me, "They must all know about Billy, huh?"

"Carl knew he was dead, but wasn't sure it was murder."

"This is much less intimidating than a police station."

"It makes me think that the police might not be truly suspicious of anyone here though."

"You never know," Tom said.

The younger men, all (I counted in my head quickly) twenty-three of them, listened intently. I spotted Carl; he caught my eye and nodded before he turned his attention back to the gentleman at the front.

Another older man, this one in a plaid shirt, stepped up and continued.

"As you all probably now know, Billy Armstrong was killed. We haven't shared the other part because the police asked us not tae until this evening—we were told that he was hit over the head with a blunt instrument, murdered. That's all we know. We are sorry for his loved ones."

The men's faces showed their disbelief and confusion, but unless one of them stood up and confessed, there would have been no way to pinpoint any of them as suspicious.

The man in plaid continued. "You don't have tae talk tae the police if you don't want tae. None of you are under arrest, which is a part of why we're here, not the police station, tonight. They asked us tae do this, but we didn't make any promises on any of your behalves; neither did we vouch for any of you. It's your choice."

None of them stood up to leave.

"We're getting company," Tom mumbled as the man in the white sweater approached us.

"Hello," he said as he pulled out a chair and sat. "Name's Dodger. The young lad, Carl, told us that we'd probably have a redhead from America come tae see us. You set off his alarms if you know what I mean. We have nothing tae hide, but I guess I'd like tae know why you're interested in us, interested in asking Carl about Billy."

"I'm sorry. I should have come and talked to you when we first got here. Yes, I am interested, but the reasons are difficult to explain."

"Please try."

With an encouraging nod from Tom, I continued, "It begins with an old friendship, a secret, and then the murder of Billy Armstrong. All of this involves people I know and care about, but I don't feel at liberty to tell you their names. I wondered if anyone knew much about the man who was killed, but it's mostly because my boss knew his father years ago. My boss is mourning this loss deeply. He would like some answers but isn't spry enough anymore to gather them on his own. Are you their supervisor?" I asked as I nodded toward the reenactors.

"I'm one of the board members. They're volunteers. Myself and a few others work together to keep things organized. We're part of a Scottish Arts board and we were assigned this task about ten years ago. We've enjoyed it so much and our tourist numbers keep increasing so we're still here."

"Sounds like you enjoy it."

"Aye. Very much so. It's mostly a group of good lads who enjoy what they do."

"Was Billy a good guy? I heard about . . . his argument with the woman with the bagpipe shop, Grizel."

Dodger rubbed his chin. "Aye. Well, I can't tell you much about Billy. He was a strange lad but not in a fearsome way. He was quiet. He loved being William Wallace. We thought sometimes a wee bit too much."

"How's that?" I asked.

"We wondered if he had a job outside of volunteering for us, but he would never tell any of us. We worried about his real self sometimes. How did he behave outside the skits? Billy was a loner from what we could see. The incident with Ms. Sheehy was beyond unfortunate. She says he didn't hurt her, but that was behavior we couldn't tolerate even if she didn't want the police tae know about it. Billy seemed to understand we couldn't have him stay. I'm sorry he was killed. He will be missed, but I can't believe that anyone from this group had anything tae do with his murder."

"You don't think it devastated him, being told he couldn't do the thing he loved to do any longer?" I said.

"If it did, I didn't see it. He knew there was no negotiation. He didn't argue."

"What about Oliver, or Carl?" I asked.

Dodger looked over to the man in plaid, who was talking to only one of the reenactors now.

"What about them?"

"Carl reported the incident to Oliver, right?"

"I believe so."

"Could that have caused them all some bad enough feelings to bring about something violent?"

"Lass, not that I could say. I still don't know all the details of Billy's murder, but I can't see how either Carl or Oliver would have wanted Billy dead. They might have been angry at him, embarrassed by him, but not filled with murderous intentions."

None of the reenactors, including Oliver, were paying us any attention. I wanted the chance to talk to all of them individually, but that seemed an unreasonable request. Even asking to speak to them as a group seemed too weird, and somehow a giant overstep.

"There are three of you who run this group. Where's the third one?" I asked.

"I'm not sure, lass, but I don't think he's a killer either. We don't always all make it tae the meetings."

"May I ask his name?"

Dodger thought for a good long half minute before he said, "Ryan is his first name."

I nodded, knowing I wasn't going to get a last name. "Did you ever see Billy with his father?"

"Not that I remember. Lass, I'm sorry I don't have more tae tell you. Tell your boss tae talk tae the police. They might be sympathetic regarding his old friendship. I think I need tae be with the lads. I suppose you could stay for the police, but that might be odd. Up tae you." Dodger stood so Tom and I did too.

"Yes, it might be odd," I said, but my attention was on Oliver, as he had moved next to a table against the far wall and studied a piece of paper he held.

Dodger shook Tom's hand, my hand, and told us to have a good evening before he walked back to the others.

"What are you looking at?" Tom asked me.

"That piece of paper looks important," I said.

"Oh, aye, maybe."

One of the reenactors approached Oliver. All I could see were the reenactor's jeans and red sweater from behind, but I could see Oliver's face as he looked up at the reenactor. Something was wrong, upsetting.

I stepped away from the table, but I still couldn't see the front of the reenactor as he guided Oliver toward a back room.

"Looks like the police are here," Tom said.

I looked toward the three approaching officers, who were serious in their demeanor. They spoke over the bar to Kate, who sent them a disappointed frown before she reached to a bell nailed to a post and rang it.

"We're closing early tonight," she announced. "See ye all tomorrow."

The officers seemed to know who they needed to keep in the pub, and the three of them lined up as if to form a barricade to keep the reenactors from leaving. I couldn't think of anything to say to them other than the fact that Gordon was alive, and I still hadn't talked to Edwin.

Besides, I was beginning to think that Gordon being alive had nothing to do with his son's murder. Too much had happened at the William Wallace monument over the last week of Billy's life, and I thought that somehow his dismissal from the role he so loved must have led to his murder. The facts as I knew them didn't make a lot of sense, but it was likely that the police had done their job well, and they were on the right track.

I hoped.

As awkward as it was, Tom and I both sent parting nods to Kate as she stood behind the bar, fists on her hips, the frown on her face even deeper.

I was glad when we were out of the pub, and I took in the fresh, cold air.

"Did you see Oliver go to the back room?" I asked.

"No, I saw him looking at the paper," Tom said. "But then I noticed the police. Did I miss something good?"

"I don't know. I couldn't tell who he went into the back room with. They all looked so much alike."

"Important, you think?"

"I have no idea," I said as I shook off the wonky feeling that had come on when I saw the look on Oliver's face. "No more murder investigation tonight though. How's that sound?"

"I like that. I have some ideas how we could fill the rest of the evening."

"Sounds perfect."

THIRTEEN

Unfortunately, things didn't go as we hoped.

As we drove toward my cottage, a surprise turn of events that had nothing to do with The King's Wark, Kate, Billy, or distractions with Tom brought the romance to a screeching halt.

Tom's employee Rodger called just as we turned onto my street. A pipe had burst and Tom's pub was flooding.

With a quick stop on the street in front of the guesthouses, and an even quicker kiss, Tom let me off at the curb and told me that he was sorry and that he'd call me in the morning.

It wasn't even eleven o'clock as I made my way around the guesthouses and Elias and Aggie's small cottage. Lights were off in the McKenna cottage, but that wasn't a surprise. They were early to bed and even earlier risers.

I played over the events of the day and decided that even if I didn't see Edwin soon, I needed to call him and ask about SPEC.

The bookshop's Sunday hours were listed on the door sign as: Sunday—sometimes we're here, sometimes not, but give us a ring if it's something urgent. And then

Edwin's phone number. There hadn't been many Sunday book emergencies, but a few over the years.

I'd go in tomorrow anyway and get some work done, with the hope that Edwin would be there and I wouldn't have to call him. He sometimes liked to hang out in the warehouse with me on Sundays and share stories.

My thoughts had moved so far away from the present moment that it took me a long minute to notice the things on the top of the small coffee table only a couple yards inside the cottage's front door. In fact, I smelled them before I saw them.

A bouquet of roses.

"Oh," I said quietly.

By nature Tom wasn't the most romantic guy but he liked to give me flowers. I liked that too.

I didn't have to read the card to know the roses were in celebration of the anniversary of our first date, though I had to count back to realize that we'd now been a "couple" for five months. I'd received this same bouquet every month.

My mobile buzzed.

The text said: *This evening didn't go quite the way I'd planned. We'll have a do-over.*

I typed back: *The flowers are perfect. Happy Five Months! Hope the pipe gets fixed. We'll talk tomorrow.*

Practical romance. It worked just fine.

I was one tired bookshop employee/murder investigator, though I'm sure I was still smiling as I drifted off to sleep.

———

Once I started looking, I was surprised by how many dirks I found on the warehouse shelves. I speculated, backed up with quick Internet searches of their maker's marks or handle designs, that at least one of them was likely much more valuable than the one I'd found on top of Castle Doune.

I discovered one tucked behind a torture device known as a heretic's fork—a wicked-looking thing that was made to force confessions through sleep deprivation. I got sidetracked and spent too much time looking up the heretic fork's history, but got back on task soon enough. I'd once asked Edwin why he'd chosen the torture devices as one of his collections, but he'd never given me a clear answer.

I found two dirks behind a stack of old, but not *very* old or valuable paperback books. And then I found one more under a wooden mug that might have been drunk from by a Scottish noble. I replaced the mug carefully on a separate shelf. My list of warehouse tasks only grew each time I explored.

My desire to search the warehouse for dirks had surprised me. I hadn't woken up with the idea, but as I'd unlocked the shop's front door with the hopes of finding Edwin inside, it seemed like the right thing to do. I found four dirks quickly and didn't search deeper for others. If there were four, there were probably more though.

One of them was obviously a replica, something made probably even later than the one I'd found at the castle. Its dark handle felt like plastic and the dull blade might not be strong enough to cut into a watermelon. I set that one to the side.

I didn't know how long it was from when they were used as weapons to when they were re-created as souvenirs, but it might not have been a stretch to think that a hundred years or so separated the versions. If a dirk wasn't something made in the twentieth century, it was probably authentic and a century or more old. If Edwin didn't realize this—and I'm sure he did but might not have given it much thought, it was my job to research the particulars and let him know.

One of the dirks had an eleven-inch blade, with a black and gold handle. Its sheath was also black and gold. I concluded that it was probably a piper's dirk made for the Black Watch, a regiment group that fought against the Highlanders first during the Jacobite rebellion. I could see no mark on it that told me it was a replica; I found no maker's mark at all. I'd show it to Joshua after I showed it to Edwin, but I suspected it was rare and probably valuable.

Carefully I held the dirk and wondered whose blood it had shed and why. As had happened with other items, I became overwhelmed by the amount of history each of these things had participated in making.

A knock sounded on the big red door.

I jumped up quickly and unlocked the deadbolt. I knew Edwin's knock.

"Hi," I said. "Come in. I'm so glad you're here."

"Working Sunday again?" Edwin said. He looked less disheveled than when I'd last seen him, but his eyes were weary and rimmed in pink. He hadn't slept much these last few nights.

"I am. I like the quiet," I said as I shut the door and turned the deadbolt.

"I do too."

"Come sit."

There was no excited anticipation between us this morning like there was most Sunday mornings. No hope to share a fun memory or old adventure today.

"Edwin, I'm so sorry for everything you're going through. I'm sorry for whatever part I played in the terrible and shocking news," I said after we were both seated.

"Lass, none of this was your fault. I'm sorry I got you involved. I should have just met with Billy myself."

"You couldn't have predicted how it would go."

Edwin pulled an ankle up to his knee, and I noticed his attire. I wondered if he ever wore jeans. Even on Sundays, Edwin dressed to the nines. Today it was pressed tan slacks and a brown sweater.

I was wearing jeans, which were acceptable on any day of the week apparently, but I couldn't bring myself to wear them to the shop any other day but Sunday.

"Oh! Dirks!" Edwin said when he noticed the items on my desk. "How lovely. What are you doing with them?"

"I found these on the shelves. One seems like a replica, a modern souvenir, but I'm looking into these others. I think this one was used by the Black Watch."

I held it toward Edwin.

"It's possible. I'm sure I acquired this from an old woman from a Highland village, though I can't remember exactly where she said she lived. She came tae the shop just tae show this tae me. She said she'd heard about my treasures, but I, of course, wouldn't confirm or deny. She wanted tae give the dirk tae me, but I insisted on paying her something. I fear I didn't give her enough if it's from the Black Watch."

"Well, I don't know for sure yet, and I need to look into these others too, but you might want to consider them all for auction."

"You might be right. We have a number of members who enjoy weapons. I didn't know I had more than a couple." Edwin leaned forward and looked at the two other dirks on the desk. The blade of the white-handled one was long and vicious. The blade of the mahogany-handled one was partially serrated and just as intimidating.

"There might be more. I'll let you know what I find," I said. "But the thing that sparked my desire to look for these this morning is something else I found. I should have told you about it but . . . well, I just didn't. And . . . I was hoping to see you today." I lifted my phone from the desk and scrolled to my pictures. "I don't think it had anything to do with Billy Armstrong's murder, but I found it near where we found him. I went up later that same night with Tom to look for any sign of the hand-written story that was supposed to be included in the book. This isn't authentic. It's a souvenir made about the mid-nineteen hundreds."

I held the phone out for Edwin to see. "It's interesting though, isn't it . . . Edwin?"

My boss's face had paled and he blinked rapidly, his eyes in the general direction of the phone but not really looking at it anymore.

I'd done it again.

I hurried around to him. "Are you okay?" I reached for my mobile to call 999.

Edwin put up his hand. "I'm fine, Delaney. No need tae call anyone. You surprised me again, that's all."

"I promise I'm going to stop doing that. Are you sure you're okay?"

"I'm sure. I'm . . . Tell me exactly where you found it." He reached for the phone on the desk but then pulled his hand back before he reached it.

"On top of Castle Doune, under the stone wall that was next to the stairs where we found Billy. I had begun to think it didn't have anything to do with his murder. Do you think it did?"

"No, please don't call anyone. I . . . don't think this has anything tae do with the boy's murder. But I do think it was meant for me, part of the message that Gordon wanted tae give me."

"What's it mean?" I said as I stood and went back to my chair. His color was returning.

Edwin shook his head. "I can't tell you, my dear. But I do promise you sincerely and deeply, I'm sure it had nothing tae do with Billy's manner of death."

"But it could have contributed to the reason he was killed?" I said, thinking as quickly as I could through his word play. He looked at me and blinked.

"No, I think it's more likely that it was dropped accidentally. There's no mistaking that this is something only Gordon and I would understand. I doubt even Billy understood the message his father was relaying to me. And, frankly, no one else would care. And I don't think it was the reason he was killed. No, that wouldn't make sense. Where's the dirk now?"

"I gave it to the police," I said. I watched him closely for another reaction.

"I see," he said, not bothered. "You've been busy."

"I have, and I'd really like to know what the dirk means to you, what the message was. Please tell me."

He stood. I thought his legs might be shaky, but they weren't.

"I will, I promise, but now I must find Gordon. I need tae talk to him."

"Edwin, there was more," I said as I picked up my phone again.

He sat in the chair again as I scrolled to the picture of the business card.

"I found this by the dirk, and I know that Billy was involved with this woman, Grizel Sheehy. They had a public argument in Stirling, where Billy volunteered. On Tuesday, he slapped her. As a result, he was asked to not come back to portray William Wallace ever again."

"Was she hurt?" Edwin asked.

"Not physically, but I'm sure the entire scene was awful."

"Aye," Edwin said as anger lit briefly in his eyes. "Unacceptable behavior, but I'm sure he was devastated about his mistake."

"I don't think the gentlemen who run the group were accepting apologies," I said. "I can't put the pieces of information together so they lead to a killer, but I think they somehow must. The police seem to be on the same trail, but they don't know about Gordon. I think you should tell them he's alive, even if that fact has nothing to do with his son's murder."

"I can't do that, Delaney. The news would devastate Fiona emotionally and financially."

"You could help her out financially if you wanted to, and she'd eventually recover emotionally," I said. "It's the only right thing to do."

"Even if Gordon is dying?"

I swallowed hard. "Yes."

I knew that exceptionally rich people were often called upon to save those who weren't their responsibility just because money could solve financial problems, and if you had so much you wouldn't miss giving some away. I never did like that line of reasoning; if I didn't think that in some old-friendship way Edwin was responsible for Fiona at least slightly, I would not have suggested he help her.

"I'm not prepared tae tell the police that," he said. "I will talk tae Gordon first, and then maybe."

"Do you think the story Gordon was talking about was written on a piece of paper, or was the dirk the story?"

Edwin cocked his head and looked at me. Slowly a sad smile overtook his features.

"Excellent, Delaney. I think you might be onto something. It hadn't occurred tae me but now I don't think there ever was a written story. The dirk says it all. Gordon would never have admitted that in front of everyone here, and I was so angry with him and so devastated by

Billy's death . . . No, there was no story, I'm sure. The annual and the dirk tell the story he wanted me tae know."

Edwin stood again and moved toward the door.

I scurried out of my chair. "May I come with you to talk to him?"

"No, not today."

"Edwin?"

"I'm sorry, lass. Forgive me, but there are some things that each of us must attend tae alone. It's just the way it is."

I nodded. I was confused and concerned. I hadn't expected these turns at all, and Edwin wasn't *just* my boss.

"I'll ring you later. After I talk tae Gordon, I will want tae talk tae someone. I will ring you," he said.

"All right," I said hopefully. "I'll keep my phone right next to me."

I locked the warehouse door behind him again but then remembered I'd forgotten to ask him about SPEC.

Hurriedly, I unlocked the door, had to lock it again because that was the rule—never, ever leave the door unlocked—ran up one side of stairs, down the other side, and then out through the front door. There was no sign of Edwin or his Citroën.

I tried to reach him on his mobile, but he didn't answer.

"Now what?" I said as I bit my bottom lip. I looked up toward Tom's pub and answered my own question.

FOURTEEN

"He just left?" Tom said from the awkward sideways position he'd taken under the back side of the bar. His face was spotted with black grease and dirt, and the wrench he held was so big that it looked more deadly than the dirks.

"Yeah. I didn't even get a chance to ask about SPEC. Can I help with that?" I said from my crouched position next to him. "I know a little plumbing. Farm girl and all."

Tom smiled up at me. "I just have tae get a couple things tightened up, but I'm not surprised you're not afraid tae get your hands a little dirty. That sounded like innuendo. Didn't mean it tae."

I smiled down at him but his attention had gone back to the pipe. I said, "Thank you for the flowers. They're beautiful."

"I'm glad you like them."

A couple of seconds later and after saying some unfamiliar words that were probably a Scots version of expletives as he looked at the pipes, Tom sat up and dropped the wrench into a toolbox on the floor in between us.

"So the dirk we found was a message from the dead man's father?" Tom said as he rested his arms on his bent knees.

"Right. Originally the story was supposed to be about the reasons Gordon faked his death. He said he wrote it all down. But I'm pretty sure Edwin thinks that the only story was the dirk. Edwin doesn't think anything was written down at all. At least that's my interpretation."

Tom nodded. "I bet you want tae talk tae Gordon. I could go with you later today, but not right now."

"That's where Edwin said he was going. Gordon works at a fish market but when I looked them up, there's more than one."

"Aye." Tom hoisted himself up and then gave me a hand too. He pulled me close and held on a little too long, but there were no customers around at the moment. "They're all down close tae the water, close tae the pub we went tae last night actually. Rodger," he said to his affable employee who was cleaning the front windows of the pub, "your da works at a fish market, right?"

"Aye."

"Where does he go when he isn't working?"

"Which pub?"

"Aye?"

"Believe it or not my dad's not a drinker. He works a full week and rests on his days off."

"Then that won't work. All right, how many fish markets are there?"

"A few? Why?"

"We're trying to find someone specific."

Rodger scratched the side of his head. "Well, I guess I'd need more information, but many of the markets are run by families. Da works with his cousin. There's a particularly big market that has a number of employees that aren't family though. Honestly, I cannae remember the name, but it's the big red barnlike building right next tae the river."

"I think I saw that last night near The King's Wark," I said.

"I think so too."

"It's not too cold. Maybe I'll take a bus over there and see what I can see. It would be pure luck to run into him, but it would give me something to do while you're busy."

"What if you run into Edwin?"

I shrugged. "I'll improvise, I guess."

"I'm sorry I'm busy. We have to get this all cleaned up and put back together before tomorrow. It's a mess. You'll be careful?"

"Yes, and don't worry about it. I'm glad you're able to get it fixed. Tonight, we'll try again?"

"Aye."

"Uh-oh, shall I close my eyes and ears?" Rodger said.

"Your choice," Tom said.

It was an awesome good-bye. If he didn't, Rodger probably should have closed his eyes.

———

I found the long red building quickly and easily. It was as simple as retracing the route to The King's Wark, but stopping about a half block sooner. Sea smells greeted me outside the building, somehow different when the air was cold, sweeter maybe. I walked over to the side of the building that was next to the water. From there I could see an inlet with a few moored and rocking boats and a couple of wake markers. The seawater wasn't too rough, but was very foamy around the shore; the cold spray hit my cheeks with a gust of wind. It wasn't below freezing but I wondered if I'd have ice drops on my face if I stayed outside long enough.

I met even stronger smells when I went inside, and not much more warmth. The market reminded me of any classic fish market I might have seen in pictures or read about in books, but it was my first in-person visit to one. Kansas fish markets were more about poles and wormy bait sunk into a river than buying anything from someplace indoors.

Rows of fish on ice filled the building. Big fish, small fish, gray fish, and even red fish. There were so many varieties, including what must have been some sort of cephalopod, but its numerous tentacles seemed alien and I found myself stepping away from it when I wondered if I saw one of its tentacles twitch.

Now that I was there, I felt lost and silly for even trying to find Gordon. I hadn't seen Edwin's Citroën anywhere nearby, but if he'd been here he could be long gone by now, which was good news. I really didn't want to run into him.

"Hello, can I help ye?"

The smiling man wiped his hands over his mostly clean apron as he approached. He also wore a very clean and very white coat with sleeves pushed up displaying heavily muscled forearms. His hair was covered with a net but that didn't take away from his dimpled smile. He was a tall man, probably close to my age, but with twinkling eyes that made him seem youthful.

"I'm not sure. I'm just looking around a little bit," I said, noting to myself that there were only two other customers in the large building and at least five other men in white coats and hairnets, though none of them immediately reminded me of Gordon.

"Certainly. I'm happy tae answer any questions or make recommendations."

"Thank you."

He smiled and stared at me a beat too long. "Do I ken ye?" he asked.

"I don't think so."

"Ye're so familiar. I felt like I ken ye."

"I'm not from around here."

"Aye. I see that. Or, I hear that, I s'pose." He wiped his hands again and extended the right one my direction and said, "I'm Liam."

"I'm Delaney."

We shook, his grip almost as strong as his arms inferred it would be.

"I'm sairy tae stare, but ye're lovely," he said.

Predictably, my cheeks reddened. "Thank you."

"If ye're new tae Edinburgh, I'd be happy tae show ye around. Been here all my life. I ken all the guid places. The bad ones too."

"Well, thank you, Liam, but I've been here a few months already, and I am seeing someone."

"Pity. Real pity."

"Delaney?"

I turned as Gordon approached. He had a box of fish over his shoulder and the edge in his voice told me he was both surprised and unhappy to see me.

"Hello," I said.

Gordon set the box of fish down. "I see ye've met our Liam."

"Aye, meebe ye leuk familiar because ye ken Barclay."

"She's never been here before. Have ye, Delaney?" "Barclay" Gordon said, his tone firm and unfriendly still.

"This is my first time. Good to see you, Barclay. I hoped to run into you today."

"Aye," Gordon said.

Liam's eyebrows lowered as he inspected Gordon and then me and then Gordon again.

"Awright. Let me know if ye need anything," Liam said before he turned and walked away.

Gordon stepped closer to me. "What are ye doing here?"

"I wanted to talk to you. I didn't know any other way to get in touch," I said. "Gor—Barclay, no one knows me. I have nothing to do with your past. No one will make any connection to Gordon," I said quietly.

"It's risky, Delaney, but ye're here now and it would leuk more suspicious if I threw ye oot. They frown on us doing such a thing tae customers. I'll talk tae ye."

I looked around. "Can you take a break or is there someplace we could go that's more private?"

Gordon gave me the most impatient look I'd ever been sent. I realized quickly that he was correct in thinking I shouldn't have come to see him. Nevertheless, I tried not to let him see my wavering confidence.

"Give me a minute," he said.

He lifted up the box of fish again and carried it to a bed of ice in the next row. With fast, sure movements he placed long gray fish, one at a time, onto the ice, making an appealing stack despite their glassy eyes and open mouths. He grabbed the empty box and walked past me toward what looked like an office space in the middle of the market.

"Follow me," he mumbled as he went by.

I did as he said, but not without noticing Liam watching our every move. He wasn't attempting to be subtle and he made me feel much more exposed than I liked. I kept my steps sure.

"In here," Gordon said as he pushed open a door.

The space was the smallest office I'd ever seen, even smaller than Joshua's converted supply closet. A messy desk and two chairs were crammed in the windowless room, and I had no desire to be packed in there with Gordon, but I'd come this far.

Once I'd sat in one chair with my knees rammed up against the desk, Gordon shut the door and wedged himself around the desk to the other chair.

He took a deep breath as he sat. "Awright, Delaney, what could ye possibly want? Ye dinnae even ken me."

"I have some questions."

He blinked. "What kind of questions?"

"About your past, about your son?"

"Why?"

"Because no one including the police can know you're alive, apparently. I think your son's killer needs to be brought to justice."

"Ye're going tae the police?"

"I might."

Gordon squinted hard.

"But I won't tell them about you, I don't think. I don't want to do that to your wife. But no promises."

"Ye ken Fiona?"

I nodded. "She came into the bookshop. She's heart-broken. Your son's killer needs to be found, for her if not for anyone else," I said. "Didn't you see Edwin earlier today?"

"No, why?"

I blinked. I wondered why Edwin hadn't done what he'd said he was going to do.

"Delaney?"

I jumped.

"The police need to find your son's killer, Gordon. I would think that would be your wish as well," I said.

"The police will find the killer. I had nothing tae do with my son's death." His jaw tightened for a brief mo-ment as if he had to work hard to contain his emotions. "I'm not important tae that equation."

"I'm sorry, but I'm not so sure." I reached into my bag and pulled out my phone, once again finding one of the pictures of the dirk. "Does this have anything to do with you?"

Any other time, place, or person facing him, maybe

Gordon would have been able to hide his surprise. But I was a stranger and I'd come to the place he'd been hiding. I'd caught him off guard and I'd already caused him some grief.

"Where . . ." He reached for the phone but then sat back again, seemingly suddenly tired to the bone. "Where did ye get this?"

"I found it close to where I found your son's body. I'm sorry. I'm sorry to keep pressing the matter, but I have to know, do you think this dirk has anything to do with Billy's death?"

Gordon shook his head slowly and said, "Not unless Edwin MacAlister is his killer."

It was my turn to be surprised, but I cleared my throat and continued on, past the sense of the walls closing in. "What do you mean?"

"I cannae tell ye more than that. I dinnae understand why this was on top 'o the castle with my son but Edwin must have been the one tae have put it there. Billy brought it with him if Edwin didn't, I suppose, but I didnae ken Billy knew aboot it." Gordon's shoulders sank and he blinked at me two hard times. "It all makes more sense now."

"What does?"

"Why he wanted Edwin tae know that I was alive."

"Please explain, Gordon. Help me understand. I know my boss didn't kill your son. He couldn't, and you probably know that too, but what's all this about?"

"I cannae tell ye, Delaney. It would be breaking a promise I swore I wouldnae break. I'm not much anymore, a liar certainly, but I cannae betray . . ."

"Who?"

"I cannae."

"What if you telling me the answer finds the killer?"

"It willnae unless it was Edwin," he said a long,

thoughtful moment later. He sat forward and touched the phone with a fingertip. "I didnae ken that Billy knew about the dirk."

"You didn't ask him to give the dirk to Edwin?"

"I never would have."

"So, you really wrote down the story of your faked demise on a piece of paper you put in an *Oor Wullie* book?"

"Aye."

"And the *Oor Wullie* comic was important to you all?"

"Aye. At one time, many years ago, it was important tae us all."

"Could you explain that, please?"

If I hadn't already shown him something that seemed to have drained him of all of his energy, he might have told me.

"Not today," he said.

"Would you write down the story for me?"

"Why? I told ye the story in person. There's nothing left tae tell. I was a drunken fool and I made a mistake in thinking I was tae blame for Leith. I wasnae. I wasnae tae blame for Billy either." Heavy tears welled in his eyes.

I reached for the phone. Gordon made a brief motion toward it but then sat back again. "Why did seeing this dirk bother Edwin so much?"

"He saw it?"

"Yes."

"Then maybe he's not guilty. He'll get over it," Gordon said with a small smile.

I put the phone back into my bag and said, "Gordon, does S-P-E-C mean anything to you?"

His smile widened for an instant but his now dry eyes remained sad as they locked onto mine. "Ye are interesting, Delaney from America, but that's another secret I'll not tell." He stood, making him seem gigantic in the small space. "I have tae get back tae work now."

"Did you know it was tattooed on the inside of Billy's wrist?"

"Of course I did." He lifted his sleeve and showed me his identical tattoo.

"A secret society from the university?" I said.

"I have tae get back tae work." He pulled down the sleeve.

A noise sounded outside the door. It was as if someone slipped on the floor and caught themselves with a stomp of their foot. Gordon and I looked at each other before he turned the knob and pushed it open. No one was in sight.

I followed him out to the market, where many more customers filled the space along with the strong sea smells. There was no obvious eavesdropper in the area, but a tall, older man next to the closest set of doors looked over at us and pulled his eyebrows together.

"My boss," Gordon muttered quietly. "We were in his office. I'll come up with an explanation."

"Thank you for your time," I said loud enough and friendly enough for the boss to hear.

But Gordon lowered his voice. "Dinnae come back here again, Delaney. We have no business together. I wouldnae want tae do anything tae put Fiona in jeopardy. Please stay away."

He turned and walked past the office and through some plastic dividers that I assumed led to an even colder part of the building where the fish went before they were displayed out front.

I smiled as I passed Liam. He smiled too and then quickly turned his attention back to the mussels he was placing on ice.

The nice day had disappeared by the time I stepped

back outside. Light rain fell with clouds that promised heavier rain before they dissipated. From the landing I peered toward the street in between the market and the river. I had an umbrella in my bag but there was a bench on the landing around from the front doors that was protected by an awning. I took a seat and pulled out my phone again, finding the bus route and time app.

A fifteen-minute wait. Not bad. I tried to call Edwin and wasn't surprised that he didn't answer. Just as the ten-minute mark ticked by, Liam came out through the door, stopping short when he saw me on the bench.

"Hi again," he said. He'd taken off the hair net, apron, and white coat, and his dimples stood out even more when you could see his short brown hair.

"Hello," I said.

"Hey, I'm sairy if I was weird in there. Ye really do leuk familiar but that's no excuse for my stalkerish behavior."

"It's okay."

"Ye waiting for Barclay?"

"No, a bus."

"Aye? Weel, I'd offer ye a ride, but after all that I'm not sure it would sound awright."

I smiled. "Thank you, but I'm okay. I like the buses."

Liam smiled and cocked his head as he looked at me. The moment went on a bit too long.

"Nice tae meet ye, Delaney," he said a beat later.

"Nice to meet you too, Liam."

"Ye ken where I work. Stop by sometime if yer personal circumstances change."

I nodded.

He started to walk away but turned again to face me. "How do ye ken Barclay?"

"A friend of a friend." I shrugged.

When I didn't offer anything else, he tipped an invisible

hat and said, "Weel, then, I'll be off." He glanced up at the door to the market so I did too. The tall, older man I'd seen, Gordon's boss, stood there. He sent Liam a distinct look of displeasure. He sent one my direction too before he went back inside. Maybe he always looked like that.

Liam turned and was gone in a flash, moving down a street I couldn't quite see from my vantage point.

The bus stopped on the corner a few seconds later. Even with the umbrella, my legs got drenched as I hurried across to catch it. Once seated I looked toward the spot where Liam had last been, but didn't see any sign of him still there. As I looked one more time at the doorway to the fish market, I noticed what I first thought was a misplaced steady snake upward of steam, but I realized I was seeing a discarded but still burning cigarette on the landing right outside the door.

The bus took a route that reminded me about someone else who might be able to answer some of my questions. Or at least help me come up with better questions.

I disembarked earlier than I originally planned.

FIFTEEN

Though all libraries, even the smallest, least stocked branches, are treasures, the library at the University of Edinburgh is a masterpiece of treasures.

The building's outside is made with modern, squared-off lines and concrete balconies, but the inside is an arched cove of nothing but architectural smarts and historical beauty. Tables, chairs, reference desks, and computers populate the main floor and shelves upon shelves of books ride up the sides, filling in the spaces between the windows and the arches and pillars. The stairways throughout are dark carved wood, and I often wondered if they were magical and moved of their own accord when the lights were out at night and no one was around.

I knew that Tom's father, Artair, had been recently spending most of his time in the art book room, cataloguing the lifespan of a specific design of ceramic bowl. It was such a micro-research project that even I, someone who was made to research, felt anxious thinking about the tediousness that must be involved.

I made my way toward Artair, keeping my footfalls as quiet as possible. As I passed by them, I enjoyed glancing at the busts of past notable university professors that lined the main room. I always wondered what they'd taught so well that they got to be honored in such a cool way.

I usually pushed my bookish voices away when I was inside the library. If I was overwhelmed and in awe, they'd probably be that way too. Today, though, I opened my mind and let them in. Maybe they could tell me what "SPEC" meant. It didn't work that way, but it was worth a shot.

We are what we pretend to be, so we must be careful what we pretend to be.

If I wasn't mistaken, that wasn't a quote from a book, but a quote from an author. I'd gone through a Kurt Vonnegut phase one semester in high school, but I didn't remember where I'd read the quote or why I was so certain the voice in my head was his.

Mr. Vonnegut was talking about Gordon, I was sure. The idea of him playing dead and hiding in plain sight couldn't continue forever, but he'd managed it so far. I was disappointed in my bookish voices for giving me something so obvious, and I was at the doorway to the art book room before I could see if they had anything more to say.

The room wasn't large and though all of the shelves on each wall were full, there was a distinct sense of organization inside it; a neatness that seemed to follow Artair wherever he went.

He sat behind a tall worktable, studying something intently. I had a misshapen view of him because the large lit magnifying glass clipped onto the side of the table was elbowed at just the right angle to make him look bug-eyed. A moment later he sensed I was at the doorway, and looked up over the glass.

"Delaney, lass, welcome! Come in, come in."

He clicked off the light, stood, and came around the table.

"How are ye, lass? Any news aboot the murder? I wanted tae call Tom, but I didnae want tae bother the lad when I heard about the broken pipe."

"A little news," I said. "And when I last left Tom, I think he was getting the pipe under control."

"Guid tae hear. What can I do for ye?"

"You have a few minutes? I have some questions, but I don't want to interrupt."

"I need a wee break anyway. Come along. We'll have some coffee and ye can tell me the news."

He led us down a hallway, and slid his ID through a slot next to a security door that opened to a dark and echo-y stairway. The break room beneath the depths of the magnificent library was disappointingly like almost any other break room, stark and boring, but today this one wasn't busy. I knew that Tom had told Artair about Gordon's visit to the bookshop, his faked death, and what we knew of his history with Edwin. Only a few people traveled in and out of the break room as I told him about Edwin's reaction to finding the dirk, but I got to the point of why I'd come to talk to him with as little preamble as possible.

"Do you know anything about something called S-P-E-C?" I spelled.

"An acronym?"

"I think it's an acronym. S-P-E-C," I repeated. "But I'm not sure. Either way, does it ring a bell? I believe it might have something to do with a university secret society."

Artair's eyebrows lifted. "Aye?"

I nodded. "It was a sticker on the glass part of the frame over Edwin's diploma from the University of Edinburgh. It didn't seem official, but like something that someone had stuck there later. Billy, the dead man, also had a tattoo of those letters on the inside of his wrist."

Artair had fallen into thought, his coffee cup halted halfway to his mouth. He didn't speak for a long moment. I waited silently.

"Delaney . . ." he began as he put the cup back on the table.

"I'm listening."

"Come with me," he said, his jaw suddenly set firm as he hurried out of the room.

"Okay."

I grabbed my cup and the one Artair seemed to have forgotten and threw them away before I followed his fast steps the other direction from the stairs and down a sloping hallway.

We took three right turns, walked down another short flight of stairs, turned left, and then entered a low-ceilinged room with shelves packed with boxes.

"A sub-basement?" I said.

"One of a few," Artair said. "I need to know what year Edwin graduated from university. Do ye remember what the diploma said?"

"No, sorry, but we can figure this out."

After some quick calculations and a few guesses, Artair grabbed a cart that was against a wall and rolled it down an aisle. He pulled one of the office boxes from a shelf, dropped it with a muffled boom onto the concrete floor next to the cart, and then lifted the lid.

"Yearbooks?" I said.

"Aye, and some other items of note from those years. Some of our archivists and librarians save things in different ways. It's . . . it's difficult to explain, but let's leuk."

Artair pulled out the two yearbooks that were on top of folders, small trophy-like trinkets, and a couple of smaller boxes. He handed me one of the books. It didn't take me long to find a picture of my boss.

"He was the *editor* of the university's paper his senior

year? I'd heard about the writing, but editor? That's a pretty big deal," I said.

"Aye," Artair said as he looked at the open book I held. "Awright. We have dates. Let's load up some boxes and move over to the microfiche machines."

He repacked the box and lifted it and then three others to the cart. We rolled over to the other side where a row of three microfiche machines were lined up against the wall. My years of experience working in libraries had given me quite a knack with these machines.

We'd found the yearbooks from the years Edwin had been at the university and then pulled out some of the smaller boxes from the bigger ones. Each small box held a roll of film that displayed the pages inside the yearbooks as well as pages from the university's newspaper.

I scrolled to a newspaper article that had a black-and-white picture of a young Edwin as the subject of the article. He'd been a well-respected editor, and had made "stylistic and content changes" to the paper that had been heralded as, among other things, "revolutionary" and "progressive."

"Handsome, huh?" I said with a smile. I enjoyed the flattering content of the article, but I couldn't help but notice the dapper style he'd had even back then. He'd reminded me of Jimmy Stewart when I'd first met him. Even more so now.

"Aye. A good lad too, from all indications. Here's something." Artair held an open folder with a short stack of papers on the table in front of me.

I took the folder and read the caption under the picture on the top of the stack. " 'Edwin MacAlister, Leith Stanton, Gordon Armstrong, and Clarissa Bellows work to create their own *Oor Wullie*–type comic strip.'

"I don't understand," I said. "This was in one of the boxes?"

"Aye, I wondered if my memory was true. Until ye mentioned SPEC, I didnae remember these things. Even now though, Edwin's involvement is a surprise. I didnae remember the names of those involved."

"What does this have to do with SPEC?"

Artair's eyebrows came together. "I'm not certain yet. I'm still putting the pieces together in my mind, but I think it was the students involved in the book like *Oor Wullie* who were part of a group called SPEC." He shook his head. "I need tae keep looking, perhaps in a different place."

I read the full article and inspected the picture.

The three men and the woman had been given a class project about mixing visual art with words, so they'd decided to create something similar to *Oor Wullie*. The editor of the Edinburgh paper that ran the *Oor Wullie* strip had heard about the project and was encouraging the students and giving them access to anything they might need at the city's presses. The picture showed the four students posed outside a university building.

Though the project and the community support were in themselves interesting, the picture was even more so.

The three men, Leith and Gordon surprisingly as dapper as Edwin, gazed at the beautiful woman they surrounded.

"From this picture, the three of these men look to be quite taken by Clarissa Bellows," I mumbled.

Artair leaned over my shoulder and readjusted the thick glasses he'd put on.

"Ye might be right, or that might just be for the photo. She's a lovely lass. Ye should ask Edwin aboot her. See what happened tae her. I cannae remember if I read aboot her specifically."

"I will," I said. "Did they ever create their book?"

"I dinnae ken yet, but I'll keep looking. These aren't

the boxes I was looking for, Delaney. I have memories of finding things much more scandalous."

I glanced at the date on the page with the picture of the four of them. "This one looks like it was taken before Edwin became editor, which according to the first year-book was his senior year. The date on this article is two years earlier, their sophomore year. Did something scandalous happen sometime during those two years? Something with SPEC?"

"I think something did, but I shouldnae have mentioned it tae ye until I knew for certain. I'll need a little more time."

"It must not have hurt Edwin much. I doubt he would have been given the position of editor if he'd been in trouble."

"Probably not," Artair said doubtfully.

I looked at him and sensed we'd spent a lot of time in the sub-basement, keeping him away from the art room. "Artair, you don't have time for all of this. If one of them would talk to me, that would give us a shortcut. I'll try that first, but I might come back and look through these records again if that's okay," I said.

"Anytime, but, Delaney, there's one more thing."

I lifted my eyebrows at his ominous tone.

"I think ye are correct about SPEC. I think it was a secret society, or at least something like that. I think there was a suicide, or someone died. It was many years ago, and I need tae find the connection again between the society and the book yer boss and his friends were making. I'll find it, but it might take me a few days, and I'm curious. We're a library and we like tae keep a record of everything, even if the manner of recording can be a wee bit hidden sometimes."

"Don't do anything to put your job in jeopardy, Artair," I said.

"I willnae. Only *some* people like tae keep secrets buried. I know others who are keen tae share them with the world. I'll find what ye're looking for, if it's tae be found."

Though he didn't act put out in the least, I felt like I'd asked too much of my pub owner's father. It suddenly seemed like I was taking advantage.

"Artair . . . thank you."

"Ye're welcome."

Unfortunately, it was against policy for Artair to leave me unattended while he got back to work. We cleaned up the mess we'd made, both of us using our precise triple-check obsessive method to make sure we put things back better than we'd found them. I realized Artair might make for a good museum companion and filed away the idea to invite him someday.

It might not have mattered if Artair and I hadn't gotten along, but I was grateful that we did.

With the thick file that held the copy of the article secure under his arm, he escorted me out of the building, telling me good-bye with a promise he'd call me soon with more details. I was torn between begging him to hurry, wanting to sneak back into the sub-basement by myself, and still feeling like I'd imposed. I kissed his cheek and told him thank you before he turned and hurried back inside.

With no rain falling, I walked back toward Grassmarket. Hopefully my pub owner would be available for dinner. And conversation.

SIXTEEN

Instead of heading directly to Tom's pub, though, I took a detour. Inspector Winters had told me specifically to not ask Grizel Sheehy questions about anything that had to do with Billy Armstrong. I hadn't forgotten that charge as I took the route to her bagpipe shop. I told myself I was just wasting time, that chances were good that the shop wouldn't be open on Sunday, and that I would only look from afar—definitely from across the street—for whatever it is I thought I needed to see, before I went to find Tom at his pub.

Gray clouds filled the darkening sky and the cold temperatures made me again think of a Kansas winter, but without the snow. It was almost four in the afternoon and the sun had mostly set. For a moment I missed the way the sun set on the distant flat Kansas horizon and longed for the smells of snow.

I wouldn't be going home for Christmas, but my family had planned a trip to Edinburgh to visit me sometime early next year. My heart ached at the thought of not spending the holiday with them, but I tried not to think about it too much.

Tom wouldn't be in Edinburgh for the holiday. He and Artair were traveling to Germany to visit friends. They were taking Tom's aunt, whose dementia was almost to the point she wouldn't be able to travel any longer. I'd been invited, but had declined, and looked forward to creating new traditions with Edwin, Rosie, Hamlet, and Hector. But, I'd miss Tom.

I'd become so lost in my thoughts that I arrived across from the bagpipe shop quickly, warmed through from my speedy pace. I did as I told myself I would do; I looked across the street at the shop.

It was open, the light from the window warm and bright. Grizel was arranging a few bagpipes behind the window. She must have sensed she was being watched because she looked up, did a double take, squinted, and then smiled with a wave, signaling me to cross over and go inside.

I didn't hesitate.

"Hello, lass," she said as I came through the front door. "Did ye wonder if the shop was open?"

"I did."

"I'm here all the time, except when I'm not," she said. It was similar to what she'd said the first time I'd been in the shop. "Now, what can we do tae find some pipes for yer friend's wife?"

"I'm not sure."

"All right. Is she a beginner? Or does she have some experience under her belt? I dinnae carry the cheap ones; they're unplayable. I have some that can be played with a good tone, and then some that have the best woodwork ye'll find anywhere. Those are the ones that sound the best and are by far the most expensive."

I stared at her without answering. She blinked and waited.

"I think I figured out how I know you," I said. "I didn't put it together when I was last here, but after we left I remembered seeing you in Stirling at the Wallace monument."

"Aye, she said. "As I said, for a short time, I did help them with some bagpipes. I'm not doing that anymore."

"Small world, huh?"

"Aye. So what about the pipes? Is the lass a beginner or does she have some experience? Do ye ken their budget?"

"I'm afraid I don't. I'm unprepared, I'm sorry, but I'll tell Elias the things he needs to know before he comes back in."

She nodded, clearly disappointed that she wasn't going to make a sale today.

I forged on. "You know, I met someone when I was at the monument who was so interesting. I didn't get his name, but he had a tattoo on his wrist. Letters, S-P-E-C, I think, but can't be sure. Would you by chance know who I'm talking about?"

Grizel thought a moment. "I think so, but I dinnae ken his name either. I remember seeing that tattoo though."

She was the best liar I had ever seen. There was nothing that gave her away; not a twitch nor any strained eye contact, no telling look up to the left. She must not have thought that Inspector Winters might have shared with me that she'd known Billy. The police usually don't share that sort of information with civilians, and she didn't know my real motive for asking her questions anyway.

"Really?" I said. "Do you know any of the guys who act the William Wallace role?"

"Oh, I ken a few of them," she said. "But not the one with a tattoo on his wrist. I've seen him, but I didnae get his name. He wasnae all that friendly," she said in a tone of warning.

"Are you sure?"

"Aye, lass, I'm sure. Now, I have no interest in talking about that group of people. Ye'll have tae get yer own dates. If ye have any bagpipe questions, let me know." She turned and lifted a set of bagpipes from a display and then walked to the back of the store, disappearing though a dark doorway.

"Okay," I said, but I doubt she heard me.

She'd probably be back out in a minute, but I couldn't think of anything else to ask her. The brilliant last-minute idea I'd had—get around to asking her if she knew what "SPEC" meant—had been thwarted by her lies of denial before I could get to the real question. Even if she didn't know the words behind the letters, she certainly knew Billy Armstrong.

I looked around the shop. Bagpipes and some of the things that go with them: tartans, sporrans, and one small rack of kilts filled the store, but nothing else. Reluctantly, and without any more conversation with Grizel, I left the bagpipe shop and made my way toward the pub.

As I turned the corner that led into Grassmarket I was glad to spy customers inside the pub. Sunday wasn't usually the busiest day for Tom, but some patrons would have been sad to miss their Sunday ritual if Tom hadn't been able to fix the pipe. It looked like this Sunday was a little more popular than others.

I crossed the street and then the square and looked inside the front window. Rodger was pouring tumblers of whisky, and Tom was leaning on the bar talking to one of the regulars. As I walked inside, Tom smiled briefly and waved at me before turning his attention back to the customer.

There wasn't much space to cover to make it to the bar, but a group of three men suddenly spread to fill a big chunk of the small space in the middle of the pub. I was behind them as another man approached from the corner.

The three men hadn't taken up the space on purpose, but their wall made me feel trapped.

"Hey, I ken ye," a voice said when the man in the corner made it around the three men.

"Oh! Hello," I said, my mind falling into one of those moments when it tried to connect dots it didn't know were there.

"Weren't ye just in the fish market today?"

"Yes, small world," I said to the man Gordon had said was his boss. His voice was deep and rough, from all the cigarettes I guessed.

He wasn't holding a drink and I couldn't determine if he was with someone else. He looked toward the bar and then back at me. "What was yer business there?"

"I was shopping, but I ran into Barclay and we're family friends. I was surprised to see him. I hadn't seen him in years." I stopped myself from continuing to talk too much more.

"Aye?"

I nodded.

He didn't tell me his name, but his eyes softened a little before he said, "Excuse me."

He walked around me and then moved hurriedly out the door.

I was left unsettled, but I wasn't exactly sure why. I shook it off and made my way to the bar.

"Who was that?" Tom said as he handed me a glass of water. I might switch to soda, but that's as crazy as I got on school nights.

"Someone I saw at the fish market today. I think we surprised each other here."

"Aye. I don't know him, but he was familiar," Tom said.

"The pipe's all fixed?" I shook off the weird moment.

"And it's even better than it was before. I'll have tae

replace a wood panel or two back behind there because
the leak came on slowly and ruined a couple, but all's
well."

"Glad to hear it. You're going to be busy for a while,
huh?" I said.

"Aye. A wee bit," Tom said. "Sorry about that. Some
of the customers are making up for the few hours of lost
time since we were closed, but it's Sunday so the crowd
will probably clear in a couple of hours. Late dinner?"

"How about a late dessert? I need to talk to Elias and
Aggie. I thought I'd make them dinner, which will probably turn into Aggie making dinner, but I'll try."

"Dessert it is," Tom said with a smile. "I look forward
tae it."

"Me too."

I weaved my way out of the pub again and hurried to
the bus stop. I had to pass the bookshop on the way, and
I glanced into the now-darkened windows, wondering
what Rosie and Hamlet had done with their Sunday just
as much as I wondered why Edwin hadn't gone to talk to
Gordon. I'd tried to call him again, but there was still no
answer. I thought about going inside the shop, but wanted
to catch Elias and Aggie before it got too late.

The light from a streetlamp glimmered off a spot next
to the window, and I stepped closer to take a look.

A shot glass sat on the tiny corner of a brick that happened to jut out slightly. I grabbed the glass, remembering
Hamlet sweeping up one he'd broken the other day. It
was just a plain shot glass, the kind used in pubs everywhere, including Tom's. I decided someone must have
created some sort of ritual of taking a shot glass and leaving it at the bookshop on their way to their next destination. It seemed harmless enough, and glasses of all sorts
were taken from pubs or broken all the time. I knew Tom
was always ordering more.

I put the glass in my bag and made it to the stop just as the bus arrived.

———

"Lass, ye're verra good with the pancakes," Elias said as he grabbed another one from the platter in the middle of the table.

"Thank you," I said.

Aggie smiled at me. She made pancakes that I'd wake up early for, but Elias liked my grandmother's recipe that included lots of vanilla. I'd given Aggie the recipe, but she vowed not to make grandma's cakes until I went back home to Kansas, a thing she hoped might never happen.

I wasn't much of a cook or a grocery shopper, but I usually had breakfast ingredients on hand, so dinner tonight was pancakes and eggs. I'd improvise dessert later when I saw Tom.

I told them both everything, which meant repeating some things and noting too many details that were probably irrelevant, but I hoped they'd offer me a new perspective or an idea. I wasn't disappointed.

"I'm certain that SPEC was a secret society," Aggie said. "But I havenae had much of a chance tae leuk up what it was about. Many of the secrets are probably still secrets. Ye could try tae find Clarissa Bellows. If she's alive she might talk tae ye. It all sounds suspicious, but it could have just been young people making their lives more adventurous than they really were. Artair will remember more in time. That will help."

"Do you think the old secrets could be tied to Billy's murder?"

Elias chewed thoughtfully a moment, swallowed, and said, "Aye. No such thing as coincidences."

I didn't disagree, but it was all so long ago and seemed unlikely now, no matter the coincidences.

"All right. After dinner, we'll look her up," I said.

After dinner, Aggie parked herself in front of my laptop on the coffee table and got to work while Elias and I did the dishes.

"She's alive, Delaney," she said from the front room. "At least I think that's the Clarissa Bellows ye're looking for. She seems the right age."

I hurried from the kitchen and sat next to her on the couch. She'd written the address on a Post-it and handed it to me.

Elias had followed me out, a dish and drying towel in his hands. He looked over my shoulder at the paper. "Brilliant. She's in Edinburgh. Not close tae here or the bookshop, but I will take ye there this evening if ye like."

"As much as I want to, I don't think we should go over this late, do you?"

Elias shrugged.

"Maybe wait until tomorrow. Ring her first if we can find her number," Aggie said.

"No! Dinnae call her first," Elias said. "Dinnae let her prepare. Catch her off guard, so she cannae be ready with a lie."

Aggie and I looked at him.

"He might have a point," Aggie said.

"Just let me know," Elias said as he turned and headed back to the kitchen. "The cab will be available."

SEVENTEEN

"Hello, lass," Rosie said as she worked to unlock the bookshop door.

"Good morning," I said as I took Hector from her so she could use both hands. He wore a blue knit sweater and a gold barrette in his bangs. "Hector, you look particularly fetching this morning." I smiled as I held him up to kiss my cheek.

"Hamlet had a test tae study for and Edwin's traveling to Glasgow today. It will just be us for a while."

"You talked to Edwin?" I asked as I followed her inside. "When?"

"No, he left a message. Must have called me in the dead of the night. Gracious, it's a cauld one today." She put her bag on the front desk and hurried to the light switch and thermostat on the wall next to the stairs. "There. We should warm up soon."

"Why is he going to Glasgow?"

"He didnae tell me."

That was the first time I'd ever heard a bitter tone in her voice when she spoke of Edwin. She'd been angry at him before but never bitter.

"You mad at him?"

"Aye, I'm wicket angry. I dinnae understand his loyalty

tae that liar. Why hasnae he gone tae the police? I guar-
antee that that . . . man had something tae do with his
son's death," she said as she went back to the desk and sat.

"Edwin hasn't gone to the police because of Fiona, but
I think he should go to the police too. It's difficult for us
to understand though. Their history together, I mean," I
said as I tucked Hector into the crook of my arm so he
could warm up until the temperature in the shop rose.

Rosie tented her fingers on the desk as she leaned forward. She looked up a moment later with pursed lips.

"I've thought about it, lass, and Fiona wouldnae be in
any long-term trouble, and . . . weel, I make it a habit not
tae advise Edwin on his *personal* finances, but he could
pay back the money for her and he wouldnae even notice
it was gone. I ken, I'm terrible tae even say it."

"Not at all," I said. "Maybe that's what will happen.
We'll see. But do you really think that Gordon had something to do with Billy's murder?"

"I dinnae mean that Gordon kil't Billy, but something
Gordon did caused his son tae be murdered. There's no
doot in my mind."

"Like what?"

"I dinnae ken."

I bit my lip and scratched behind Hector's ears.

"Rosie," I said a moment later. "Do you know anything about a secret society at the university, S-P-E-C?"

"Aye, I might remember something." She said it so
quickly that I wondered if she'd been thinking about it
specifically, maybe waiting for me to ask or at least the
right moment to slip it into the conversation.

"Can you tell me more about it and if Edwin ever mentioned any trouble with it?"

Rosie removed the scarf from around her neck. It was
red and orange and she'd crocheted it herself. She folded
it and put it on the corner of the desk. Hector squirmed

so I put him on the desk, and he trotted over to the scarf, where he curled and blinked up at me. Rosie removed her coat and let it fall over the back of the chair. She rubbed her arms but it was already warming up.

"Aye." She looked at the front door. There would be no customers this early. "There was trouble. It was a muckle—a lot of trouble—and Edwin, Gordon Armstrong, and Leith Stanton were at the center of it all."

"Okay." I was afraid to move. I didn't want to give her too much time to reconsider telling me stories she'd originally said she wouldn't, couldn't.

She sighed deeply and said, "Grab a chair, Delaney. I'll tell ye."

In the spirit of not breaking her stride, I hurriedly got a chair from the back corner table and brought it up to the front desk.

Hector stood, considered his options, and then jumped to my lap as Rosie began.

"They started the society, the three of them. Edwin, Gordon, and Leith. I dinnae remember what the letters stood for, but Edwin told me. Anyway, it was their idea. They were proud of themselves and their silly, youthful need tae be exclusive and secretive. Edwin admits now that they were stupid, or he did back when he told me aboot it when he thought both Gordon and Leith were dead. Back at university they thought they were something special. They thought they would create something that others would want tae be a part of, something that would automatically make anyone special." She shook her head.

"They were that arrogant?" I said.

"They were, aye, but mostly young and without life experience."

"What happened that was so terrible?"

"Someone got kil't, Delaney. It might have been an accident tae be sure, but it was a tragedy just the same."

"How?"

"A boat. A night's adventure. Too much whisky." She shook her head again. "And a girl."

"I see." I suspected the girl was Clarissa Bellows, but I didn't ask yet.

"Aye. The one girl welcomed into SPEC was the object of their affection. All of them. Edwin, Gordon, and Leith loved her. There's a reason Edwin never married, Delaney. Clarissa, but I cannae remember her last name. She broke his heart. She broke all their hearts." Rosie looked at the door again. Still no customers. "She's the one who kil't the man. It was an accident, but it was her dirk that did the deed."

"Dirk?"

"Aye, part of being a member of SPEC was the carrying of dirks. They were supposed tae be for show, but the blades were anything but dull. Even many of the souvenirs have real blades."

"How did she kill him?" I swallowed. "Accidentally, I mean?"

"They were out on the sea, all of them used tae love the sea, and Edwin's family had boats. They were all sold off, shortly after the accident, Edwin told me." Rosie sighed. "It was a late spring night, the society members were oot on the boat. Seven young men and Clarissa. Having too much fun, being too young. Edwin couldnae bear tae give me the exact details, but one of the men who had just joined the society was complaining aboot Clarissa being the only female allowed in. His complaints turned intae an argument between him and Leith. It got physical. Clarissa got scared so she pulled her dirk oot of the scabbard and told them tae stop fighting. She meant it only as a threat, maybe just tae get their attention, but as boats will do, this one rocked on a dark wave and the blade went intae the man's heart."

"That's horrible," I said as surprise tears filled my eyes. I blinked them away.

"Aye, 'twas. The body went overboard. The police found it though."

"Did the police think he drowned?"

"No, Edwin and the others told the police he'd been accidentally stabbed, but they told the police that it was Leith's dirk that kil't the man. They all protected Clarissa, even the men who had just joined the club. No one ever said it was anyone but Leith."

"What happened to Leith?"

"He served some time in prison. Ye ken he became successful later. I suspect Edwin played a part in his release and his later success."

"And Gordon was with the victims both times they were killed on the water, the man from back then and Leith. Strange." I'd heard plenty of people say it, probably read it many times, but at the moment the voice that spoke the loudest in my mind was Elias's from the night before: *no such thing as coincidences.*

Rosie shrugged. "Aye, 'tis, and Gordon's always the common denominator. Edwin thought he was dead. I thought he was gone from the chance to ruin Edwin's life, and now he's not. No matter what, he's up tae no good, Delaney, and the people in his life seem tae be in danger. Ye see why I dinnae like the man? I dinnae trust him, and I think he had something tae do with Leith's death and that's why he went into hiding. I dinnae ken how, but many things are amiss, and he's at the center of them all."

I'd dropped my bag on the floor. I reached into it now and pulled out my phone, finding the dirk pictures again.

"Does this mean anything?" I handed her the phone.

"'Tis a dirk," Rosie said as she took it from me. "Where did it come from?"

"I went back to the castle that night with Tom and his

father and we found it, close to where Billy's body had been. Do you think it was Clarissa's, the murder weapon from long ago?"

"No idea." She put her glasses on and looked at the pictures again. "It's lovely. We can research the maker's mark."

"I did; a friend at the museum helped. It's not a valuable piece, but Edwin was bothered by it when I showed him the picture. I took the dirk to the police."

"Guid! Maybe that will help them tae somehow find Gordon." Rosie turned the camera and enlarged the picture with her fingers. "Ah, here. Did ye see this?"

She held the phone toward me. Along the top ridge of the dirk's handle, in very small letters, it looked like "SPEC" had been carved. If the letters hadn't been on my mind specifically I might have just thought it was a mar.

"It might be S-P, but I cannae tell for certain. Maybe it was part of S-P-E-C, but it's not easy tae know," Rosie said.

"Possibly. You don't remember what the letters stood for?"

"Big, pretentious words, meebe, but I cannae remember what Edwin said."

"Secrets everywhere."

"Aye. A paunchie of them, and I dinnae like secrets. I like everything oot there for everyone tae see. I dinnae like secrets, Delaney."

"Me neither," I said.

The bell above the door jingled. It was time to put away phones and secrets for now and get to work.

EIGHTEEN

"Hi, yes, I'm looking for—" She glanced at the piece of paper in her hand. "—Hamlet. At least that's the name I was given. Perhaps it's some sort of code or something."

"We do have someone named Hamlet working here, though he's not here at the moment. May I help you?" I said as Rosie put Hector on her lap and sent a welcoming smile to the customer.

She had an American accent, pretty green eyes, and boyishly short brown hair that looked feminine on her tanned face. Other than the accent, the tan gave her away as not being from Scotland. It was difficult to get a tan in the summer in Scotland, and tans in November were impossible.

"Sure. You're from the States?" She smiled.

"Kansas. I'm Delaney."

"Really? I'm from Florida. Ellen."

"Welcome to Scotland, Ellen."

"It's good to be here. Or it will be when I get all the errands done. I'm a nanny and the family I work for is touring the castle up there while I came to get the book Mr. Kramer ordered."

"I can help. I know where Hamlet keeps the orders. Back here."

I turned and led the way to the back corner.

"Ooh, this is so perfectly perfect," Ellen said when we reached Hamlet's table. "It's an adorable bookshop in Scotland, next to a castle. Is it all real? I mean, are the books really books or is this just for show, some setup to hook the tourists?" She laughed.

"It's real," I said. "And it's definitely perfect."

"I'd like to see a few more kilts, you know?"

"I do know. You'll see some, but there aren't as many as I expected either, which makes them even better when you do see one."

"How fun." She lowered her voice and leaned closer. "Was that a real dog in a sweater and a barrette?"

I lowered my voice too. "It was, and he's very friendly, likes to be scratched, mostly behind his right ear. I'll introduce you on the way out."

"Cool."

"What's the book you're here for?"

"I have no idea." She handed me the piece of paper. "It's something I can't even begin to pronounce."

Silently, I read the note. *Aonghas Pàdraig Caimbeul- An Oidhche Mus Do Sheòl Sinn.*

"It's in some old language," Ellen said.

"Scottish Gaelic," I said. No one from the book spoke in my head. I couldn't read Gaelic, hadn't even tried to have Hamlet (who actually knew a little Gaelic) help me through a page or two, but I'd heard about the book. "Not many books are published in Gaelic anymore. It's a big story about a family who lived during the twentieth century. Hamlet was telling me about it just the other day, probably when Mr. Kramer placed the order."

I looked at the shelf behind Hamlet's table. A pristine copy of the book sat on the top shelf with a Post-it noting the new owner's name and the fact that he'd paid in full. It wasn't an old book, having been published first in 2003, but it would have been difficult to find in the United States.

"The title translated is *The Night Before We Sailed*," I said. "I've heard it's quite beautiful." It was rare when I held a book and didn't even hear a low mumble of the characters inside. The language barrier made them the quietest group of bookish voices I'd ever known. Hamlet wrapped books in brown paper and tied them with string, but I hadn't had enough practice wrapping quickly yet, so I put it in a brown paper bag and folded the top over.

"Gaelic? Hmm."

"Not many people speak it anymore, but there's a school in Scotland trying to revive the language. I'm not sure how that will go."

"It looks like a jumble of letters to me," Ellen said as she carefully took the bag. "Thank you." She hesitated as she looked at me. "I'm sorry I didn't get to meet someone who's truly named Hamlet. Please tell me he looks like a Hamlet."

"He looks exactly like a Shakespearean character. You would not be disappointed. You and the Kramer family should try to stop by the shop again. I'm sure he'd love to meet you all."

"Good idea. I'll ask. Thanks." She pulled a knit cap out of her coat pocket and slipped it on, covering her short hair except for one end of a curl that stuck out from the side. The moment pinged something in my memory but I didn't know what it was specifically.

"What?" Ellen asked. "Did I put it on funny?"

"No, I'm sorry. It's a cute hat. I was admiring it," I said.

"Okay. Well, thanks," she said, putting her fingertips on a spot next to her ear. The cap was simple black knit.

There was nothing unique or interesting about it. She smiled. "I'm going to go pet the dog now."

"Sounds good."

I introduced her to Rosie and Hector, who melted appropriately as Ellen scratched behind his right ear.

"I think this might be even better than all the books," she said. "Thanks."

"Anytime," both Rosie and I said.

As she left, I leaned into the front window and watched her turn left to make her way up and around to the castle.

"A delightful American," Rosie said from the desk. "You liked her hat?"

"It was fine," I said a beat later.

"Delaney?"

"Sorry, Rosie, I was trying to remember something, but it's not coming back to me."

"S'awright. Excuse me, Delaney, I need tae grab something from my office. Ye'll be up front here a moment? I think Regg is bringing some coffee. Can ye watch Hector and the shop?"

"Sure."

Hector, still on the desk, and ever suspicious of my drifty moments, shifted as he looked my direction. I wanted to tell him that it wasn't the bookish voices this time, but I just nodded instead. He relaxed his head on his paws, seemingly content with my communication.

After Rosie disappeared through the door at the top of the stairs, I looked out the front window again and pushed my mind to work double-time. What had Ellen's hat reminded me of? I was a breath away from the memory coming clear, but that breath seemed to expand farther away with each passing second. I relaxed and hoped my instincts would kick in. *Talk to me.*

Love Jo all your days, if you choose, but don't let it

spoil you, for it's wicked to throw away so many good gifts because you can't have the one you want.

"*Little Women*?" I said aloud, albeit quietly, to myself.

It was Amy talking to Laurie. She knew he would always love Jo, but she didn't want him to miss the love she had to give him. I hadn't read anything by Louisa May Alcott in years.

Only after a person has their heart broken does the world appear as it truly is.

I'd read *Perfected Sinfulness* by British writer Michael Gilbert only recently, a recommendation from Hamlet.

"Okay, I get it," I muttered. "I'm supposed to be paying attention to the hearts that got broken."

Sometimes the bookish voices really did dig deep into my subconscious and dredge up something I hadn't quite zeroed in on yet. I needed to find and talk to Clarissa, I was sure. There was no other answer at the moment. I pulled out the Post-it Aggie had given me and looked at it.

The bell jingled again as two more customers and Regg, holding a tray full of coffee cups, walked in.

I'd have to attend to Clarissa later.

———

"I ken ye'd want tae call on Ms. Bellows at the end of yer workday," Elias said from the driver's seat. He'd answered his phone on the first ring when I'd called. "I was ready for yer call."

"It took you a whole thirty seconds to come get me."

"Aye. I was parked just over there. Had tae pull out into traffic was all."

"Thanks, Elias."

"Glad tae be of service. I know the way. Aggie and I looked at the map on the computer before I left, but I ken Edinburgh weel enough tae get there on my own."

"Aggie likes her computer."

"She does, even if I think it's the devil of a thing. It's been more good than bad though, I suppose."

Elias was gifted at small talk. He could bring up the most mundane topic and make it seem both interesting and curious at the same time. I credited his accent and his sense of humor. We made interesting small talk about refinishing the floors in the guesthouses as he drove, and by the time we turned onto a narrow street lined with shortish trees, I had a passing desire to sand and varnish something.

"Here we are," he said as he parked. He nodded across the street.

The bottom of the two-story house was hidden by a large row of mostly leaf-free shrubbery, but the second story was visible above the bushes. About ten feet back from the bordering plants sat a stately, light-colored, squarish home. It was difficult to see it clearly with only the streetlights' illumination and all the plants blocking the lower story.

"Should I just go and knock on the door?" I said.

"Aye. Cannae think of a better way," Elias said. "I'll come with ye."

There was no other traffic to impede us, no rain. As we searched for an opening in the wall of plants no cars drove by, no pedestrians spotted us. It was dark and cold and quiet.

We found a short gate at an opening on the side of the property around the corner. Elias swung it in with a squeak and then let me lead the way into the small front garden, now cut back for winter, but showing signs that there would be an abundance of flowers and plants come spring. The garden spread back and around the main focal point—a tall, now empty concrete fountain and birdbath.

"Charming," I said.

"Aye," Elias said suspiciously.

"What?"

"Not a fan of the funtains. Something jubous about people with funtains."

"Jubous?"

"Suspicious."

"Suspicious, how?"

"Dinnae ken." He shrugged. "Just how they make me feel."

"Okay."

"Help ye?" a voice cracked from the dark corner on the other side of the fountain.

Elias and I both jumped.

"Och, sairy I scairt ye," she said as she came into view. She was older than time maybe, bent over and shriveled. Even though the dog on the end of the leash she held was a small poodle, I thought the animal could pull her over if it tugged too hard.

"We should have announced ourselves better. Clarissa Bellows?" I said.

"Heavens no, I'm not Clarissa," she said as she peered up from under the brim of a straw hat that seemed more appropriate to summer gardening than winter nights walking the dog.

After a beat of strained silence, Elias spoke. "We've stopped by tae pay a visit tae Ms. Clarissa Bellows. Does she live here?"

"Aye, Clarissa Bellows McIntyre does reside here. Shall I gather her for ye?"

Elias and I shared a look before I said, "Can we help you inside?"

"No, not a'tall," she said as she shuffled toward the door, the dog keeping his steps slow and even with watchful sideways glances at her feet.

A long few moments later she stepped through the front doorway and turned toward us.

"Names?" she said.

We gave them to her.

"Ye're with?"

"Uh. I work at a local bookshop."

"Wait here." She shut the door and disappeared.

"We could be here a long while," Elias said quietly as he lifted and then replaced his cap.

I smiled and wrapped my arms around myself.

Much to our surprise, the door swung open only a couple of seconds later.

"Do I know you? Please tell me you're not here tae sell me something, because I would have to shoot you if that's the case."

There was no mistaking that this was Clarissa Bellows, now McIntyre. The woman looked almost exactly like the version of herself I'd seen in the university newspaper picture. As my Kansas grandmother would have said, and though it was an expression that always got under my skin, it seemed wildly appropriate at the moment: this woman was "well preserved."

"We're . . ." I began.

"You dinnae ken us," Elias said as he put his hands up in a surrender gesture. "But we're not here tae sell ye anything. Just here for a moment of yer time."

Clarissa cocked her head, squinted, seemed to like what she saw, and then smiled. "All right. Come in. Mind yourselves though. I can still shoot you if you make me mad enough."

"Will do," I said.

I followed her inside and Elias followed me as I became transfixed by the wavering hem of her blue silk robe and the authoritative noise her hard-soled slippers made on the polished wood floor. She moved quickly, giving me no real time to peek into the two rooms we passed. She finally turned into a room on our left and reached around the wall to flip a switch.

"Have a seat and make it quick. I have a good book on my nightstand that's calling tae me at this very moment."

"Okay," I said as I sat on a red-and-yellow-floral-patterned wingback chair. Elias sat next to me on a matching one as Clarissa took a seat on the spotless white Victorian couch. She sat with such a flourish of her blue robe that I sensed she'd taken on the pose for a photograph at one time.

The room was homey, complete with a fireplace mantel and a baby grand piano, both covered in family pictures. Considering what I knew about all the men who had been in love with her in the past I wished for the chance to look over the pictures, or better yet meet her husband. Who had won this beautiful woman's heart?

"Your name is Delaney. Are you from America?" Clarissa asked, her tone so friendly and welcoming now that I did a double take.

"I am. I'm working here, though, at a bookshop called The Cracked Spine."

Clarissa's smile fell quickly and I wished I hadn't mentioned the bookshop part so quickly. Her eyebrows came together and I braced myself for the chance she'd shoot.

"I see," she said. "Edwin send you here?"

"No, not at all. I'm here on my own. Elias is a friend," I said as I nodded toward him.

She didn't look at Elias. She didn't look anywhere but directly at me.

"What can I do for you?" she asked, not meaning it.

"I guess I have some questions about your time in school with Edwin, Gordon Armstrong, and Leith Stanton."

"Why?"

I cleared my throat. I should have rehearsed this better, but I hadn't. I had, however, thought about my approach and decided that the honest, most direct route was truly the only way to go, but that didn't change the fact that the words didn't want to be easily or quickly spoken. "There's been a . . . tragedy."

"What happened?"

"A murder."

"Who?"

"Gordon Armstrong's son. Billy."

I'd never seen the sequence of her next actions before. Clarissa gasped, stood up, started to cry, and then fainted, all in only a few brief seconds.

Fortunately, Elias was quickly up and out of his chair to catch her.

"Oh, no! Not again. This has got to stop," I said, more to myself than anyone.

"Call for an ambulance, lass," he said to me as he held Clarissa in his arms.

NINETEEN

The conversation with Clarissa Bellows Mc-Intyre did not resume, but fortunately she regained consciousness. The paramedics weren't happy with her heart rhythm so she was carted away, off to hospital, leaving Elias and me in a wake of concern and guilt.

Elias and I had been trying to stay out of the way but still answer the questions the medical professionals had. After the ambulance left and everyone was sure we hadn't purposefully done something to harm Clarissa, we set out down the hallway to leave too. We were surprised when the older woman appeared from a back room.

"I'm Liza Marie," she said. "Clarissa's cousin. What did ye want with her?"

The hat had been removed and she stood up much straighter than before. Her gray hair was pulled back into a tight bun and her blue eyes were much clearer than I would have predicted.

"We wanted to ask her some questions. We didn't know we would be so upsetting but maybe we should have predicted as much. I don't know. We're sorry," I said.

"What did ye say?"

I repeated the short conversation as best I could.

"Och, those were long-ago days that she wouldnae want tae be reminded of. Circumstances did not go well. It took her some time tae move forward. She met her husband, God rest his soul, and she managed tae put the bad memories behind her. I suppose ye stirred up some ghosts she'd rather hadnae been bothered."

"We're very sorry," I said again, disappointment over her now dead husband adding to the guilt I felt. If he were still here, he could comfort her at least.

"She'll be fine. Tell me more about the lad Billy Armstrong. What happened tae him?"

"He wasn't a young man," I said. "Almost fifty I guess. All I really know is that he was murdered and they haven't found the killer."

She frowned as she nodded.

I bit my bottom lip, looked at Elias and then back at Liza Marie. "There was an *Oor Wullie* book and a dirk involved. Do you know anything about those or about the secret society that Clarissa was a part of back at university?"

"No. All I really ken aboot is a man who died on a boat. It was a tragedy that Clarissa never quite got over."

"What happened to the man on the boat?"

"She was on the boat with other men. A man went over the side and drowned, but it has been the nightmare that's haunted her all these years. It's why she never finished school, why she left Scotland for a time. She had much healing tae do."

"Drowned?" I asked.

"Aye."

"It sounds like it was rough."

"I suppose t'would be difficult for anyone tae get much past that." She smoothed her already smooth hair. "Why was it yer job tae tell her about the murder?"

"I guess I made it my job," I said. "I care for my boss, and he's upset about Billy too."

"Ye said ye worked at the bookshop, but who's yer boss?"

"Edwin MacAlister."

I could tell she knew that we hadn't intended to upset Clarissa, particularly to the point of being ill. She nodded thoughtfully but not suspiciously.

"I have one suggestion for ye," she said.

"Anything."

"Tell yer boss tae stop by the hospital and see her tomorrow morning. She'll be there until at least the afternoon, since they'll admit her. I think it would do her some good."

I looked at Liza Marie and realized she knew much more than she was sharing. It was at that moment, as I looked at her beautiful but wrinkled face, that it became distinctly clear to me how old all these secrets were. Decades, about half a century. Ancient, considering a life span. No one had wanted these memories brought back to the surface, and old bad memories probably hurt worse than new bad memories. Did bad memories that old ever really die?

"I will," I said.

And I would, no matter how weird it would be.

———

I started the next day with a call to Hamlet. I tried Rosie's mobile but didn't get an answer.

"I'll be a little late this morning," I said.

"Thanks for letting me know," Hamlet said. "I'll tell Rosie when she gets here."

"Do you know if Edwin will be in today?"

"I believe so. Rosie said yesterday that she expected him today."

"Good. I shouldn't be too late. Would you mind asking him to wait for me if he gets there before I do?"

"No problem. Everything all right?"

"Fine, but I need to talk to him."

"Certainly. Oh, there was a note taped to the front door for you."

"From?"

"I don't know. It smells like fish though."

"Would you mind opening it and reading it to me?"

"Aye. Hang on. Let me grab it." The sound of paper tearing came through the phone. "From Gordon Armstrong. He'd like you tae meet him tomorrow evening, at the fish market."

"Really?"

"Aye. You're not going, are you?"

"Not alone at least. I saw him two days ago and he told me to stay away, so I'm curious."

"Delaney?" Hamlet said.

"I'll tell you all about it later today, but I promise I won't go by myself to meet the man who's pretending to be dead, particularly at night. Not a chance. I just have one quick errand to run before I come in this morning."

"Should I tell Edwin about the note?"

"No, I'll tell him."

"All right. You're not doing anything stupid, are you?"

"Not completely."

"That's at least something. Be careful, Delaney. If you're not in by ten I'm showing Edwin and Rosie the note and calling . . . Tom, that's who I'll call."

I smiled. "Okay, but I'll be in."

"See you soon," he said with a hopeful caution.

The bus I took was the same one I always took to work, but today instead of disembarking at Grassmarket, I rode it up the hill to the Royal Mile and then down toward the sea. I'd created a superstitious personal tradition of nodding toward the wall at the bottom of the hill that enclosed the World's End Pub. The wall used to mark the border of Edinburgh, back in the day when the tens of thousands of residents were all cramped onto the long road that was topped off by the castle, living in small rooms piled high and fighting terrible deadly diseases. I was glad to live in current times.

Whenever I passed that wall I knew I was leaving behind a huge population of ghosts. I didn't sense them, really, except for a weighty loss each time I left them behind. Like sometimes in the warehouse, it felt a little like time travel.

The police station was at the bottom of the hill, housed in an old building with a small clock tower in the middle. Inspector Winters and I hadn't gotten off to the greatest of starts, but once the murder of Edwin's sister had been solved we'd formed a friendship. I'd lied to him when he'd first asked me about a secret room full of treasures that Edwin kept; I told him it didn't exist. I hadn't righted the lie, and there were moments I thought he was still so curious about the possibility of its existence that he did things like tell me more about Grizel than he should have with the hope I'd spill the beans about the room. I never would.

"Help you?" a young girl behind the front desk asked with a smile.

"Inspector Winters in?" I said.

"What's yer name and why do ye need tae talk tae him?"

"Delaney Nichols, and I have some questions about the dirk."

Her eyebrows lifted. "One minute." She lifted the handpiece from the old phone on her mostly clean desk.

A magazine lay open in the middle, displaying pictures of what I assumed were celebrities, but I didn't get a close look.

Inspector Winters swung his head around the side wall almost as the young woman hung up the phone.

"Delaney?" he said.

"Hi. Am I interrupting anything?"

"Not really. Come on back."

I followed him directly to the small interview room I'd been in before. He closed the door behind us and sat only after I did.

"As I mentioned, we didn't find any prints on the dirk or the business card, but thank you for bringing them tae me. We're going tae keep them until the murder is solved but it looks like you will get the dirk back if we don't find an owner."

"I'm disappointed there were no prints that might help."

"The items had been outside. I didn't expect much. Is that what you came to ask me about?"

"Not exactly."

I hadn't gone to the police station to spill the beans about Gordon, though I was getting closer to doing exactly that. I was still concerned about the other ramifications for Fiona. It was more than the money. Gordon had committed an immeasurable betrayal, and I didn't think Fiona needed that right now. Nevertheless, I was getting close to not caring much about the ramifications of bringing Gordon's lie to light. I just wasn't all the way there quite yet.

"I have a question about something that happened a long time ago."

"All right." He pulled out the notebook and pen he kept in his shirt pocket and placed them on the table, but he didn't ready himself to write anything and his eyes squinted suspiciously. I imagine the secret room mystery was wearing thin for him. "I'll do my best tae answer."

"There was a tragedy back when Edwin was at university. He was on a boat with friends and someone died," I said.

"Drowned?"

"Maybe, or was killed, I think accidentally, with . . . a dirk." I paused as his eyes squinted even more suspiciously. "Right, anyway, I think the police had to fish the body out of the water."

"Maybe like the dirk you brought in here?"

"It's the dirk that brought back the memory. Coincidence. Timing."

"Sounds terrible."

"I know."

"And what information would you like from me?"

"Can you tell me anything about that old case? Maybe there's something in a file somewhere. Also, is there a chance you know anything about a secret society at the university? Something called SPEC. Maybe something that was somehow a part of the death of the man on the boat?"

Inspector Winters took a deep breath and let it out. "I don't know what information I can get from a long-ago tragedy, but being that it was so long ago, perhaps it will be easy. Either the case is closed or cold. If it's cold, are you saying you might have some information tae help solve it?"

"No, I'm afraid not. It's just . . . well, Edwin is so secretive. A person from his past has come back into his life. Rosie's upset. I'm trying to get a clear story so I can smooth troubled waters," I said. So far I hadn't exactly lied.

He gathered the pen and notepad and put them back into his pocket as he stood.

"Who's the friend?" he asked. "Perhaps someone who

is also tied tae the dead man's father who died in the fire a couple years ago?"

"No, it's someone else from his university days." Still not really lying, but getting much closer. If he'd ask if the person who'd come into Edwin's life was Gordon, it would have been a complete lie, but Inspector Winters thought Gordon was dead.

He bit his bottom lip and looked at me. "I need tae know if you have any information about a crime, Delaney."

"I know. I brought the dirk and the business card right to you."

"You did. All right, give me a minute. I need tae ring someone."

I wasn't alone for long. It seemed like only a few minutes before he came back.

"I'm afraid I don't have any immediate answers. I made a call, but I'll need some time, and searching for the answers won't be a big priority. We're busy with current cases. Now, if you had something that might help us solve something old, I could get information more quickly." He rubbed his chin. He was slightly overweight, giving his features a pleasant roundness.

"Thank you for making the call, Inspector Winters," I said.

"Aye. You're welcome. Thank you for bringing me the items you found at the castle."

"You're welcome."

The air was never so thick with untold truths, on both our parts probably.

I stood and he escorted me out of the station.

"Thank you," I said again.

"Stay in touch, Delaney from Kansas in America. And be careful."

"I will."

Though I got out of the police station without telling Inspector Winters that Gordon Armstrong was still alive, I felt so guilty about my attempt at manipulating him for answers that I wondered if he'd put the pieces together on his own. If he saw through my elusiveness, our friendship might soon come to an end.

That would be disappointing.

TWENTY

"Delaney," Edwin said, the disappointment thick in his voice even with just that one word.

I nodded but I didn't apologize. There were many reasons I didn't utter the words, "I'm sorry," but mostly just because I wasn't sorry that I'd disappointed my boss.

"I know, Edwin, I've dredged up a lot of things, but Clarissa's reaction when I told her about Billy was one of the worst moments of my life, worse even than what I've done to you this week. I can't believe I was responsible for putting her in the hospital. Maybe I shouldn't have gone to talk to her, but I did. You need to go see her; at least that's what her cousin said to do."

Edwin nodded. "I will go see Clarissa. I wish I could have been the one tae tell her about Billy. It would have been better coming from me. I should have found her immediately."

"What's Clarissa's tie to you all, to Billy Armstrong?" I asked.

We were in the warehouse. I'd double-checked the lock because I didn't want there to be any chance we would be interrupted. Nevertheless, Edwin stood up and moved to the door. He checked the deadbolt and the knob.

As he sat down again I tried not to look too quizzical, but I doubt I pulled it off.

"Delaney, Billy Armstrong was Clarissa's biological son," he said after he folded his hands on his lap.

"Oh, crap," I said. My heart sank. Briefly, I had wondered about that. I'd hoped it wasn't true, hoped that the strangely mixed friendship of the three men and Clarissa hadn't somehow led to Billy. Everything else in me sank with my heart. I'd surprised a woman with the news that her son had died, had been killed. "Oh, oh, oh, crap."

"Aye." Edwin blinked at my blanching face and said, "She hadn't known him, lass. She gave birth tae the boy, and Gordon and Fiona raised him from that moment. The news was terrible for her, I'm certain, but not what you might think, perhaps."

"Oh no," I said. "Who was Billy's biological father?"

Edwin sighed. "We didn't know."

"As in, she didn't tell you?" I asked.

Edwin's mouth formed a straight, hard line. "I'm afraid it wasn't that simple. The father—well, the father could have been one of three different men, or at least that was what she said back then."

"You, Leith, and Gordon?" I said.

"I'm ashamed tae say it, but aye, we were the three. She claimed tae love all three of us, Delaney. We all . . . well, looking back I know that she was just trying to confuse the matter." He sighed again. "The story makes us all sound like terrible and careless people. We weren't. We were young, perhaps a wee bit careless, and Clarissa didn't want tae keep the child. We think she wanted the father's identity tae be unclear. She manipulated all of us, but we all went along with the manipulations. We never understood why she did what she did, but it was most likely because she was a frightened young woman. Back then, single women simply didn't have and raise children.

I haven't seen her in almost fifty years, lass. None of us have. We broke ties after Billy was born."

"But how did Gordon come to raise Billy?"

"Gordon and Fiona were already married, married young, before university actually. Fiona thought Clarissa was a friend of all of ours, and she was going tae give up the baby. Fiona couldn't have children, so she took Billy in and was the best mother any child could hope for."

"Fiona didn't know that Gordon might be Billy's biological father?"

"I don't think he ever told her about his infidelity. I wouldn't know for certain though."

I thought back to Billy. Had he looked like Edwin or Gordon or Leith, who I'd only seen briefly in the old newspaper picture? I realized that Billy looked more like Clarissa than any of the men.

"He might have been yours?" I said, my voice cracking.

"Aye."

"I'm so sorry, Edwin." I *was* sorry about that part. Tears filled my eyes.

"Lass, I'm heartbroken about his death, but it's been a long time since I considered that I might have fathered him. I tried tae give money tae Gordon and Fiona, tried tae help them, but Gordon wouldn't hear of it. They raised the boy as their own." He swallowed hard. "My heart hurts, but it's their heartbreak we should be considering."

His heartbreak was pretty evident to me. "Not Clarissa's?"

"Weel, she's tae get some sympathy too. She was a lovely young woman who handled a delicate situation in the wrong way. She wasn't . . . Lass, it's difficult tae tell you the story of the time as it was. Aye, there might have been three potential fathers, and that sounds disgraceful on the surface, but you'll have tae trust me that it wasn't

disgraceful. It was just . . . it was just many poor decisions. It all worked out for the best though, it truly did.
Until recent events at least."

"I believe you, but maybe Billy was killed because of
that past?"

"I have no idea how, lass. It was rough, but we were
all happy with the final outcome. Leith is gone and I
would never have hurt any of them. They were friends,
dear friends at one time. You understand why we had tae
part ways, but at one time I loved them like family."

"What about the man on the boat that Clarissa accidentally killed?"

"Delaney, that wasn't Clarissa. I don't know where you
got the information, but she didn't kill him. He fell overboard, that's all. There was no mystery."

"No knife? No dirk that killed him first, accidentally
even?"

Edwin's eyebrows came together. "No, lass. We were
all wearing dirks, but there was no foul play, even accidentally. The lad had had too much tae drink. We all had. It
was terrible, but that's not what tore apart our friendship."

I believed him, but I was momentarily rocked by
the fact that I'd been given the wrong information by
Rosie.

"I thought Leith served some time in prison for the
death," I said.

"No, not for that. Leith spent some time in jail but not
for anything that terrible. I believe his crimes were along
the lines of drunk and disorderly. How did you come by
this information?"

I smiled weakly. "Rosie."

Edwin's smile matched mine. "I see. Rosie is good at
embellishing and mixing up stories, but there was no
murder. She means no harm, but she's not the most reliable

source. I didn't know you were dredging up these old events or I would have talked tae you sooner, before you'd spoken tae Rosie."

He could have returned my calls, but I didn't point that out.

"What's S-P-E-C?" I said.

He thought a moment. "Our secret society?"

"Yes."

"My goodness, lass, you have been busy. How do you know about SPEC? No matter. It disbanded after the drowning."

"Why is the sticker on your diploma? It's in your office, up against the wall."

"I'd forgotten all about that. I put the sticker on the glass decades ago, tae remind me of the better days at university and, I suppose, the lessons that needed tae be learned by the bad days. I pulled the diploma out from behind my file cabinet shortly after you got back from the castle and told me about Billy. Anyway, by the time I graduated, we'd gone our separate ways and Clarissa was long gone tae us all, having run away tae have the baby and then never returning tae school. I ran into her some years later once but didn't keep tabs on her."

"What do the letters stand for?"

"S-P-E-C?"

"Yes."

"Society, propriety, excellence, and calling. We meant it tae mean that we honor society, we behave with propriety, we strive for excellence, and we search for and follow our calling, whatever that might be." Edwin smiled sadly. "We thought we were so special, more honorable than the next lads. We were wrong and we learned our lesson quickly, Delaney. It was a tough lesson for some of us tae learn."

They weren't *big words* like Rosie had remembered.

"Were the lessons tough for you too?" I asked.

"Well, despite my wealthy upbringing, my parents tried to instill some humility in me." He smiled again, a little less sadly. "We weren't a part of something that had any sort of history to it. We created it. It wasn't meant tae be something done out of arrogance, but it felt that way after what we went through. We felt stupid and arrogant."

"You know, lots of university-aged kids do crazy or stupid things that don't necessarily dictate their futures. I'm sorry you all weren't that fortunate."

Edwin brought his eyebrows together and he studied me a moment.

"All of what we are talking about took place a very long time ago. Another lifetime, really. None of us forgot the pain from that time, particularly the death of the lad, but we were happy with what happened to Billy. Despite my feelings for Gordon now and his lies, Billy had a lovely family. I'm sure even Clarissa was happy with that outcome."

"But it's all so . . . suspicious, Edwin. Leith is dead. Gordon has been playing dead. Billy was killed. All coincidences?"

"I think so. Sad coincidences they may be."

"Why did the dirk upset you so much?"

"It brought back those days, the drowning, Clarissa's manipulations. The handle made me think it was her dirk at one time. As I mentioned, we were all wearing dirks on the boat. It was part of SPEC, tae wear the dirks. I hadn't seen that one in years, but it brought back the memories; even more than Gordon coming into the shop, that dirk took me back tae those days."

It was only because I'd sensed that he'd been mostly telling me the truth before that I knew this statement was a lie, or at least partly a lie, but I nodded. Why would Gordon have said the dirk indicated that Edwin could be

Billy's killer? Then again, Gordon's life seemed to be one big lie.

"Why did you go to Glasgow yesterday?" I asked.

"Well, that's business for another day. I looked at a portrait I'd like to buy and sell at auction. I needed the time alone or I would have taken you. We'll talk about it another day. For now, I think I should go see Clarissa."

"May I come with you?" I asked.

"Aye, Delaney. Come along."

———

"I am fine. Please stop all of this . . ." Clarissa said to the nurse who seemed to be trying to take her blood pressure.

The woman I'd caused to faint to the floor looked no worse for the wear as she sat up in the hospital bed. I was momentarily jolted by the hospital gown and its noticeable lack of high style, but her hair and makeup were in place and she felt well enough to argue with the nurse. I took all of those behaviors as good signs.

On the way up to the hospital room Edwin prepared me for the fact that even though Clarissa's cousin might think he should visit Clarissa, Clarissa herself might not be all that happy to see him. And even if she was happy, there would be at least an undercurrent of unhappy riding with it.

We had stopped by the nurse's station to ask if it would be okay to visit the patient. Edwin admitted to the fact that she might experience a raised blood pressure at seeing him. The nurse had smiled, looked around to see if anyone was listening, and then told us Clarissa's heart was fine and that she would probably be released within a few hours.

Nevertheless, I worried briefly as I saw the look on Clarissa's face when she noticed Edwin.

"I guess I should have predicted I might see you soon," she said as she sat up straighter in the bed. She smoothed the front of the hospital gown and pinched her earlobe as if she was checking on an earring. Her mouth fell into a straight line and color bloomed on her cheeks.

"Hello, Clarissa," Edwin said with a smile.

He approached the bed and took her hand in both of his.

"You are still beautiful," he said.

She didn't buy into the compliment but at least she didn't roll her eyes as she gently pulled her hand away.

"Hello," she said to me.

"I'm so very sorry," I said. "I didn't know."

"Of course not."

"But I told her the story," Edwin said.

"I work for him," I said.

"You mentioned that," she said.

"Aye, Delaney is a good friend. She cares for all of us at The Cracked Spine. Sometimes perhaps a bit too enthusiastically." He smiled at me before turning back to Clarissa. "She didn't know about the secrets from a long time ago before she came to visit you. She does now. I told her about me, Gordon, and Leith."

Clarissa blinked, nodded, and then looked at me, her mouth still a straight line. I had listened hard to Edwin's tone. I didn't want to believe that he was trying to send Clarissa a signal as to the version of the story he'd told me, but that's exactly what I'd heard. I wouldn't call them on it, but continue to listen and hopefully figure out the truth at some point.

"Much happened that I'm not proud of, but it was a long time ago and we all did the best we could even if it doesn't seem like it," she said.

I shook my head. "I'm just sorry for the way I handled everything when I came to see you. I hope you're feeling better."

"I'm fine. My heart's fine. Well . . ." She put her hand over her heart as if to see if it really was fine. She removed it a second later and sat up even straighter. "My heart hurts but not because it is sick. I'm sorry tae hear about Billy Armstrong. It's sad news."

"Devastating," Edwin agreed. He cleared his throat.

"Did you know him well, Edwin? Billy?" Clarissa asked.

"I knew him a wee bit as a boy and young man mostly. I hadn't seen him much over the last thirty years. But through Gordon and Fiona I knew he was fine. He was always happy, always kind."

"Gordon and Leith died two years ago. Now Billy. I regret . . . It doesn't matter."

"There's no need tae regret anything. You did right by him."

Edwin and Clarissa looked at each other a long moment. There was no indication that Edwin was going to tell her that Gordon had not died with Leith. She looked at me.

"If you know the story, I must sound like quite the tart tae you, Delaney," Clarissa said.

"Not at all. Things happen. I understand that nothing is as simple as it might sound. Ever."

"True."

Again she and Edwin gazed at each other. They both looked like slightly older versions of the newspaper picture I'd seen, sepia tones turning to full color right in front of me. They'd aged well. I felt like I needed to give them some time alone. Clarissa hadn't been angry. I sensed that she was happy to see Edwin and he felt the same to see her.

As I was going to excuse myself, she spoke again.

"I have had a good life. My husband was a good man," she said.

"I'm sorry he's gone, Clari," Edwin said.

"Thank you, Edwin." Clarissa turned to me again. "My husband passed last year, didn't wake up one morning. His lungs. He'd lived a good long life, but it was the cigarettes that did him in. A bad way tae go."

"Did you two have any kids?"

"Aye. One son. He's a lovely man. He lives in Glasgow."

"I'm sorry for your loss," I said. Glasgow was where Edwin had claimed to go yesterday. Was this another piece of the puzzle or another coincidence?

"Excuse me. I'll wait outside for you," I said to Edwin. I turned to Clarissa. "I hope you feel better, and again I'm so very sorry."

She nodded and hinted at a smile.

Once in the hallway I stepped out of the way of a hurried group of medical personnel. The nurse who'd been trying to get Clarissa's blood pressure smiled at me from behind the nurse's station. I smiled back and approached the station.

"She's fine, huh?" I said.

"Oh, aye, she'll go home soon. Ye a family member?"

"No, a friend of a friend. Has her son come by to visit?"

"No, she wouldnae give us any family names. She didn't want tae worry anyone. An older lady stopped by earlier this morning, but she didn't stay long."

I didn't know if Scottish laws were similar to American medical privacy laws, but I couldn't imagine that Clarissa's health was any of my business or important to my growing list of questions.

The passing of almost fifty years hadn't completely diffused the spark between Edwin and Clarissa. I felt it when they looked at each other. How in the world had those dynamics worked? Three men smitten with the same woman. That had to have gotten ugly.

Maybe she had loved all of them or maybe she'd not

loved any of them. I would have liked to truly travel back in time just for a moment to better understand their complicated relationships.

Fifty years ago. The mid-1960s. Had Scotland seen any of the hippie counterculture movement? I didn't think it had, though Hamlet had said something recently about that time period. I was curious enough to wonder. I'd have to ask someone.

I just had to figure out who.

TWENTY-ONE

Turned out my problem was easily solved. Artair knew almost everything about everything, and he was one of my dinner dates that evening.

Tom had prepared dinner for the two of us, which turned out to be the three of us. He made his famous seafood pasta and invited his father to join us. Artair had told him he had some information he wanted to pass along to me.

Tom lived by the sea. In a small blue house that was from another time. It was squeaky and drafty and held one of my favorite places in the entire world: a big old chair by a front window and a fireplace, from which could be seen a view of the North Sea while one lounged, under a quilt preferably, and read book after book.

The old two-story house was tucked between two larger, also older, buildings that had been turned into apartments. Artair had purchased the house when he and Tom's now deceased mother had first gotten married. The garden in front of the house was as close to a magical garden as I'd ever seen. No one had ever requested that the house be torn down to make way for other, taller buildings that could hold more people or bring in more money.

Artair had eventually aged to the point that it was more work than enjoyment for him, so he gave the house to Tom and moved to a flat closer to the university library, where he spent most of his time anyway. Tom had proved to have just as green a thumb as his father, but the lines of the garden had apparently changed, become somehow more modern. I hadn't seen it pre-Tom so I didn't quite understand what that meant, but he and Artair had spoken about it a few times, neither of them giving way to how they thought a garden should look. Their garden stubbornness was only one of the many things they had in common.

"No, we didnae experience the 1960s the same way ye Americans did," Artair said. "However . . ." He scratched his cheek as he sat across the small kitchen table from me. "No, the rebelliousness that came along with yer hippies didn't happen here, but something else did. There was an undercurrent of change that would happen more in the 1970s and that could be seen and felt mostly with the literature of the time, the poetry too. Counterculture was quieter here, citizens finding their explorations in books or quiet clubs. I knew of a club in Glasgow. Can't remember the name offhand, but I went a time or two."

"Who were some of the writers of the time?" I asked.

"If I remember correctly, and I can look it up for you, I believe a group of them were given some sort of title like 'justified sinners of the sixties,' even if their words didn't become imbedded deeply enough to cause any sort of large movement. John Calder, Jim Haynes, Ian Finlay . . ."

"Someone recently brought a first-edition Ian Finlay into the bookshop," I interrupted.

"Aye? Weel, meebe there's still hope that the books will be read and thought about, but it's been a long time."

I looked at Tom before I continued. I didn't sense that Artair was as conservative as my parents back home. I didn't want to say anything too scandalous, but I couldn't think of a more delicate way to phrase my question.

"So, if a woman back then was uncertain of which man of three was the father of her child, how would that have been received?" I said.

Artair laughed. "Not weel at all. No woman in her right mind would have admitted tae such a thing. And if she wasnae married, she'd be smart tae get married before the pregnancy showed. No, that wouldnae have gone over weel. It was a different time tae be sure. I remember the sense of wild freedom that we saw coming from America. I believe many of us found it interesting, but also somewhat frightening. No love and peace here. 'Twas a much more conservative time for us." He held up two fingers in an arthritic peace sign.

The pose didn't seem awkward on the older man with the slightly too-long hair and bushy eyebrows. Tom and I shared a smile.

Clarissa and the three men in her life had been faced with a difficult situation. She'd given her child to the man who might have been the biological father, but there must have been so much more involved. Big emotions, big feelings, ultimately more painful than joyous.

But the group of friends had been faced with at least one other difficult situation too. The death of their fellow society member.

"Artair, I found out what 'SPEC' means." I shared Edwin's definition and his explanation of the group's intended motives. "It was a short-lived secret society that Edwin and his friends started. The letters stood for society, propriety, excellence, and calling. Does it sound more familiar?"

"Aye, now it does. I did a little research."

"They had a member fall off a boat and drown."

Artair nodded. "There was some suspicion around the death though. That's what I found."

"Oh?" I said.

He leaned over and pulled a file up from out of a bag he'd placed on the floor beside his chair.

"It was ultimately covered up, I think. That's what's bothered me the most when ye first mentioned it."

"Covered up?" I said.

"Aye, or mistakenly reported."

Tom and I shared a curious look before I took the pieces of paper that Artair handed me. He kept hold of them too for a moment and looked me in the eye. Artair was a playful man with a kindness that overlapped into everything he did. I'd never seen such a serious expression on his face. I gave him my undivided attention.

"Delaney, the only reason I knew tae look for this is because I've been at the library a long time, over thirty years. But when I first started working there, I was curious, energetic, and ambitious. I'm still curious." He half smiled. "Deep in the archives I came upon something that made me wonder—had someone gotten away with murder? It leuks as if that moment, that time when I sat on a cold floor with open boxes around me and a mind tae put them in order, has come full circle, and here we are.

"All those years ago, I read a story about a man who had died on a boat, had been stabbed on accident by a dirk and then had gone over the side, his body being retrieved not too much later."

"So he *was* stabbed?" I said.

"The top paper is a copy of that story."

The article wasn't from the university newspaper, but from *The Scotsman*. It was short and to the point. University students had been out on the water, there had been a tragic accident, and charges were expected to be filed, but no names were being released until further facts could be verified.

I flipped to the next page. It was an article from the university paper. It stated that there was a mistake in *The Scotsman*'s report that a stabbing had occurred. None had occurred. The accident was a drowning, that was all.

"You think it got covered up from one story to the next?" I said.

"Leuk at the last page," Artair said.

It was another article from *The Scotsman*. Again it was short and to the point, claiming that the publisher of the paper stood by the reporter who first reported about the stabbing. They believed that the university was trying to cover up the event, but they had no further proof and the police weren't cooperating. They would continue to try to gather more evidence or proof.

I looked at Artair. "Any other reports?"

"Not that I could find."

"So a stabbing would be murder, a drowning an accident."

"Even if the stabbing had been accidental, someone might have had tae pay the price for their carelessness. As it was, the story could have been that the young man fell off the boat of his own accord."

"Well, this is certainly suspicious," I said. "The contradictions, I mean."

Who'd either lied or been mistaken, Edwin or Rosie?

"Aye. More memories came back after I started searching. This box was hidden in the depths of the library and when I brought it up so that I might ask questions all those decades ago I was told tae put it back where I found it. Quickly, at that."

"Why wasn't it all just destroyed?"

Artair smiled and lifted his eyebrows. "Like I

mentioned tae ye at the library, we like tae keep a record of everything, us librarians, even if we're told tae hide it away. Someone back then wanted the facts tae remain somewhere, I suppose. Probably wanted someone like me tae find them someday."

I nodded. Proof was in front of me that something murderous or accidentally homicidal might have happened many years ago. But, other than Edwin and Rosie's differing stories, what more did that mean—particularly to Billy Armstrong's murder?

I had no idea.

"Do you think this ties in with Billy Armstrong?" I said.

Again, Artair shrugged. "Dinnae ken. It's just something tae keep in mind for now."

"I've got something else you might want tae keep in mind, Delaney," Tom added.

Artair and I watched him as he stood and walked around the corner and into the front room. He brought back his own file folder.

"I have something I want tae show you," he said as he opened the file. "I would not have found this on my own, of course. Da's the one for research. But Rodger overheard us talking about William Wallace and the reenactments. He had this at his home and brought it tae me."

Tom handed me the paper over the table. I held it so Artair could see it too.

"Another article," I said. "From three years ago."

"Rodger's brother was a William Wallace reenactor back then," Tom said. "Something happened."

Artair and I read silently.

William Wallace Reenactor Gilroy Wyly was killed yesterday at the William Wallace monument in Stirling.

> In what witnesses say was an accident, Wyly was
> killed by a dirk. Witnesses say some of the reenac-
> tors were "playing around" with the dirks and this
> one accidentally stabbed Gilroy in the heart. The in-
> cident is under investigation.
>
> Additionally, it was noted by the reenactors that
> the dirks weren't used for the reenactments. The
> use of dirks would have been historically inaccurate.

"Well, that's terrible," I said. "And oddly similar to the
boating story, or at least one of them."

"Look at the picture of the group of reenactors," Tom
said.

In another less tragic setting the picture might have
been comical; a group of almost identically dressed men
standing together and looking equally circumspect and
confused. There were no names under the picture but I
recognized Billy Armstrong. I couldn't help but feel a
sense of loss yet again for the man. He had been handsome with intriguing eyes. I pushed away a wave of sorrow.

"Okay, now look at the bottom picture," Tom said.

The smaller inlaid picture was a dirk.

"It looks like the dirk I found," I said. "Maybe."

"Aye, the picture is fuzzy," Artair said.

"It might be," Tom said. "I have no idea what that
might mean except I think it's something that might be
of interest tae someone, maybe the police, but maybe not.
Here's something else Rodger gave me. You might understand his interest in collecting these stories after you
see this one."

It was a copy of another short newspaper article. This
one talked about another William Wallace reenactor
named Donnan Lawson and the automobile crash that

killed him. There were signs his vehicle had been tampered with, and Lawson's death was also under investigation.

"Do you know the results of the investigation?" I asked.

"Rodger didn't know and I didn't take the time tae try to search. Da?" Tom said.

"I think we can look more closely at this too," Artair said.

"Some sort of conspiracy?" I said. "Against reenactors?"

"Meebe," Artair said with a shrug. "It's worth a leuk."

"And it might be an angle the police haven't considered."

Tom and Artair looked at me.

"Someone who has something against William Wallace and what he stood for? Maybe?" I said.

They looked at each other; in tandem their spines straightened and their mouths formed hard lines.

"They wouldna be a Scot then," Artair said.

"Right," I said. That Scottish pride again. I cleared my throat.

"Do ye ken the angles the police have considered?" Artair asked.

"No. Inspector Winters wouldn't tell me much."

"I had a feeling you'd talked to him." Tom smiled.

"I did. Just today, actually."

"Let's do some research first thing tomorrow," Artair said.

"I'll be there," I said.

We put away the files, ate dinner, and then moved on to more pleasant subjects for the rest of the evening. Artair told me stories about Tom as a child, which were funny and appropriately embarrassing, but my mind was never fully in the current moment. Was the past to blame for Billy Armstrong's death? Could there possibly be some sort of conspiracy against the reenactors? Was Edwin lying, and did that matter?

Artair left soon after dinner with the promise that he'd see me in the morning and a wink toward his son. I liked those winks, and I hoped I'd get to pretend I didn't see them for a very long time to come.

TWENTY-TWO

As seemed to be happening lately, my morning didn't go exactly as planned. Though I had intended to meet Artair first thing, I decided to stop by the bookshop first just to make sure there was nothing pressing that needed my attention.

I was also out of sorts about Edwin and hoped to see him, since he wasn't answering his phone, again. Either he wasn't being truthful with me or he didn't remember or know what *The Scotsman* articles had claimed. I thought there was a chance he didn't know about them, had been too caught up in the tragedy to pay attention, but if Edwin was anything it was informed and observant.

The first indication that something was wrong inside the shop, or at least wasn't right, occurred to me as a million bookish voices came at me when I walked through the front door. They caught me off guard, but instead of trying to sort them out, I pushed them away when I noticed that Fiona was in the shop, speaking to Rosie as they stood on opposite sides of the desk.

"Delaney?" Rosie said.

Fiona cleared her throat and I noticed her red cheeks. Her voice had been raised; I realized I'd heard it through the other voices.

I cleared my throat too and made my way to the desk. "Is everything okay?"

"Fine. How are ye, dear lass?" Rosie asked, but I could tell she was trying to regain her composure.

"What's going on?" I asked.

"Wanted tae get some work done," Rosie said. "Came in a bit ago."

"What's up?" I asked Fiona.

"I've come tae talk tae Edwin," Fiona said.

"He's rarely in this early," I said.

"That's what I told her," Rosie said.

"That's what she said," Fiona said. "But I have a hard time believing it. I thought I saw his car around the corner."

"He's not here," I said tersely. "Do you need something that only Edwin can help you with?"

"Aye."

"We can have him call you, or you're welcome to come back in later," I said.

Fiona's eyes clouded and I remembered that not only had she been raising her voice at Rosie, she was a mourning mother who'd also lost her husband. She didn't need people speaking to her like this, no matter what.

"I'm sorry, Fiona, but he really isn't here. He keeps odd hours," I said more evenly.

"He always has," she said quietly and sadly. "He called me and asked tae see me, but has not answered my calls since. His tone sounded . . . like he had something important tae tell me. I'd rather not have to hunt him down."

"I'll be happy to have him call you," I said again.

"Yes, please do. As soon as possible," she said.

I stepped out of her way but I sensed that she walked too close to me on purpose, as if she wanted to accidentally run into me.

I turned and watched her leave and then faced Rosie again.

The inside of the shop was warm, comfortable, meaning that Rosie had been there a good hour, or . . .

I looked at her as her lips pursed and her eyes avoided mine. The back table light had been switched on, and a copy of *The Scotsman* sat on the corner of her desk.

"Oh," I said. "Edwin is here, isn't he?"

"Aye, but excellent job playing along, lass," Rosie said cheerfully. Moments of contention rarely bothered her for long, particularly when she was pretending.

"I didn't mean to . . . What's up? Why didn't Edwin want to see her?" I said.

"He was here when I arrived. He was peeking out the front window, hiding. He told me that Hamlet, ye, and I were the only people he wanted tae see today, but he wanted tae talk tae ye specifically. He's either in his office or the warehouse, waiting."

"Is he okay?" I asked.

"No, of course not. Edwin's not a hider, he's not one tae peek out the window. He faces things head on. Something must be terribly wrong. It's up tae ye, dear lass, tae figure it out. And then come tell me." She lifted her eyebrows.

"I'll find him right away," I said. Artair would know I'd get there when I could.

I hurried over to the dark side. I didn't check his office but went directly to the warehouse. He wouldn't be anywhere else.

It was colder over here and I rubbed my arms as I descended the stairs, and then was startled as I turned the corner and saw the warehouse door open. It was never supposed to be left open, even when someone was inside. I approached slowly.

Edwin stood in front of shelves I'd designated only for books. Though I hadn't scratched the surface of inventorying all the items in the warehouse, I had at least straightened some of the books.

"Edwin?" I said as I came into the room.

"Delaney, lass, did you see Rosie?" Edwin asked as he turned. Even in the midst of the tragedy of his sister's murder I'd never seen such dark circles under his eyes.

"I did. You okay?"

"No, I'm afraid I'm not. I need your help. Could you close the door, please? I left it open tae warm it up."

The creaking door and heavy deadbolt were more foreboding today, but I closed and locked quickly.

"What's wrong?" I said as we each took a seat. "Fiona was out there. I told her you'd call her."

He took a deep pull of oxygen and then placed his folded hands on his lap as he released a heavy breath.

"I will call her later. However, I think my friend killed his son," he said perfunctorily.

The idea had crossed my mind, more than once, but it was most definitely the angle I didn't want to be true.

"You think Gordon killed Billy? Why?"

"He might have killed Leith too. I think he would like to kill me. I think he tried tae last night."

"Edwin, we need to call the police," I said, fumbling for my phone in my bag before he could tell me any more.

"Wait," he said gently as he leaned forward and placed his hand on the edge of the desk. "I don't know if we should."

"Why?" I said, but the answer glimmered in my mind. At least a ghost of the answer. Edwin had done something wrong along the way, perhaps far back in the past, and he didn't want that deed to come to light.

This really had nothing to do with protecting Fiona's

money. For an instant I felt like a fool, but I pushed it away. I needed to understand and not assume, not put my faith in ghosts of answers, but get the real ones.

"Because, Delaney, I think I can handle it, with your help, and I've already thought about it."

I appreciated the fact that he'd thought about it, but it would have been impossible for any of this to be free of danger. Still, I wanted to help. I wanted to understand. I wanted to know all the secrets.

"Tell me, but I'm not promising I won't call the police."

"All right."

"Start with why you think Gordon killed Billy."

Edwin nodded. "The dirk you found."

I nodded him forward.

"It was mine." He swallowed hard. "I believe it was representative of the true identity of William's biological father."

"You?"

"Aye."

My eyes filled with tears but I blinked them away. Edwin's new pain was palpable.

"I'm sorry," I said.

He nodded and then blinked away something too, but I couldn't be sure if it was tears or just a cyclone of emotion that he must surely be dealing with.

"I cared for the lad deeply anyway, but I didn't believe he was my son. I'm not one hundred percent sure still, but . . . When he was a child I knew him well. Now, it's just . . . different I suppose. There are more regrets. I should have worked harder to stay in touch with the lad."

"I'm sure you tried. You said that Gordon and Fiona raised him well, that events happened as they were supposed to. Edwin, I went to talk to Gordon. I found him at the fish market two days ago. You left here and said you were going to go talk to him. He said you didn't."

"No, I realized that I didn't want Gordon to know that I knew about the dirk. Not yet, at least. When I left you I decided that he would never have wanted me to have the dirk, that it wasn't *his* message. He would not have wanted me tae know that Billy was my son. That was all Billy's doing, and . . . well, whoever told Billy the meaning behind the dirk."

I nodded, sensing I might have just come upon at least a nugget of more truth. However, Gordon had at least acted surprised to see the dirk too, and I'd told him I'd shown the pictures to Edwin. If he'd killed Billy because of the dirk, he would have known about it before. Had he simply been surprised that I knew about it? He'd also said he thought it indicated that Edwin was the killer, but maybe this was a case of two sides of the same coin. Or dirk, as it was.

"How would Billy have gotten the dirk then? Where has it been? There's a part missing from your idea."

"I know. I've been trying tae put it together. I can speculate, of course, but there are just too many possibilities. I'm working on it."

"But, Edwin. Gordon raised Billy as his own. Surely he couldn't kill his own son," I said.

"I think that me knowing the truth was the most devastating thing for Gordon. I think his pride couldn't handle it. Yes, we were very good friends at one time, but Gordon's feelings for me must have soured tae the point that he didn't want tae share his son. If there was a story written down about Gordon still being alive, it didn't include Billy's parentage; Gordon wouldn't have included that. But somehow, Billy found the truth and he wanted me tae know, so he brought the dirk with him tae the castle. I can't come tae any other conclusion. I've tried."

"I just don't know," I said.

"Possible, aye?"

I nodded. "Why were you hiding from Fiona? She said you called her," I said.

"I did. I was going tae tell her about Gordon still being alive, but that was before last night. Now, I don't want tae tell her yet. It might put her in danger."

"Last night?"

"I heard noises. I have a security system, but you know I never turn it on. I heard noises outside the back window of my study. When I went to investigate, I saw footprints and . . . a pack of cigarettes, the same kind Gordon brought in with him that day."

"One of your groundskeepers?" I said.

"I don't think so. The pack was dry, the only wet part was a corner. If it had been there on the ground for much more than a few minutes it would have been soaked."

"Edwin, we have to call the police."

"Not yet, lass. Please."

"Why? You could pay the money back for Fiona."

"Of course I could. It's never been about the money."

"Then what is it about?"

"It's about a girl, Delaney, and my love for her. And a tragic situation a long time ago. More than one tragedy, actually."

I swallowed, even more certain now that Edwin had done something he was afraid for the police to know about. I was torn between curiosity and not wanting to know. "But that couldn't have anything to do with Billy Armstrong's death. I believe you said it yourself, that was a whole other lifetime ago. Why does that need to even be part of what we tell the police?"

Edwin sighed. "Because now I believe it has everything tae do with Billy's murder. I might not have it figured out exactly, but I will. I think there's no need tae

hurt someone that made such a long-ago mistake, someone otherwise innocent and good. I can't tell you more
than that, but I have a plan." He looked at me a long moment. "I need your help though. Can you trust me enough
tae do me a wee small favor?"

"Of course."

"Send me the pictures of that dirk, and do not say a
word more tae anyone yet?"

A long moment later, I nodded, and texted him the
pictures.

TWENTY-THREE

My energy was drained after meeting with Edwin, but I still needed to see Artair. On another day, in another setting perhaps, Edwin's furtive moves of searching out the window and then looking both ways before leaving the bookshop might have been comical. Today, they just made Rosie's eyebrows come together, Hector whine, and Hamlet, who'd arrived late, ask what he'd missed since being so busy with school lately.

I told both Hamlet and Rosie that I'd fill them in after my morning meeting at the university. They watched me leave with almost the same curiosity we'd all watched Edwin.

Not only had the buses and I become comfortable with each other, I had also become familiar with a couple of the bus drivers.

Finn had come to Edinburgh from Germany. He'd become smitten with Gretchen, a "pretty Scottish lass" who'd taken a holiday trip to Berlin about ten years ago. They'd met in front of a museum as she took pictures of the building, and his heart couldn't let her go. He'd followed her to Scotland only a week after she'd returned. They now lived close to the university and had three wee 'uns, which was always interesting to hear being said with a German accent.

"Delaney, the fraulein from America. How are you today?" Finn asked as I took the seat directly behind him.

"Fine," I said, but he must not have believed me. I saw his raised eyebrows as he glanced at me in the wide rearview mirror.

I laughed. "It's been an interesting few days, and I need some answers."

"Can I be of any assistance?"

"You get me where I need to go. That always helps."

The eyebrows were still together. "Going to the university today?"

"Yes, the library."

"Research?"

"Yes, a few things: William Wallace, dirks, and some old stories."

"I see. Libraries are the best places for old stories. Gretchen is from Paisley, that's about all I know about William Wallace."

"Paisley?"

"That's where William Wallace was born."

"I didn't know that," I said.

"He was a hero, died a martyr for the cause," he said, pride lining his words. Scottish history was seeping into his blood too. I supposed it was inevitable.

I looked out the window as the meeting with Edwin played again in my mind. I believed most of what he had told me. In fact, I thought that he'd said everything in the complete spirit of being honest even if dishonesty still shadowed his words, but I wasn't ready to agree with him that Gordon Armstrong was a killer. Not yet. I didn't like the man and trusted him even less, but I couldn't wrap my brain around the idea that he could kill his child.

I'd told Edwin about the possible conspiracy against the William Wallace reenactors, but he wasn't impressed by the idea. That might have been my fault though. As I'd said "William Wallace reenactor conspiracy" out loud I'd felt silly. There'd been no conviction to my words. I hoped Artair had found something to give them some conviction. I would rather the killer be a conspirator than someone from the half-century-old boating tragedy that Edwin and Billy's father had somehow been involved in.

William Wallace had died a martyr. Maybe so had Billy Armstrong. Maybe there was some strange similarity there because of their names and the role that Billy had played. On the surface that idea seemed even sillier than a conspiracy, but it might be worth more thought.

"Thanks, Finn," I said. "You might have realigned my perspective a little."

The eyebrows relaxed. "Always glad to be of service."

Once off the bus, I hurried through the cold and into the library, today not worrying about my noisy footfalls or looking at the honorary busts. I'd left a message on his phone, but like Edwin, Artair wasn't all that in tune with his mobile. I found him in the art book room again, this time holding a magnifying glass over a document as the arm attached to the table was bent out of the way.

"I'm sorry I'm a little later than I thought I would be," I said breathlessly.

He put down the magnifier and came around the table. "I knew ye'd be here when ye could. Not tae worry, lass, I've always got something tae occupy my time. However, I'm verra glad tae see ye. I found a few things that might be of interest. Over here," he said excitedly.

It wasn't a large room, but he'd placed two folding chairs and a card table in a corner.

"Have a seat," he said as he pulled out a chair for me.

As he sat down he smiled slyly. "I found some interesting things, lass. Here, right here. Let's start with this."
He placed an open book in front of me.

"What is this?" I said.

"It's a copy of a comic book, though I dinnae think
that's what folks these days call them. It's an early version of a comic book. I dinnae want ye tae see the cover
yet. First, leuk inside. It's not completely professional,
though the sketches are quite good and the story is silly
enough tae bring a smile."

There were only a few pages beyond the cover, each
of them with their own eight-panel story about Millie, a
character much like Wullie, full of attitude while meeting challenges of her everyday extra-challenging life. The
sketches were good and I wondered which of the group
of friends was the artist. On the last page, I saw a quickly
written "Bellows" at the bottom of the panels, answering
my question.

"They parodied *Oor Wullie*?" I said. "Wasn't *Oor Wullie* already kind of a parody?"

The stories the strips told, though delightful and
charming, did not give me anything I would consider a
clue.

"Awright, now leuk at the cover." He closed the book.

The cover was also done in pencil. The authors were
listed in this order: Clarissa Bellows, Edwin MacAlister,
Leith Stanton, and Gordon Armstrong. They'd titled it
Oor Millie, but underneath the block-lettered type, someone had hurriedly written "working title." The only illustration on the cover was a young girl with freckles and
two dark pigtails that curled perfectly. She was cute and
reminded me of Pippi Longstocking.

"Here, I think this is an important part," Artair said
as he pointed.

Someone had written a short note on the bottom corner of the cover. "Love—Wullie for a boy, Millie for a girl?"

It very well could have been Edwin's handwriting, but I couldn't be sure. I didn't have Gordon's or Leith's to compare it to. Even if Edwin had written the note I didn't think it told me much, but it might lead to something at some point.

"Where did you find this?" I said. "This was in the library? I can't understand why."

"Aye. There's more."

Artair looked toward the door. He hurried over to it and closed it before he retrieved a small box from under his worktable. With a glance toward the closed door, he finally placed the box onto the table.

"I dinnae ken why these were in the library, lass, but like I said before, someone wanted them hidden but not destroyed. I couldnae begin tae guess who. It's that box I found long ago and buried deep away, part of some stacks of boxes that have never been inventoried or catalogued. After I left Tom's it took some time, but I finally remembered exactly where I'd seen it. I came into the library early this morning and with the help of a security lad and his keys, I found it in the same place I'd found it all those years ago. The exact same place."

He pulled out the items from the box.

"I dinnae ken if there are important things, but I want tae be careful just in case," he said as he handed me a piece of paper.

I immediately recognized this handwriting as belonging to the same person who'd written "Bellows" under the comic strip.

"I, Clarissa Brennan Bellows, being of sound mind and body do bequeath my entire fortune, which consists of the contents in my room and about thirty pounds, to

Mr. Edwin MacAlister." A space was left in the middle of the page and more writing followed: "Forgive me for my sins."

I looked at Artair.

"Taken out of context, this is strange. Maybe taken in context, it's nothing but more silly college fun," I said.

"Aye, but I wanted ye tae see the heart she drew by yer boss's name. I think that's more important than whatever she was going on aboot. Meebe."

I hadn't noticed the heart, but I did now.

"Right, considering everything, this isn't too big a surprise, but I don't see anything suspicious," I said.

"This," Artair said as he handed me the next item, "is a wee bit more intriguing, and the item I find the most important."

"A passport?"

"Aye."

"Moray Persley?" I said. "I don't know that name. Is it Scottish?"

"Aye. He was the man who died on the boat, either drowned or killed."

"He was unnamed in the articles you showed me."

"Exactly. He was unnamed in *all* the articles. I had to dig through some death notice records tae piece together who the victim was once I had the passport. I wasnae too surprised tae find a match. And this," he handed me another piece of paper that was a copy of another article, "is dated the day after the first small article we found in *The Scotsman*. It wasnae with the others. Look at the picture."

Not only was the victim unnamed, so were the other people in the picture above the article. They were a frightened, forlorn, and wet group. Except . . .

"I recognize Edwin," I said. "His clothes are dry."

"Aye." Artair smiled again. "Ye have a good eye,

Delaney. I noticed that too. He's dressed more nicely than the rest of them too."

"He wasn't with them on the boat?" I said.

"Or he was and he was dressed up and didnae go into the water like the rest of them seemed tae do."

There was no doubt in my mind that Edwin would have gone into the water if it had meant trying to save someone, no matter what he was wearing.

"That wouldn't jibe with his personality," I said.

"I agree, something's amiss," Artair said.

I looked at the picture again, remembered how he'd insisted to me that the drowning had been an accident, and noticed now how he stood separate from his other wet friends, none of them looking toward him.

"I guess it's a possibility," I said quietly as I glanced toward the door. There was no reason to think anyone could put together the pieces as Artair and I might have just done, but like Artair, I'd become paranoid and protective of whatever this information we were finding might turn out to prove. "Why is the passport the most interesting to you?"

"Right. Here." He opened the passport to the signature page. "Leuk."

"I see. It's his signature."

"Now, leuk, here."

Artair scooted the comic book in front of me again and pointed at the note on the cover. There was no doubt at all that the handwriting on both of these belonged to the same person.

"Who in the world was Moray Persley?" Or had Edwin written both the note as well as forged the passport signature?

"I have no idea, lass. I havenae found him anywhere but in one small police report about the identification of the dead body and a city death record. Nowhere else."

My heart sank as I came to a shaky point. Maybe Edwin hadn't told me any truths, ghostly or not. Maybe he'd told me more lies, and maybe they were meant to cover all the other lies.

TWENTY-FOUR

"I cannae tell ye how many times seemingly insignificant facts have ended up being the answer tae some mystery I was trying tae uncover. Ye need tae remember everything," Artair said as he handed me a cup of coffee.

After we went through the items in the box, he gathered a short stack of papers from a shelf. The papers were copies of notes or other articles that highlighted notably deadly endings for the William Wallace reenactors.

Artair's conclusion was that there probably wasn't a conspiracy against William Wallace reenactors, but there might be a curse.

In the last ten years, seven Stirling monument reenactors had died. Billy Armstrong's death seemed to be the only murder, but the others were unexpected. Two car accidents, both found not to have included foul play, one food poisoning, one slip off "a craggy mountainside," and two heart attacks. They'd all been investigated. For a brief time, authorities suspected more was behind the mountainside accident, but ultimately no foul play was found to have occurred.

I made a list of the reenactors and their causes of death

just in case, but there didn't seem to be anything there to point out to the police.

After our coffee break, I helped Artair clean up, but we were both a little slower today, getting lost in our thoughts more than we normally would. I hugged and thanked him before I left the library and, because it wasn't too cold, took the mostly downhill trek back to the bookshop.

My thoughts turned over and moved in so many directions that I couldn't wrangle any of them in long enough for a longer contemplation. The time and journey passed quickly, and before I registered where I was I'd come upon Grassmarket, and as I looked up toward the bookshop I thought I saw someone familiar.

It looked like Gordon's boss, the big older man from the fish market who had a permanent frown on his face, the man I'd run into at Tom's pub, was leaving the bookshop. He was at the other end of the square; it was too far to yell or try to flag him down. I was curious enough about the reason behind his visit to set off in a run.

There were other pedestrians and lots of other traffic in my way, but I dodged well. The man turned the corner, the one in the shadow of the castle. There weren't storefronts around that corner, but it was an often-used thoroughfare, either to move farther west into downtown or up a winding hill to the castle at the top of the Royal Mile. He could be going in either direction, but I'd have to set a record pace to see which way he chose.

By the time I made it to the corner, I was breathing heavily, and he'd disappeared from sight. I had a 50 percent chance of guessing the path he'd taken, which meant I had a 50 percent chance of being wrong. The fish market wasn't nearby, so I couldn't even make an educated guess.

After a moment's contemplation with my hands plopped on my hips and my breathing returning to normal, I made my way back to the bookshop. Suddenly, I remembered the note that Hamlet had told me about, the one from Gordon that had asked me to meet him at the fish market tonight. I had completely forgotten about it, forgotten to even tell anyone else about it. How had it so completely slipped my mind? The only quick conclusion that I could come to was that the request had been so ridiculous that I'd put it out of my mind. Did the man I'd seen leave the shop know about the request for a meeting? Had he come to see if I was going to show up?

"Delaney, ye just missed a caller," Rosie said as I went through the front door.

"I think I saw him. Big guy, older? Did he give his name, leave a message?"

"That's the one, but no, he didnae give his name. He said he has some information for ye, but he wouldnae tell me what it was. He shopped and bought a book while he waited for ye and told me he'd find ye later. He was anxious tae talk tae ye, but not enough tae leave a message. Did ye recognize him?"

"I think he works at the same fish market that Gordon Armstrong works at."

"Do ye think he has something tae tell ye aboot Gordon?"

"I don't know. As far as I can tell he doesn't know Gordon is Gordon. He thinks he's Barclay."

"Interesting. Anything ye want tae share with me? I'm available tae listen."

"I don't know anything really. Or, the more I learn the more I think I don't know. Things keep getting worse and more confusing. I can't imagine why that man came to the bookshop, or how he knew to find me here."

"Weel, ye ken what I say?"

"No."

"Pulling on a string of bad news can only unravel a whole ball of it. Be careful with yerself. Tell me what ye can tell me when ye feel like ye can. I'm here."

"I'll be careful."

Rosie smiled. "Guid, and a wee bit of being scairt will keep ye safe."

"Edwin's not in is he?"

"No, I'm afraid not," she said, her tone having now gone from bitter to sad and possibly hurt.

"It's going to be okay, Rosie."

She waved away my concern. "Oh, I ken."

"What book did the man buy?"

"A copy of *The Old Man and the Sea*. Not expensive, but in guid condition."

"The sea again, huh?"

"*The Old Man* and *the Sea*," Rosie corrected.

I listened hard for the bookish voices. I knew I must be missing something important because of the overload of information I was mulling through. I hoped the bookish voices would pick up on anything that might offer clarity. I was befuddled, my thoughts noisy in my head. But the bookish voices responded to my confusion by being stone-cold silent.

Hector barked.

I smiled at the perceptive dog. "I'm going to get to work. I'd like to talk to Edwin. Would you send him over if he comes in, please?"

"Aye. Right away."

——

I first tried to call the fish market. Once connected I could press numbers to hear the fresh catch of the day, get the address or directions to the fish market, but there was no option to talk to a live person. I'd have to stop by to talk

to the man who'd come to see me, but I didn't want to
do that, and I wasn't going to meet Gordon there, no matter the request.

I was grateful that I had work to do, and even though
work was usually a good distraction, something in the
universe seemed bound and determined to keep me on
the trail of trying to find Billy Armstrong's killer. I pulled
out the letter that Edwin's friend Birk had asked me to
try to authenticate as something written by the Scottish
historical figure Rob Roy.

Rob Roy MacGreagor was a Jacobite and cattleman
who had fought many battles over his lifetime, but ultimately died in his bed at the old age of sixty-three, of
natural causes. Birk didn't want to sell the letter at auction. He wanted to donate it to either a library or some
other historical collection, but only if it was a real letter
from the real Rob Roy MacGreagor.

I hadn't done one thing toward its authentication, but
I was ready to give it some attention, if only to distract me
from everything else. I began with the Internet. I looked
up some facts and their historical timing to see if the letter
that Roy had allegedly written regarding a question about
his cows would jibe with the happenings of the time.
The timing seemed feasible.

I looked for Rob Roy's signature, and found a match—
though a quick search-and-find on the Internet wasn't
nearly enough to be completely certain, or uncertain for
that matter. More research needed to be done, though I
got as far as *not* ruling out the letter's authenticity, which
was a good step in the right direction. Lots of written
documents out in the world were forgeries, and lots could
be so determined with a quick Internet search. But some
couldn't. It took a good eye, the ability to dig deep, and
then the access to equipment that could tell the age of

paper and ink. I still had a couple more steps to go before I'd need to use equipment.

Birk's letter was sealed in something similar to laminated plastic, but the material was made specifically for document preservation. There were no harmful chemicals touching the almost three-hundred-year-old parchment—if that's what it turned out to be.

After checking the signature, I quickly came upon a number of mentions about the Stirling Council's archives and Web site that each month highlighted a document they deemed their "document of the month." One of the other bits of information I came across on their site also discussed Rob Roy's cattle—the cattle that were spoken about in my letter and that ultimately led to his downfall. Sometime after the Jacobite uprising, Rob Roy became a cattleman; at the time cattle rustling and selling protection against theft were commonplace. He borrowed money to expand his herd, but when his chief herder, who had been entrusted with the money, disappeared, Rob Roy defaulted on his loan and became an outlaw. His house was burned down and though he evaded capture for a long time, he did spend some time in prison. The information I found was from an original certificate of ownership stating that Robroy's (as it was spelled on the certificate) cattle belonged to John Oge Campbell, and Robroy's creditors had no claim to the livestock. It was dated April 5, 1716.

The Stirling Council had a number of offices in Stirling, probably each one manned with someone who would be able to help me with the next step of validation.

Coincidentally, Stirling was right there next to the William Wallace monument, where the reenactors hung out. It wouldn't hurt to get their take on the conspiracy or curse angle, and ask them more about Armstrong. It

all seemed like a valid excuse and a gigantic nudge from
the universe that I should go back to Stirling.

However, I didn't want to bother Elias for another long
trip, and Tom was working.

I had yet to ride the train, but I knew how to take the
bus that would get me to the train station. I told Rosie
the specifics of my plan and asked her to have people call
me on my cell phone if any questions arose.

The ride to Stirling did not disappoint. Scotland was
not short on pretty views, and the passing sights out the
train window only raised the tally on places that made me
wish I knew how to paint or had a really good camera.

Once off the train at Stirling I had to break my rule and
ride in a cab other than Elias's. The council office building was three miles away from the train station, and it
was more like an American office building than any I'd
been in so far, though it still seemed to have a certain
style about its angles and corners.

I was directed to the appropriate document room,
where I found a short line of people waiting for two patient employees behind the counter. I had the Rob Roy
letter in my bag, further protected by a thick cardboard
folder. I wasn't going to show anyone the letter, just a
copy of the signature, but I thought I should have it with
me just in case I changed my mind.

"Hi," I said when it was my turn to approach the
counter. "I was hoping to see and perhaps photograph
an authentic Rob Roy signature."

"Looking tae forge something, are we?" the ancient
woman said as she pushed the glasses up on her nose and
pursed her lips. Her wrinkles ran deep, her short hair was
as steely gray as it could get, but her blue eyes twinkled
with intelligence and playfulness layered with a practiced
accusatory glance from behind the modern pink reading
glasses adorned with sparkles.

"No." I smiled and then leaned forward. "Just trying to see if someone who wants me to buy something has been up to no good doing some of their own forging."

This wasn't my document to show, and you never knew who was listening or what might happen if you spilled the beans to the wrong person.

"I understand." She smiled, happy to see I didn't cower from her accusation or turn defensive. I'd played this game a time or two. I kept on my toes though; she had a few more games under her belt than I did.

"Ye know ye could find one on the Internet?" she said.

"I know, but you can't always trust what you see there. I want to make absolutely sure, and I heard this is the place to come for that."

She gave me a nod of respect. I wondered, if I lied and told her I didn't like Wikipedia, would she invite me over for dinner?

"One minute." She turned and walked back toward a desk, where her long red fingernails skipped expertly over the keyboard. Without so much as a slight hitch in her step, she walked over to a printer, grabbed a piece of paper, and made her way back to me.

"Here ye go, lass." She handed me the piece of paper that had a visible watermark to make sure I didn't try to pass it off as something genuine. "Ye can't get more authentic than this one."

"Thank you!" I said. "It looks just like the one that's being shown to me."

"Aye?" she said doubtfully. "Just make sure ye look closely at the Rs. We find the most forgeries in the way the Rs are sloped."

"That's good to know. Thanks again. What do I owe you?" I said.

"Nothing at all." She waved away my question. "Except . . ."

"Yes?"

"Will ye promise tae come see me again if ye have any document questions? Ye remind me of myself back when I was curious enough to lie about some things I wanted tae know."

"I will." I blushed.

"Name's Audrey Hackburn, like Hepburn, but not quite." She extended a hand over the counter.

"Delaney Nichols," I said. "I'm in Edinburgh for a while, working at a bookshop. I hope to see you again."

"Me too, Delaney Nichols."

I smiled again and then turned to leave. I heard her say "next" as I went through the document room door.

My task had been accomplished quickly and easily. I could have done the same thing somewhere in Edinburgh, but with my ulterior motive for coming to Stirling in mind, I got back into my waiting cab.

I had to remind myself that it was just a cab ride, not an act of betrayal. Still, I felt myself try not to be too friendly as I asked the driver to take me to the reenactment site.

He matched my unsociable attitude, silent moment for silent moment.

He parked the cab at the top of the hill Elias and I had trudged down when we'd been there before. It was just after three in the afternoon and the sun was low in the sky, casting cold gray shadows over the large crowd below. I saw the group of actors, along with many pockets of engrossed and winter-wear bundled-up tourists.

Amidst the crowd, I was sure I saw Oliver and Dodger. I thought it good luck they were there.

"Could you just wait here again?" I said as I handed the cabdriver two large bills.

"No, lass, I'm off shift." He handed me back one of the

bills. "I have to head back with the cab, but I'll send another driver out directly. It won't be long."

"Oh. Okay. Thank you."

"Aye." He looked at the bill he kept. "Thank ye."

I stepped out into the cold wind and felt a brief moment of regret as I looked down the hill and then toward the retreating cab. In my almost thirty years I'd done plenty of things alone, but I was not only far from home, I was far from both homes; Kansas and Edinburgh. The inside of the cab was warm and could take me back to the train station. I hoped the other one would be there soon.

"Don't be silly," I muttered to myself before I moved down the hill.

The skit was almost over; the speech about Wallace's gruesome death held the audience's full attention. I caught the eyes of a couple of the actors off to the side, but I didn't immediately see Carl. However, Oliver and I shared a nod—mine with a smile, his with a surprised smile. Nevertheless, he made his way toward me.

"Hello, lass," he said as he closed the distance between us. "Dodger told me you wanted tae talk tae me the other evening. I'm sorry I was otherwise occupied. He said you were a delightful lass who seemed tae care about Billy. I'd be happy tae talk tae ye."

"Thank you. I have even more questions now though."

Oliver looked back toward his group. Most of the men weren't looking at us, but a few were.

"I have a few minutes," he said.

"Can I buy you a coffee or something?"

"I don't have quite that much time. The skit is almost over and then we're having a brief gathering in the car park. Are you cold?"

"A little, but I'll be okay." I was more than a little cold.

"What questions do ye have?"

I nodded as a gust of wind blew my hair back.

"Did you and Billy Armstrong have any issues, other than the obvious one of him slapping the woman from the bagpipe shop?"

"You do get tae the point."

"I lied. In fact, I'm very cold."

Oliver's eyebrows came together. He glanced up the hill toward the coffee shop and then back at me.

"I suppose I did have issues with him," he said. "I told the police. But, aye, about a week before he was killed, things got worse. I always thought Billy was a good man, but he took his role so seriously. I had to tell him many times that we weren't hired tae walk around the grounds and talk tae the tourists in costume, that we didn't have to tae stay in character after the skits and up by the monument. None of those were angry conversations though, just frustrated on my part, a wee bit stubborn on his part, until the week before he was killed. I talked tae him again, but that time, he didn't take it well. He was having a rough week, I thought, but then when he slapped Grizel . . . I could have put up with telling him not tae take his role so seriously forever, but I couldn't tolerate violent behavior."

"Oliver, forgive me for sounding uncharitable, but was there something wrong with him?"

"I don't know about his mental health in general, but he had obsessive tendencies. Here, when he was in costume. I wouldn't know how he was outside of here. He rarely attended the meetings and the pub social events, and when he did, he was quiet, kept tae himself. I'd heard he didn't have another job but I never asked him."

"He and Grizel dated, right?"

"Aye, I believe so. I don't think it was a good idea. I think he was so used tae being alone, that someone else in his life was too much tae handle. It was when I learned about the two of them that he started to change, brood more maybe, until it got worse." Oliver looked up toward the coffee shop again. "She just came back today. I saw her a wee bit ago. She's agreed tae bring back the bagpipes. They're a nice addition to the skits."

"She's here?" I said as I looked up the hill too.

"She was. She might have left by now."

"Did Billy carry a dirk with him?"

"Oh. Not that I ever saw. We use longswords here, but they're dulled props."

I nodded. "Did you know about the SPEC tattoo on Billy's wrist?"

"No, what's that?"

"It's not important."

"I've seen tattoos on the lads, but I don't pay much attention tae them."

"Who were you talking to at The King's Wark? The reenactor who wore a red sweater?"

Oliver rubbed his chin and looked over toward the group of reenactors. "I have no idea, lass. I talked tae many individually, I think."

"He showed you something on a piece of paper and you looked upset?"

"The complaint?"

"I don't know."

"One of the lads showed me a letter. A tourist complained about the lack of kilts on the men here. I didn't mean tae look upset. It's a common complaint. Perhaps you mistook my impatience for being angry? It's a tiresome complaint tae deal with."

"It's possible. You know, your group has seen quite a few tragedies in the last ten years. Car accidents, cliff falls. Do you think there might be something up with that and Billy Armstrong's death?"

Oliver looked at me a long moment, confusion in his eyes. "A conspiracy or something?"

"Yes."

"No." He hesitated. "No, I don't think so. I never thought about it that way. Any tragedy is terrible of course, but I don't know that our group has seen more than our fair share. I need tae think about that."

"What do you think happened to Billy?" As I asked the question, I thought I noticed Carl in the group behind Oliver. I hoped to talk to him too, but when I looked again I didn't see him.

"I have no idea, but he was an odd one, lass. Here at least. Maybe his oddness spread tae another part of his life. I'm sorry for him. I'm sorry for his loved ones."

"Me too."

The skit had ended and the shadows had deepened, the sun setting very quickly now and the air cooling even more. The tourists began their quick exit, and the group of actors seemed to move in tandem toward the parking lot.

Oliver looked over toward them, then back at me. "Anything else?"

I shook my head. "Could I call you if I have any other questions?"

"Certainly."

Oliver gave me his phone number and then turned to follow the actors' path, leaving me a distracted and grumbled farewell.

As he moved out of sight, I realized that everyone else had too; the small valley had cleared quickly. It was far too cold for anyone to have any extra questions. I looked up the hill and saw a few people here and there now mostly in silhouette, but no cab, and no one looking my direction. I saw the silhouette of a woman carrying a set

of bagpipes. I was sure it was Grizel, and she was by herself, trudging up the hill.

The wind picked up and was loud in my ears as I
moved to try to catch up to her.

The next seconds would forever stretch into something
bizarre and slow speed, but I would always think I got
the sequence of events correct.

Someone ran toward Grizel, someone big and moving as if he meant to tackle her.

I halted, studying what I thought I was seeing in the
shadowed darkness. She held the bagpipes so they blocked
her from seeing the force coming toward her, and she
seemed totally unaware of any threat.

"Grizel!" I yelled, but I could tell my voice got carried the other direction by the wind.

It wasn't easy to see the specifics, but I thought the
man tackled her and then straddled her a second later,
his fist lifted in the air.

My feet flew up the hill and I closed the distance between us quickly.

"Grizel!" I yelled again as I propelled myself at the
dark, violent figure. I couldn't see his face, but even in
the midst of the horror I could tell I surprised him by the
way his head snapped my direction and his fist moved in
front of himself to block my tackle.

I put my head down and rammed into him. We turned
into a mess of limbs and curse words as I knocked him
off Grizel. He pushed me off him and I landed on my
back next to Grizel, air whomphing out of my lungs.

"Mind your own business," a deep male voice said. I
couldn't see his face, just his outline as he scrambled to
stand. He turned and ran up the hill.

I hadn't caught my breath as I tried to pull myself up
to inspect Grizel.

"Grizel," I tried to say, but it came out as a croak. "Grizel."

She moaned but didn't speak.

Good enough, I thought. I couldn't see that anyone had noticed the ruckus on the side of the hill. No one was coming to our aid; we were in darkness and it was only getting darker.

I pulled out my phone and somehow managed to call for help.

TWENTY-FIVE

"Ms. Nichols, wake up."

"Tom?"

"No, it's Dr. Preston. You fell asleep. Wake up."

I'd forgotten I was in a hospital. I opened my eyes wide and shot out of the chair. I'd fallen asleep with my head against a wall in the waiting room.

"Is she okay?" I asked with a sleep-graveled voice.

"She's fine. A concussion, but not a bad one. You probably saved her life." A short man with Einstein hair and friendly eyes, Dr. Preston had a calm demeanor that must have served his physician role well.

"I . . . I'm glad she's okay."

"We're going tae keep her overnight but she'll be released early tomorrow morning."

"May I talk to her?" I said.

"Yes. She just finished with the police and asked about you. She'd like to talk to you too, but I wanted to make sure you also talked to the police before they left."

"I already did. I'm sorry I fell asleep out here."

I'd told the police only about the attack, sticking to a minimum of details, and like the police at the castle, they assumed I was simply visiting the monument as a tourist. I wasn't trying to protect Edwin or anyone.

"Fatigue can be a normal reaction to all the stress. You show no sign of serious injury but you'll be sore tomorrow. You need to get home and get more rest, but it's okay to take a few minutes with Ms. Sheehy. She's in room 201."

"Thank you," I said as Dr. Preston smiled and then made his way down the hallway.

I grabbed my bag and flung it over my shoulder. I'd already confirmed that the Rob Roy letter was still safe inside it. Not that the letter was nearly as important as Grizel's or my well-being, but I was glad I hadn't lost it in the scuffle.

The wait for help hadn't been long, and the ambulance ride had been speedy. I'd been fine once my breathing returned to normal, but Grizel said her shoulder hurt. I'd made her stay still as I covered her in my coat, but we were found and helped off the side of the hill quickly enough that I didn't have a chance to get much colder. The paramedics had been careful with Grizel, but I was able to walk on my own. They insisted I come with them to the hospital, mostly, I thought, because they knew I didn't have another ride. I rode in the back of the ambulance and sat next to one of the paramedics, who assured me that Grizel wasn't badly injured. Once I'd been examined again at the hospital, I sat in the waiting room with the hope I could make sure Grizel really was okay before I went home. I didn't even remember being tired enough to fall asleep.

I knocked on the door of room 201.

"Come in," Grizel said.

The window curtains were open wide to the inky darkness outside. This side of the hospital must have faced the countryside since there were only a few lights dotting the view.

"Lass, thank ye for saving my life, but who in the name

of the almighty above are ye and why were ye there?"
Grizel said as I came into the room.

Her cheek was more swollen and bruised than it had
been earlier and I held back a gasp. Her arm was in a
sling but I didn't see a cast or any other injuries.

I closed the door behind me.

"Well, I'm not exactly who I pretended to be," I said.

"No kidding? Tell me what's going on."

I told her. I started with finding Billy Armstrong's
body on the roof of the castle, and then her business card
and the dirk; told her he was the son of a friend of my
boss's; wondered if a mystery from long ago had been the
reason Billy had been killed. I *didn't* tell her Gordon was
still alive. I gave her a big picture of the story, not a version with lots of details, but enough.

"Ye and yer friend pretended tae want some bagpipes?
Why didn't ye just ask me about Billy?" she said.

"I'd delivered the dirk and your card to the police the
night before. Remember the police officer who had just
talked to you as we were coming in?"

"Aye."

"He told me to mind my own business, and it truly was
none of my business anyway."

She smiled and then cringed at the pain in her cheek.

"Aye, none of yer business tae be sure. Nevertheless,
there's not much tae tell. Billy and I dated briefly, very
briefly, lass; only two dates. He was a strange lad, but I
tend tae like strange. Anyway, I told him I didn't think it
was going tae work. He got angry and slapped me. I got
angry at the whole lot of them and took my bagpipes and
went home. However, and no disrespect to Billy, I enjoyed
being at the monument, so I went back today tae tell them
I regretted leaving. I'd left some bagpipes there that
needed to be fixed. I grabbed them from a small storage
shed and was walking up the hill when I was tackled. It

was dark. I assumed it was someone taking advantage of a lone female in the darkness. Thank goodness ye were there tae save me."

I cleared my throat. "Why did you lie about the SPEC tattoo on Billy's wrist?"

"I didn't lie! I never saw that tattoo on Billy's wrist. It was only two dates, and he wore sleeves, I suppose. I just didn't see it, if there was one there."

"But you said you saw it on someone."

"Aye, I did. In fact, today I asked about it. Your question had me wondering. When I was talking to the lads, I asked who had the tattoo. None of them remembered."

"Do you remember which guys you were talking to? Did you tell the police?"

"Not specifically, no. It didn't occur tae me tae tell the police."

"Try hard to remember," I said.

"Why?"

"I don't have any idea how it all fits together, Grizel, but if one of the reenactors other than Billy has that tattoo, I would not be surprised if he was Billy's killer. And the one who attacked you too."

Grizel blinked and shook her head "I don't even know all their names."

"Just try to remember, and then tell the police. I'm sure they can show you pictures. I'll talk to the police too. I'll tell them they need to round up the reenactors right away and look for the one with the tattoo."

She nodded. "I didn't think it was important tae give them that detail."

"I think it's the most important thing now."

"All right. I will. I'll call them right away."

I handed her her phone from the nightstand, and then pulled mine out of my bag. I didn't know exactly who to call first; I chose Inspector Winters.

TWENTY-SIX

After a call to Inspector Winters that started out confusing but was ultimately successful, I called everyone else. The only one I woke up was Rosie, but she was just as willing as the others were to meet me for a middle-of-the-night meeting at the bookshop. Inspector Winters would confer with other officers and they would round up the reenactors to check wrists for tattoos.

We sat around the back corner table as I told Rosie (a sleepy Hector on her lap), Tom, Elias, Aggie, Hamlet, and Edwin (who'd answered the late-night call I'd made probably because late-night calls can't be ignored as easily as daytime calls) about what had happened in Stirling, and then I rehashed everything else. It was a bigger than normal crowd for the small bookshop, but the members listened with rapt attention.

―

As I spoke, I couldn't help but notice Elias as he crossed his arms in front of himself and anger took over his features.

I knew I should have asked him for a ride. I sent him an apologetic smile and Aggie patted his shoulder. He sighed and shook his head before he uncrossed his arms and blinked away some of the anger.

Tom was the only one not sitting down. He stood with his hands on his hips, and worked hard to contain his concern, and probably some unpleasant words for Edwin. I smiled at him too, but it didn't help.

Rosie cried a little and Hamlet seemed perplexed, but I went through every single detail with them. I thought I'd shared almost everything with them all, but I wanted them there together to make sure I didn't leave things out individually.

"Enough is enough," Edwin said when I'd finished. "I will call the police and tell them everything."

"I hoped you'd feel that way. Inspector Winters will be here soon," I said.

"Aye," Edwin said with a nod. "I'm glad ye asked him here."

If he was angry he hid it well. For the others, I'd said the magic words, and their anger and tears mostly went away. I hadn't yet told Inspector Winters *all* the details. I was leaving that up to Edwin, mostly because I didn't want Rosie and Hamlet to get in trouble for knowing that Gordon was alive and not telling the police. I knew Fiona had more terrible things ahead, but we'd help her through it. However, if Edwin didn't tell Inspector Winters about Gordon, I would.

"I will tell him everything, Rosie," Edwin said. "Everything."

"Aye," she said with a sniff.

Ten minutes later Inspector Winters joined us. He wore jeans and a dress shirt and a demeanor of grave seriousness.

"Evening," he said as his focus landed on me, bringing his eyebrows together. "You okay, Delaney?"

"Fine. You get people rounded up?"

"We're working on it."

Inspector Winters declined the offer of coffee, and pulled out his notebook and pen as Edwin began talking. I was pleased that Edwin did, in fact, tell him everything. Kind of. He did say that Gordon was not dead and had come into the bookshop, but he didn't mention that Hamlet, Rosie, and I had been there too. He also talked about SPEC and a long-ago boating tragedy. He said that finding the man with the SPEC tattoo might lead to the killer and Grizel's attacker, but the decades-ago tragedy was fuzzy in his memory. He promised to try to remember more clearly.

No one could figure out why another reenactor might want to kill Billy Armstrong, but the pieces of the puzzle certainly seemed to lead to the distinct possibility. For their part, Inspector Winters said the police had some difficulty finding someone to give them the names and addresses of all the reenactors, but they'd finally found a board member who was mostly helpful. He didn't know how long it would take, but the police would be inspecting wrists until they found what they were looking for.

I'd been inside the shop, the warehouse, at midnight before. Grassmarket always saw some pedestrian activity at this time of night, but rarely were the lights on this late in this part of the bookshop. The glow from the old fixtures was warm and welcoming and invited passersby to peek inside. We were all mostly hidden in the back corner, but Elias sat off to the side and could see out the front window. Every now and then he'd send glares that unmistakably told anyone looking in that the shop was closed, and not to bother knocking.

"Edwin, when you were contacted about the *Oor Wullie* annual, are you sure it was Billy Armstrong who contacted you, not Gordon Armstrong?" Inspector Winters asked.

"I don't think it was Gordon. He has a distinctive voice, and though I might not have recognized it at the time, I would have known it was an old man calling me. He claims he's sick, possibly dying. You can hear the decades of cigarettes in his voice," Edwin said.

I noticed one of Inspector Winters's eyebrows rise before he wrote another note. He rested the notebook on the table and looked at Edwin again.

"I heard about the boating tragedy and I did some research. Your clothes weren't wet," Inspector Winters said.

He'd seen the same picture I had. I hid my surprise with a swallow and by crossing my arms in front of myself.

"I didn't go into the water," Edwin said, nonplussed.

"Everyone else seemed to have."

"I was the only one who didn't go into the water all the way when the lad went over."

"Why didn't you?" Inspector Winters asked.

"Because I was busy trying to keep someone else from jumping in. I succeeded until we were almost ashore. My shoes were in fact wet, but barely any of the hem of my pants. The police questioned me specifically about that—was my answer not in the file?"

Inspector Winters didn't answer, but waited patiently for Edwin to continue.

Edwin shrugged and sent me a look I couldn't quite interpret. "There was so much happening that night."

"Who were you trying to keep from going into the water?" Inspector Winters asked.

"Clarissa Bellows."

Inspector Winters wrote in his notebook. "Who was she? Why didn't you want her to go into the water?"

"She was the only woman invited into SPEC, and I knew she was pregnant. I was the first one she told. She was pregnant with Billy Armstrong, Inspector. She gave the baby to Gordon and his wife Fiona to raise, and they named him."

"I see." Inspector Winters looked at me briefly. I had no idea what to say or do so I just looked back at him silently. He turned back to Edwin. "But ultimately she did get in the water to try to get the man who'd gone overboard?"

"Aye. As we were close to shore, she managed to get in all the way, I managed to stay on my feet and help her out of the water."

"Excuse me, Inspector Winters," Rosie said. "Whose knife—dirk—killed the man?"

"There was no knife. He fell overboard," Inspector Winters said.

I noted to myself that though Inspector Winters had seen the picture, he must not have seen *all* the articles. I said to Rosie, "What made you think there was a dirk?"

"I thought that's what Edwin told me long ago," she said absently, zeroing in on whatever past moment that conversation had taken place.

"Edwin?" Inspector Winters said.

"No dirk," Edwin said. He smiled wearily but supportively at Rosie. "I'm sorry if I gave you that impression."

"Och, it was long ago when ye told me. I'm sorry I'm not remembering it correctly."

"In the police report, there's no mention of a weapon of any sort," Inspector Winters said to Rosie. "Stories change over time, even sometimes in our own minds."

"Aye," she said doubtfully. "Aye," she repeated with confidence this time. "I've heard so many a story over the years that I probably confused it with something else."

Her words didn't seem to send anyone else a big wallop of suspicion, but she had spoken with too high a pitch for me to think she believed what she was saying. If he caught it, Inspector Winters didn't give any indication. I worked hard not to slant my eyes toward her. I was just about to mention Artair's sub-basement research when a voice sounded in my mind.

Then you shouldn't talk.

It was the Mad Hatter from *Alice in Wonderland* responding to "I don't think . . ."

I had no idea why my intuition suddenly and adamantly told me to keep quiet, but I listened to it.

"The next step for the police is tae find someone with a SPEC tattoo and tae track down Gordon Armstrong. Do you have any idea where he lives?" Inspector Winters asked.

"A room near the fish market," Edwin said. "But I don't know exactly. I was at the market today, but no one would tell me where he lives. My questions might have put him in a bad position, and the manager might not be pleasant tae him the next time he sees him. If you don't get tae him soon, I might have scared him away."

I looked at Rosie and remembered that I hadn't told anyone about someone possibly from the fish market stopping by the bookshop. She nodded.

"Excuse me," I said, but I waited a moment to see if any bookish voices wanted to suggest that I keep quiet. I didn't hear anything. "It seems like there is something I forgot."

Tom had been silent, but took a supportive step closer to me as Rosie and I told everyone about the customer who'd purchased *The Old Man and the Sea* as well as the meeting I'd missed that evening. Hamlet had put the note into the drawer in the back table. He gathered it and gave it to Inspector Winters who held it so I could read it too.

"I guess it's not clear that it's from Gordon," Hamlet said. "I'm sorry, but I just assumed."

The note might have been signed with a quickly scrawled G, but it was difficult to know. Inspector Winters asked Edwin if he would recognize Gordon's handwriting. He said that after all these years, he wouldn't.

If the bookish voices hadn't told me to keep quiet about Artair's research, I could have added that he might be able to round up a sample of Gordon's handwriting, at least from long ago. I filed away the idea for later.

"I'm taking this," Inspector Winters said as he put the note into his pocket.

I nodded. Inspector Winters also said he'd follow up with a conversation with the manager but he was glad that I hadn't attempted to meet Gordon on my own.

"Edwin," Inspector Winters said. "Do you find it strange at all that the fish market is close to the place where your young friend fell from the boat years ago? And then perhaps a man who 'died' is living close by there too?"

Edwin blinked. "I hadn't thought about it that way."

He and Edwin held a gaze for a moment, before Inspector Winters continued, "Well, I need tae attend to the matter of Gordon Armstrong. If ye'll all excuse me." He stood.

"Edwin's not in trouble for keeping the secret about Gordon being alive?" Rosie asked.

"I wouldn't say that, but he's come clean now. That's a good start. I'm sure we'll talk again though."

His voice was stern, but he reached over and scratched Hector's ears as he spoke. I didn't think he realized how likable and un-stern that made him. Tom and I shared a small knowing and slightly relieved smile.

"I'll walk you tae the door," Tom said to Inspector Winters.

The door wasn't far away, but as they stepped away from the rest of us, it seemed they'd gone miles away.

"I'm sorry," I said to Edwin.

"For what?"

"So many things," I said.

"Och, lass, maybe I'm too tired, but I'm not angry at you in the least." He shook his head and then continued, "In fact you might be the most level-headed one among us. I'm glad tae have ye here, and I'm the one who is sorry. I thought I could take care of things without more pain tae Fiona, or anyone else, for that matter. I should have known better."

"I'm glad to be here."

"Now, you should be resting. Take the day off. Tom," Edwin said as Tom rejoined us, "take her home, feed her soup, and make sure she rests."

"Absolutely."

"I'm in charge of the soup," Aggie added.

"I'm in charge of driving," Elias said. "Come with me and I'll deliver Tom wherever he needs tae go later."

"Och, it's a late one," Rosie said.

"We'll all take the day off," Edwin said. "Rosie, I'll see you home."

Hamlet smiled. "I'll come in later. I only need a couple hours' rest and I'll be good tae go."

"Thank you, Hamlet," Edwin said.

We dispersed into the cold night air. Our shared sense of relief was palpable. The truth was in the proper hands of the authorities. It was not up to us anymore to keep big and harmful secrets, and getting them out in the open felt good and right.

It was only later that I remembered that even though we felt like we'd done our part, not one of us seemed to give much thought to the fact that a killer was still on the loose and that killer might have been the person who'd hurt Grizel and me. Maybe something worse could have happened. Maybe something worse could happen to any of us.

If the characters in the books on the shop's overstuffed shelves were trying to tell me something else, perhaps send me a warning, I didn't hear it.

Silence from the bookish voices, along with some soup, was just the right way to end the night.

TWENTY-SEVEN

"Sore. I think that's my word for the day," I said as I walked into the kitchen.

"I'm sure," Tom said. He poured me a cup of coffee and joined me at the table. "There is breakfast food tae feed an army keeping warm in the cooker and cold in the fridge, depending."

"Aggie?"

"And Elias," Tom said with a smile over the rim of his mug. "He's vacillating between being angry at you and wanting tae dote over you."

I cringed. "I didn't even think I was being stupid."

"You weren't. Something happened, it wasn't good, but it could have been a lot worse. You're all right."

"Yeah." I sipped a big gulp of guilt along with the coffee. I wouldn't say Tom was angry with me, but he was upset. He was trying to hide it but I could hear it in his voice. I put my hand over his as he held his own mug. "Sorry."

He twined his fingers with mine and smiled again. "Ye have a shiner," he said a beat later.

"I know. It didn't appear until this morning. I don't remember getting hit there, but everything was such a flurry. It's not terrible. What's black and white and red,"

I pointed to my eye, my unharmed cheek, and then my messy bed hair, "all over?"

Tom laughed. "Aye."

"What time do you have to go to work?" I asked.

"Soon, but I don't have tae stay all day. Is there anything you'd like tae do? You only slept a few hours. You should sleep more."

"I can't sleep, and I can't think of what I want to do."

Tom cocked his head. "Any chance you'd like tae go over what happened last night again? I know you told the police, and then you told all of us, but I wouldn't mind hearing it again. Sometimes things come back with a rested mind."

I nodded, but before I could begin, my phone buzzed across the kitchen counter.

"Rosie," I said to Tom when I looked at it. "Hello?"

"Delaney, lass, have ye heard?" Rosie asked.

"I don't think so. What's up?"

"Gordon Armstrong is missing, and . . . well, Edwin just rang and told me the news, but he also said the police are trying tae track down Clarissa. They cannae find her either. Edwin is with the police. He wanted me tae let ye know, and he wants ye tae be careful, be aware."

"Of course," I said. "Where are you?"

"At the shop. I couldnae sleep anyway. Ham's here too, with Hector and myself."

"Thanks for calling. I'll see you soon." We ended the call and I turned to Tom. "Should we ask Elias if he'll take us both to work?"

"I think he'd like that."

———

Elias dropped Tom off first, in front of his pub, and then drove the short distance back to the bookshop. Neither of them were happy I was going into work, but they didn't argue too much. I told them I felt much, much better. They pretended to believe me.

"Lass, ye'll go nowhere without me, understood?" Elias said. "Not until this mess is cleared up."

"I promise."

"Not even tae the corner. I'll come get ye and take ye."

"But it's an easy bus trip anywhere."

"No; frankly, Aggie will have my hide if ye step one foot oot of that shop without me."

I smiled. "You have more to do with your day than just take care of me."

"I'll keep close by. Ring me if ye need me."

"You can come in."

"No, I'll just be in the area."

"Thanks, Elias." I leaned over and kissed his cheek. I'd never done that before.

"Get on with ye, lass," he said as he tried to hide a smile.

I squeezed his arm once gently before I got out.

If Rosie and Hamlet had wanted to spend time being worried about anything, they'd been properly diverted.

Ellen, the young woman who'd come in earlier to pick up the Gaelic book for her employer, stood on the edge of the crowd gathered around the front desk. I assumed the people with her were the family she worked for.

There was such a murmur of conversation that no one heard the bell jingle as I came through. My eyes landed on Ellen and I remembered that something from her last visit had given me pause, perhaps a moment of question. What had it been? Her cap?

"Delaney, hello," Hamlet said as he came around the group to meet me at the door. He glanced back at the group. He pointed to his own eye and silently mouthed the words *you okay?* to me.

I nodded.

"Lordy be, what happened to you?" a middle-aged and pretty woman asked.

"I'm fine, but I was in a bit of an accident last night. I hope I don't look too scary." I tried a smile.

"Not at all." The woman approached and put her hands on my arms, and bored her concerned eyes into mine. She was very tall and the maneuver made me uncomfortable but I tried not to show it. "Ice. I think you should be icing that. Nolan, shouldn't she be icing this?"

Before my eyes landed on Nolan, they skimmed over Ellen's eyes. She was more uncomfortable than I was and she sent me an apologetic frown.

"Well, dear, I'm sure she's seen a doctor," Nolan said. He was a tall, round man with an almost completely bald head and heavy glasses that hung on the tip of his nose. There was something appealing about him, approachable maybe.

I nodded at the woman.

She didn't care. "Nolan's a doctor. He'll have a closer look at that if you want."

"I'm doing much better. I iced it a little and took some ibuprofen," I lied.

"There, you see," Nolan said with a pleasant and welcoming smile. I bet he had a great bedside manner.

"All right."

She let go of my arms and propelled a hand in my direction.

"Gretchen Kramer. Ellen said Delaney was the one to help her with Nolan's book. That you?"

"It is." I shook her hand. "It's a pleasure to meet you all."

There were also two children, both of them under five, but I wasn't good at guessing any closer than that. They each held one of Ellen's hands; the little girl kept wide eyes on Hector on the edge of the desk and the little boy looked around at everything else.

"And this shop," Gretchen continued. "Ellen said it was as storybook charming as any place we'd ever been into. She was so right. You're from the States, she also said."

"I am. Kansas."

"Oh, how I love Kansas. It's a beautiful state." Gretchen smiled politely.

"Thank you," I said. I looked at Nolan. "Do you read or speak Gaelic?"

He laughed. "I do a little bit, but it'll take me a year or two to read a chapter in that book. I just wanted it for my collection. We were coming to Edinburgh, and it seemed perfect."

"I'm glad you came back in," I said to Ellen.

"Me too," she said as she pulled her attention up from the little boy.

I stared at her. I didn't mean to and I didn't know why I did. I caught myself before the moment went on too long.

"I was just going to offer our visitors some coffee," Rosie said.

"Oh, no, we couldn't," Nolan said. "Just wanted to thank Delaney and the young man Hamlet here, and see the shop. Thanks for your hospitality though."

"We have so much more to do," Gretchen said. "But thank you anyway."

"Verra weel." Rosie smiled. If she hadn't had so much on her mind, the Kramer family wouldn't have gotten away so easily. Rosie would have insisted on coffee and conversation. In fact, the Kramers would be seated and drinking coffee before they even realized they'd been invited.

The kids followed their parents through the front door as Ellen hung back.

"Thank you," she said to Rosie. She smiled shyly at Hamlet before she joined me by the door.

"You were right," she said quietly. "He looks just like a Hamlet."

I saw the blush on her cheeks. She was going back to Florida, and Hamlet wasn't leaving Scotland anytime soon. As selfish as it was, I couldn't help but be glad that my visit to Scotland was a little longer than just a few days.

"He does." I smiled.

She sent one more shy smile back his direction. He waved and smiled too. He didn't do it on purpose but he had such a classic look about him that women, even some men, of all ages couldn't help but look his direction. He never wearied from offering a friendly smile, even if he accidentally melted a few hearts along the way.

I heard Ellen's slight sigh before she turned and left the store.

As she hurried to catch up to the rest of the family, I watched her closely and wondered what in the world it was about her that made me want to stare at her, figure out the question to whatever answer she so clearly must be.

"It's not clear to me," I muttered.

The books weren't talking either, at least not right away. As Ellen took the boy's hand again and then tousled his hair with her free hand, the words finally came.

Yes, to pay a fine for a periwig, and recover the lost hair of another man.

It was Dromio of Syracuse from Shakespeare's *Comedy of Errors*. He was speaking with another character about how some men can't avoid becoming bald. The characters conclude that some men have more hair than intelligence.

I had no idea what Dromio was trying to tell me, unless to notice that Mr. Kramer was bald and that didn't make any sense. Had it just been all the recent Hamlet/

Shakespeare talk that had prompted him to speak, not my subconscious working to find the answer?

"Delaney." Hamlet, the one I worked with, had stepped up next to me. "You okay?"

I blinked. "Yes, actually, I'm great. I feel much better and I'm ready to get to work or help Edwin. What does he need?"

The four of us conferred; Hector took his role seriously and offered comfort to each of us, somehow sensing when one of us experienced an upward tick of anxiety. He moved from lap to lap and calmed us as best he could as Rosie told us that Edwin had been awakened at about three o'clock and taken into the station. She said that he hadn't been arrested, but the police didn't seem to want to give him an option as to whether or not to go with them. He had been asked to stay there.

"They found the room where Gordon Armstrong was staying but it's been cleared oot, no sign of the man t'all. Then, because yer police friend is so good at his job meebe, they went tae check on some other folks mentioned. Fiona Armstrong was fine and I dinnae ken if they told her aboot Gordon, but Clarissa was not home, which was odd," Rosie said.

"Was her cousin home?" I asked.

"I dinnae ken anything aboot her cousin so I dinnae think tae ask."

I nodded. I didn't have their phone number, but Elias had driven me to Clarissa's house once before. That trip hadn't gone well, but I wondered if he'd be interested in trying again. I wasn't even sure why I wanted to go, except that it was something to do. If I found Clarissa, would I tell her about Gordon Armstrong being alive or just that she needed to let the police know she was okay? I didn't want to risk causing her another hospital visit.

"Rosie, I need to ask you something," I said.

She nodded and leaned forward so Hector could lick her cheek. "Aye?"

"I know you remember something different about what you were told regarding the night of the boating accident. A dirk, right?"

"Oh, aye, there *was* something else." She sat up straight, disappointing Hector. He trotted across the desk to Hamlet, who lifted the dog to his lap.

"What?"

"Edwin told me the man had accidentally been stabbed with the dirk."

"At least, that's what you remember?" I said.

"Aye, but I'm sure my memory isnae off. I was too tired last night when he took me home tae remember tae ask why he wanted me tae lie, but I will ask him next time I see him. He'll tell me."

"You're sure?"

"Aye. It was a horrible story and stuck with me."

"And it was Clarissa's dirk?"

Rosie nodded, then paused. "I'm not sure he told me whose dirk it was."

"It's not in the police record that way," I said. "However, Tom's father might have found some old articles to corroborate what you're saying."

Hamlet shrugged. "Maybe Edwin or his family paid off the police."

I blinked and looked at Hamlet, and so did Rosie, but not with as much surprise as I had done.

"What?" I said.

"It could have happened," Hamlet said.

I looked at Rosie. She lifted her eyebrows and shrugged too.

"Do you think that's a possibility?" I said to her. She leveled her gaze at me. "Did they do that other times?"

"Delaney, it sounds like something terrible on the

surface, of course, but remember Edwin's sister and all her problems? If the family didnae have a relationship with the police, they might not have managed tae keep her oot of jail as much as they did."

Sometimes I was too naive for my own good.

"I wonder if Inspector Winters can look into this?" I said.

"I doubt it," Hamlet said. "We'll have to get the truth from Edwin himself."

"Or Clarissa," I said.

"If she's okay, the poor dear," Rosie said.

Frustration, real and ripe, worked its way through my gut. We'd thought we'd told the police the truth. Hopefully, Edwin was telling them the rest of it.

I took a deep breath and let it out slowly.

"Delaney?" Rosie said.

My eyes snapped back up to her. "Do you think what happened all those years ago on the boat has anything to do with Billy Armstrong's murder?"

"I dinnae ken really, but I wouldnae be surprised. Edwin will do the right thing, Delaney. He always does," she said.

I looked at Hamlet.

"I don't have any idea. We'll talk to Edwin when he gets back," Hamlet said.

"Right. Well, actually." I pulled out my mobile and punched a button.

"I'll be out front in a minute," Elias said as he answered.

"Thanks."

I disconnected the call.

"You two okay here without me?" I said.

"Absolutely," Hamlet said. "But . . ."

"If ye stay right by Elias's side, lass, then I'm okay with it. Dinnae even think about letting him oot of yer sight."

"I won't, I promise," I said as I stood.

From Hamlet's lap, Hector barked. He was a dog of few words, so it was always surprising to hear his ferocity.

I crouched and scratched his ears.

"I promise," I said.

He panted agreeably.

Elias was true to his word and was outside by the time I was there.

"Where're we going, lass?"

"The university library, please."

"Awright. Tell me aboot Edwin on the way," he said as he pulled out into traffic.

TWENTY-EIGHT

"I found a few other pictures and articles that might be of interest, but I couldnae find anything else aboot the man who was killed on the boat," Artair said as he closed the art room door. "I rang a friend at *The Scotsman* and he couldae find anything else either, but he said he'd look deeper."

"Nothing more that mentions a stabbing, accident or not?" I said.

"Nothing. Not that stabbing, at least. I did find another article about the accidental stabbing of the William Wallace reenactor," Artair said as he made his way toward the card table.

I'd all but forgotten about the conspiracy angle. I switched my mind's gears as Elias and I followed Artair and watched as he sorted through stacks that weren't there the last time I was.

"Do ye really think the truth aboot what happened back then has something tae do with Billy Armstrong's murder?" Artair asked.

"Honestly, I have no idea," I said.

"Here it is," Artair said as he handed me a copy of an article with a picture: "William Wallace Reenactor Accidentally Killed by a Dirk." The article outlined the circumstances behind the accidental dirk stabbing of Gilroy Wyly. I skimmed the tragic story, and then zeroed in on the picture.

Billy Armstrong was there, but Carl wasn't. Carl had said he hadn't been a part of the group for more than a year or so, and Gilroy's death took place three years ago. All of the reenactors were bigger men; at least they weren't small. But the part of them that gave me pause all of a sudden was their hair.

"Do lots of men around here have naturally long hair?" I said as I looked up at Artair and Elias.

They both looked perplexed at my question. I doubted either of them paid much attention to current fashion trends or the length of Edinburgh men's hair.

"I dinnae ken, lass," Elias said.

"Me either," Artair said.

"Do you have a magnifying glass?" I asked Artair.

"Of course." He grabbed the large, long-handled magnifying glass from his worktable and brought it to me.

I held it over the picture and looked at the faces of the reenactors.

"I think . . ." I said. "No, it can't be."

"What?" Artair and Elias said.

I sat in the chair because my knees went weak with the revelation. I looked at my two Watsons.

"In answer to your earlier question, actually no, I don't think what happened on that boat all those years ago had one thing to do with Billy Armstrong's murder. I also don't think Gordon killed his son, or anyone, for that matter. I can't understand why I'm seeing what I'm seeing, but it's just too much of a coincidence," I said.

"What?" they said again, more exasperated this time.

"I'm sorry. Thank you, Artair. I'll tell you everything this afternoon. Right now . . . Elias, can you take me to the fish market?" I said.

"Aye?"

"Aye. Right away," I said.

———

I knew this type of warm; the warm before the storm. I'd often felt it in Kansas. Sometimes, when there's a snowstorm on the way, the clouds come low and keep the air cocooned and at a temperature higher than when the sky is clear.

"It feels like snow," I said as Elias steered the cab toward the fish market.

"We dinnae get much of that. Are ye sure?"

"No." I smiled.

A small wave of homesickness rolled in my belly. For the moment I had to push it away, but I filed a mental note to call my parents soon.

"Lass, why are we going to the fish market?" Elias asked.

"I think one of Gordon's coworkers is also a William Wallace reenactor."

I watched Elias's profile. His eyebrows first came together and then together even more. He frowned and scratched behind his ear.

"And ye think that he might be the killer?"

"Maybe."

"Then, perhaps, lass, we should call the police."

"We will. There's a chance the police are already talking to him. I just want to see. I was also hoping to talk to the man who came into the bookshop looking for me.

Elias gave me a quick look. "When are we going tae call the police?"

"As soon as I confirm."

"Lass?"

"It's a public place, Elias. If I'm wrong, let's not bother the police. You won't believe this, but it's all in the hair, which is really making me wonder if my idea isn't a little harebrained."

"Explain, please."

"My subconscious has been trying to tell me something about hair, specifically the length of hair. I think I finally understand. In the picture of the William Wallace actors that we were looking at, there's a man who looks like someone at the fish market, but the man at the market has short hair. Of course, a wig would make his hair long.

"I'd like to get another look at him to confirm. His name is Liam. I'm not going to approach him, just take a look if he's there. I think I'll know with a quick glance."

"How would that also make him a killer?" Elias asked.

"Good question. That's another reason we're not calling the police yet. I still don't know enough to connect all the dots."

"Liam? Another William name." Elias shook his head. I looked at him. "Liam is short for William?"

"Weel, I believe it can be."

"I had no idea," I said, but I suspected that fact only solidified my idea.

"Awright, I'll stick tae ye side like glue."

"I have no doubt."

There was much more to this than the length of his hair or the use of a wig. Things had been happening in my periphery, things I might not have completely noticed but a part of me had and that part had been processing those things, perhaps waiting for the right moment to bring everything together.

I didn't tell Elias about the night that Tom and I had gone back to the castle, when Tom had been jostled by a big guy coming out of his pub. I didn't bring up the shot glasses either, because there was nothing to indicate they'd been left outside the bookshop by Liam, except I thought that one night as I was leaving the shop late, I noticed a big guy in a coat watching me from the Grass-market Square as he took a drink from what could have been a shot glass. When my eyes scanned a second time, I couldn't find him.

I hadn't seen the front of the man in the red sweater as he talked to Oliver at the King's Wark, but I'd seen the back of his shoulders, his build, his short hair.

When I saw Artair's new picture, it was as if all those moments, seeing bits and pieces and different angles, came together and my gut told me that Liam had been the man I'd kept *sort of* seeing.

Even Kurt Vonnegut's bookish words about pretending to be what you weren't were about Liam, I was sure now. They weren't about Gordon like I originally thought.

There was a good chance that I was so desperate for an answer that I was misinterpreting it all, but I didn't think so.

When I'd met Liam at the market, he'd seemed so taken with me. It was too much, really, overboard. I'd blushed and laughed away the moment, but now, from this vantage point, his behavior could easily be interpreted as overacting.

Truly, how the dots connected was beyond anything I could firmly grasp, but I couldn't help but sense that they did connect. If Liam was at the market, and if I could get a good look at him, I thought I'd know if he was one of the reenactors I'd seen in the picture.

It was still pre-storm warm when Elias parked in front of the fish market. There were cars parked in improvised spaces around the building. Elias pulled the cab as close to the building as he could and parked next to the stairs.

"Expecting a quick getaway?" I asked.

He shrugged. "Ye never know."

The market was much busier than it had been before.

Shoppers strolled up and down the two wide aisles, looking at the fish and other food from the sea that had been placed on ice. There was no obvious police presence but I wondered if there were any undercover officers looking for or waiting around for Gordon. Maybe his faked death wasn't as important to them as I thought it might be.

"I don't see Liam. He'll be in a white coat and a hairnet like the others, but he's a big guy. If he really is a re-enactor too, he might be in Stirling or the police might have contacted him already."

"Let's walk up and down once," Elias said.

It was crowded, but not enough to slow us down too much. I still didn't spot Liam among the many guys in white coats and hairnets.

I stopped at the back and peeked around toward the office I'd been in with Gordon, but the door was closed and no one was in sight. For a brief instant I thought about going into the office, but it seemed far too off-limits.

"Let's ask someone when Liam works next," I finally said.

"Awright. I'll do the asking," Elias said.

As we approached a young man who was finishing up with a customer, the man I thought had come into the shop looking for me and had purchased *Old Man and the Sea* walked through the front door. He stood inside with his hands on his hips and frowned as he surveyed the market. It took him only an instant to spot me. He held up a hand asking me to wait and then took fast steps in our direction.

"Someone's coming over to talk to us," I said as I grabbed Elias's sleeve.

Elias positioned himself in front of me, but I tried to angle myself so we didn't seem overly threatening.

"Name's Delaney, right?" the man said as he eyed

Elias and then looked at me. The smell of cigarette smoke wafted so heavily around him that there was no question as to what he'd been doing.

"Aye, what can we do for ye?" Elias said.

"Did you get my note?"

"I didn't know it was from you."

"Aye. I didn't think you'd know who I was, so I didn't sign it. I thought maybe you'd think it was your friend and you'd actually come meet him."

"No," I looked at Elias, "I gave you the wrong impression. Barclay isn't my friend."

"Well, knowing that would have saved us all a bundle of trouble. That's good tae hear, lass. I'm Osgar, I run this place," he said with a rough cigarette voice that reminded me of Gordon's.

"Osgar, you came into the shop and bought a book too, right?"

"Aye. *The Old Man and the Sea.*"

I nodded. "I would have called you back, but you didn't leave a name or a number and the fish market phone is just a message tree."

Osgar frowned at Elias and then turned to me again. "I didn't even think about that. I'm sorry."

"What did you want to talk about?" I asked.

"That Barclay fellow. I wanted tae tell you tae steer clear of him. I was also concerned about the other lad, Liam. Your life is none of my business, lass, but if you were my daughter, I wouldn't want you around either of those two, and I got a feeling maybe you were . . . friends or becoming friends or something."

"Why should I stay away from them?"

"Barclay's been odd since he started working here, secretive. And there's something about Liam. I've seen anger. And, that night I ran into you at the pub, I had been following him. I just had a feeling that he was up tae no good. He left the pub just before you got there. After I saw you and then I left the pub, I tried to find him. I thought I saw him down by that bookshop, but then I lost him," Osgar said. "I just sensed he was following you. It didn't feel right."

"I see. Did Barclay tell you that I worked at the bookshop?"

"Aye, when he was trying tae explain why he needed a private meeting with ye. He mumbled on about a book he was buying and I asked him where ye worked. When I followed Liam and figured he was following you I tried tae get in touch with ye. I should have just called, I suppose."

"You said that Barclay is odd. Is that why you want me to stay away from him?"

Osgar shrugged. "Those two are always talking. I have a bad feeling about them both, and the police left me a message aboot both of them too. The police want me tae call them. Stay away from those men, lass. They're no good."

"I will. Thank you, but do you think they're friends?"

Osgar breathed once in and out of his nose. "No, not friends, just always talking."

Elias and I looked at each other.

"Do you know what Barclay and Liam were always talking about?" I asked.

"No, I don't, but it seems as though you were suspicious enough. Maybe I didn't need tae track you down. I'm glad to hear it."

"Did you know if Liam volunteered to act as William Wallace at the Stirling monument?"

"Oh, aye, he would go on and on about it."

"Did you mention that to the police?"

"No, I need to call them back. Why?"

"Is the Wallace gig something he and Gordon talked about?" I asked.

"I don't have any idea what they talked about; they were always just talking when they should have been working."

Elias cleared his throat. "Ye should call the police and tell them all of this."

"You think so?" Osgar asked.

"Seems odd, aye," Elias said.

"I'll call them right away," Osgar said.

"Thank you for trying to warn me," I said as he turned and started down the aisle. "Wait!"

I closed the distance between us and Osgar as Elias stayed next to me.

"Did Liam have a tattoo on the inside of his wrist? SPEC, or something?"

"Aye, so did Barclay. Neither would tell me what it meant. Maybe that's why they talked tae each other so much."

"But you said they weren't friends?"

Osgar shrugged again. "I guess it's hard tae explain, but no, they didn't seem like friends. I don't think they liked each other, but they talked way too much, seemed tae be conspiring maybe. That's the best I can tell you."

"What's Liam's last name, his address?" I asked.

"McIntyre. Liam McIntyre. He's been living with his mother," Osgar said and then he listed the street both Elias and I had once visited.

Elias and I looked at each other with wide eyes.

"Ye need tae call the police, this number," Elias pulled one of Inspector Winters's cards from his pocket, "tell him the lad's last name and address and aboot the tattoo, meebe about the strange relationship between him and Barclay. Right away."

Osgar looked at the card and then at Elias. "All right. I'll make the call."

"Guid. Let's go, Delaney," Elias said as he motioned me to go ahead of him.

"Thank you again," I said to Osgar as we hurried away.

But he was already moving to the back of the market, his footsteps quick and his focus on the business card.

TWENTY-NINE

Once we were back in the cab I called Inspector Winters's cell phone. He didn't answer, but I left a message with as many details as possible, including the fact that I had also heard that Clarissa's son lived in Glasgow. I couldn't know for sure that Liam was her son, but that's what it seemed like at the moment. I told him I knew the police had been searching for Clarissa and that Elias and I were going to drive by her house, mostly to check on her cousin.

"Can we drive by Clarissa's? If Clarissa isn't home yet, Liza Marie might be there, and I'd like to make sure she's okay," I told Elias after he'd already heard me leave the message.

"I'll drive by, but I'd like ye to call the police station too. I'm sure Winters will get yer message, but let's cover all our bases."

"Makes sense."

I made another call to the station, speaking first to a young officer on duty, and then to someone who was familiar with the case. She said she'd make sure Inspector Winters and the other police officers now involved got the information.

"What do ye think is going on, Delaney?" Elias asked after I disconnected again.

"I have no idea," I said. "No, that's not true. I do have an idea. It seems like Gordon and Liam are in on something together. I don't want to admit out loud that they might have conspired together to kill Billy. I can't understand why."

"The money from Gordon's insurance? Did Billy have a healthy bank account?"

"I don't know. Maybe. It seems that Billy didn't have a real job. But how would Gordon and Liam have access to that money after Billy died?"

"Guid question."

I blinked as a splat hit the windshield. "Snow."

"Looks that way." Elias flipped on the windshield wipers.

We were at the beginning of what might turn into a real storm. Big, wet flakes seemed to make everything wet quickly and accumulate along the edges of curbs and perimeters of grass patches. The closer we got to Clarissa's house, the heavier it got and the more it reminded me of Kansas, and fireplaces and hot chocolate.

As Elias turned the corner onto Clarissa's street we hit a slick patch sending the cab sliding sideways so that when Elias got it under control we were stopped directly in front of Clarissa's garden gate. The cab stalled with the maneuver and fell as silent as the snow that now began to build rapidly on the windshield.

"Hang on, lass," Elias said as he turned the key. The engine remained silent. "Stay in the cab."

He put the hood up, and for a few moments I heard tinkering and pounding, but when it became quiet again I expected him to come back into the cab. He didn't. I craned my neck to try to see around the hood, but couldn't see past it.

I opened my door. "Elias?"

No answer.

I got out of the cab, my feet slipping on the slushy road as I came around. There was no Elias.

"Elias?" I said. "How did you just disappear?" I moved to the front of the cab and bent over to look under it. He wasn't there either. "Elias?"

"Over here, lass," he said, from somewhere.

I looked in all directions but couldn't immediately spot him. I realized that the only place he could have gone without me seeing was through the garden gate. It slowly swung back and forth.

As quickly as I could over the slick ground, I made my way through the gate and finally found him.

"Lass, call the police. Ask for an ambulance. Quickly," he said as he pointed to what I hoped was not a dead body. "I think she fell and maybe hit her head or something."

Instead of doing as he asked, I rushed to them.

"Liza Marie?" I said.

"Aye. I saw her feet from oot there, just like at the castle, but she's alive, still breathing, though barely. Call nine-nine-nine, and get an ambulance here. She's soaked tae the bone. It might be a risk tae move her, but I've got tae get her inside and warmed up."

"I'll help."

"Aye," he said. It was clear that helping Liza Marie was now a much higher priority than staying out of the house.

We lifted her, and I pulled open the unlocked front door. After we put her on a couch, I found my cell phone, but it didn't work.

"Elias, I don't have service. The snow maybe."

All at the same time he pulled his phone from his

pocket, handed it to me, and grabbed a quilt from the back of a chair.

"Your phone isn't working either," I said.

"Look for a house phone," he said.

"Got it," I said.

The house seemed empty. Only one lamp was on in the living room. I hurried around and flipped switches, looking in the places you would think you could find a phone but didn't see any.

I made my way to the back of the house, panic building inside me. As I flipped on the light switch in the vast kitchen I almost cried from relief when I finally spotted a phone, modern but still plugged into the wall. I heard a dial tone immediately when I picked up the handset.

Just as I was about to press the third 9, my world went dark and I couldn't breathe. Someone's hand was over my face, covering my mouth, nose, and eyes. I tried to scream but the noise I made was too muffled for Elias to have heard it from the faraway front room. I flailed my arms and legs, but they only moved through the air. Until they didn't.

I sensed I'd been transported through a doorway, the door then being closed behind me.

"Hush," a man's voice said in my ear. "Hush and I won't hurt ye or yer friend."

My heart beat like thunder in my head and I made loud slurp noises as I tried to find a way to pull in some breaths.

"Hush now," he said.

Things I couldn't control were controlling me. The panic, the inability to breathe; I tried to calm down but I couldn't.

"We're going down some stairs now. If you don't calm down, we'll both fall and break our necks. We don't want that, do we?"

His neck breaking wouldn't be so bad.

I shook my head.

He kept his hand over my mouth, but freed my eyes. He was to my back and he wouldn't let me turn my neck enough to see him, but I could see the stairs leading down and smell the musty basement odors.

"Good. Let's go. I've locked the door behind us. Your friend won't hear us."

But Elias would figure out what was going on, I was sure. He'd check the basement. Inspector Winters would check the basement. I just hoped at least one of them would do it in time.

We moved down the stairs. He lifted and carried me more than I walked. He was obviously a big man and his voice was familiar. Liam, I was pretty sure.

Once down the stairs, he moved quickly down a narrow hallway space and then stopped in front of a door, or I thought it was a door. It was around a corner and blended in enough with the old plaster and lath that it could be overlooked, missed by searching cabdrivers and police inspectors.

I tried to squirm out of his grip and scream behind his hand, but both the sound and I went nowhere.

He opened the door and shoved me through, sending me to my knees in the small and crowded space. He shut the door behind him and turned a lock that secured a long bolt.

"Now no one will hear you," Liam said.

"Don't be stupid. They'll find us. They'll search everywhere," I said as tears of panic and fear started to roll down my cheeks and my whole body began to shake uncontrollably.

Liam laughed. "They didn't find us when they searched before, did they, Mom?"

The room had two other occupants: Clarissa and

Gordon. They were in terrible shape, but at least Clarissa was conscious. She sat upright in a chair with her arms tied behind her back and her ankles tied to the legs of the chair. Her face was dirty and her hair disheveled, but she didn't look on the verge of passing out, or dying.

She looked up at Liam and glared.

"Not happy, Mother? Well, I'm used to that," Liam said.

I scooted over to Gordon, who was on the floor, on his back. I put my finger to his neck and felt a light pulse.

"You haven't killed anyone yet," I said, though by now I was pretty sure he'd killed Billy Armstrong. "Let us out of here. Let's get some help for Gordon."

"Sure. Let's do that," he said with a bored blink. "Not going tae happen. These two aren't going tae survive. Your boss is next. I haven't decided what I'm going tae do with you, though. If you're nice tae me I might let you live."

My stomach curdled. For a moment I had no words.

"Why Edwin?" I finally said.

"They all have to go. Those men, such horrible men." Liam took two fast and deep breaths, but he didn't calm. "I'd have gotten away with it all too, if you hadn't said something tae that idiot with the bagpipes about the tattoos. Her asking if I was the one with the tattoo on my wrist, acting like she knew something." He slammed his hand into the wall and looked at Clarissa. "It wasn't enough for you that I tried tae honor you by marking myself! What was I thinking?"

"I don't understand, Liam. Why?" I said, glad he was yelling so someone in the house above might hear, but I also wanted to divert what I thought was an oncoming violent move toward his mother.

"Ha! Look around, Miss Kansas. I bet ye can figure it out."

His accent wasn't nearly as strong as it had been be-fore. That fact hadn't soaked in until I started to look around what I realized was an old bedroom.

It reminded me of any high schooler's room—messy with an unmade bed, a few books and games, and an old video game console. He was far from high school age, though.

But the big difference between his room and that of high schoolers I'd grown up with was that instead of band or car posters, the walls were plastered with *Oor Wullie* comic strips and annual book covers.

"I still don't understand," I said.

"Why would I have so many *Oor Wullie* things in my room?"

I shrugged. "Because you like the comic?"

"Or someone else does."

I looked at Clarissa. "Okay, so your mother likes the comic strip. Why is that such a bad thing?"

Liam looked at me as if he couldn't believe I didn't understand. "She tricked me, don't you see?"

I blinked at him, but didn't want to admit that I couldn't understand how comic book covers tricked him or how they could possibly lead to what he'd done.

"This stupid character, these comic strips—of all things—reminded her of her past. When she shared her love of them with me, it was as if she was trying to turn me into the son she gave away! I knew I was never enough for her! When I figured out what she was doing . . . don't you see? I had no choice!" he yelled as spit flew from his mouth.

I looked at Clarissa. Tears rolled down her cheeks and she shook her head slowly.

"I never meant . . ." she said.

"Shut up, Mother!" Liam yelled again.

I didn't understand whatever was inside him that had

made him jealous enough of his mother's past that he'd done what he'd done. But I understood that his perception was the only one that mattered at the moment. I didn't know what to do. I didn't have any training in hostage crises. If there were bookish voices at the ready to guide me, I was too scared to hear them.

"But . . ." I said. "She kept *you*."

He looked at me, studied me for so long that I wondered if I'd said something that made sense to him.

I hadn't.

"And that fool," he nodded at Gordon, "thought I'd help him. He had no idea I was just using him tae get tae understand all of them, once I figured out what really happened." He shook his head. "Can you believe that both of Clarissa's sons ended up reenacting William Wallace? It wasn't planned! It was Gordon who figured it all out. He came tae me and asked me tae try tae bring us all together after he starting putting pieces together, and he had no clue that I could kill my own brother. What a fool! What a complete fool!"

"That is pretty amazing," I said, though my voice still wavered.

"And we were both named after that stupid character." He glared at the covers on his wall.

From somewhere I didn't notice, Liam picked up a baseball bat and held it as he charged the short distance to Gordon. He lifted the bat as high as his height and the low ceiling would allow.

"She was going to give them everything! Everything!" he yelled before he swung the bat down toward Gordon's head.

I didn't even think about what I was doing as I threw myself over Gordon, protecting his head as best I could. The bat landed squarely on my arm, equidistant between my shoulder and my elbow. I yelled out in pain even though it took a good long second to really feel it. I was filled with adrenaline so it was most likely dulled—for the time being.

The arm still worked though, or the rest of me did. I didn't think about what I was doing as I propelled myself up and grabbed on to the bat with both hands.

In a weirdly awkward pose, I leveraged my body against Liam's and then after a bizarre rhythmic side-to-side struggle, was able to yank so hard on the bat that I got it out of his hands. I landed on my backside on the floor. No one was more surprised than me, but I didn't waste a moment as I swung the bat at his knees. I swung it hard.

He didn't go down easy. He dodged the bat twice before it hit a sweet spot and took him to a screaming mess on the floor.

I didn't want to leave Clarissa and Gordon, but I didn't think I had any choice as I unlocked the bolt and hurried down the hall toward the stairs to try and get help.

I wasn't quite in my right mind as I lifted the bat to ward off what I perceived as the new approaching dangers coming down the stairs.

"Delaney! It's me," Inspector Winters said.

"Lass, put the bat down," Elias said from behind the police officers.

I put the bat down, and the only thought that went through my mind was made of my voice only: *Of course Elias didn't let Inspector Winters come down the stairs by himself.*

After Inspector Winters and two other officers I hadn't even noticed followed my tremoring arm point down the hallway, I collapsed, a crying, shaking heap, into Elias's arms and let him take care of everything else.

THIRTY

"Did the weather slow you down getting to Clarissa's?" I asked Inspector Winters as Hamlet handed me a mug of coffee and Rosie pulled the blanket up around my shoulders.

My Cracked Spine family was turning into my own personal group of nurses, but we weren't in a hospital, we were at the bookshop, surrounded by the overstuffed shelves that were a part of the place that had become so much more than just a place to work. Elias, Rosie, Hector, Hamlet, and I had gathered. Inspector Winters joined us about an hour after Elias brought me back to the shop. My arm wasn't broken. It was severely bruised and would hurt for some time, but I was going to be fine. I told Elias and Inspector Winters that I would run away and into the sea if they even tried to put me in an ambulance. They saw that all my limbs moved normally so they didn't push it.

Edwin wasn't with us. He still needed to spend some time with the police, apparently. I'd told Rosie not to call Tom yet, and Elias not to bother Aggie, since I was going to be okay.

"Aye, my car slipped off the road and got stuck in a most peculiar position. I called for others tae get tae you, but they arrived after I did. The snow caused us all some slowdowns, took down some mobiles, caught us off guard," Inspector Winters replied.

Elias had already told me that they'd found the basement door quickly, and couldn't think of any other place I might have gone.

"Had the police searched that back basement room for Clarissa before?" I asked.

"I don't think so. Her cousin, Liza Marie, told them Clarissa had stepped out and hadn't come home. Liza Marie was convincing and didn't seem worried. Liam had apparently threatened tae harm her if she gave him up in any way. He told her tae stay upstairs and act normal. Nevertheless, she tried to get away from the house so she could call the police, and she fell. She didn't hit her head but she just couldn't get up and lost consciousness. She's going to be fine, thanks to you and Elias. There was a dog too, and he's fine as well. He was hiding in the bushes."

"Elias saved Liza Marie," I said.

"It was pure luck that the car slid tae a stop in front of the garden gate. The police would have found her when they arrived," Elias added.

"She'll be fine, but even a few moments more might have been too late," Inspector Winters said.

"And the police thought Clarissa was missing?" I said.

"That's what Edwin told me," Rosie said.

"I don't think the officers who brought Edwin in were worried about Clarissa at that point," Inspector Winters said. "Edwin asked them tae check on her. They must have told him they didn't talk tae her and he relayed the message to Rosie as she was missing. I'm glad the communication got mixed up the way it did, or that he sensed there might be something else wrong. I don't know how much longer she and Gordon had down there. Liam was unhinging quickly."

We were silent, sharing a moment of relief that Liza Marie and Clarissa were going to be fine. I knew about the latter because she insisted upon thanking and hugging me before they put her in the ambulance.

"What about Gordon?" Hamlet asked.

"We just don't know. Before Delaney got there, he was hit over the head, just like his son was. The doctors weren't sure yet," Inspector Winters said with a slow shrug.

"Will he be arrested?" I asked.

"Already has been, in a manner of speaking. He's in hospital though, getting the care he needs. If he comes tae, his circumstances will be made clear tae him."

"What happened, Inspector Winters? Why did all of this happen?" I asked.

Even Rosie, who had been dabbing her eyes, turned her full attention to Inspector Winters as he stood next to the front desk, his coat still on and his demeanor both concerned and contrite. He felt responsible for me getting hurt, and I didn't know how to ease his mind from that other than to act fine. I was going to be fine.

"Tae the best of our understanding, about a year ago Liam found some old things his mother had been keeping, articles and journals, and a dirk. He took the items tae his mother, and she broke down because of the sad and happy memories she claimed the items brought her. *Oor Wullie* comics had always been something they shared together, and amongst the things were some annuals. At that point apparently Liam liked that his mother had made something from her past a part of his life. However, when Liam got a SPEC tattoo like some of the men his mother spoke about, they ended up having a heated argument and she told Liam about the baby she gave away. Liam was always a complicated and difficult person, mentally ill I'm certain, but we'll need a doctor tae confirm. It was during this heated argument that Clarissa not only told him about the baby, but said cruel things tae Liam, and told him that if he continued tae behave 'so daft and mad,' her words she claimed, she would not leave him any of her money. She would make sure tae give everything tae her other child."

"Not a guid mother, a'tall," Rosie said.

"Maybe he pushed her beyond her limits. It sounds like it was an unhappy house for a long time. She didn't even know Liam was living in Edinburgh, working at the fish market, or volunteering in Stirling. She thought he was in Glasgow," Inspector Winters said.

"Osgar at the fish market had Clarissa's address for Liam."

Inspector Winters shrugged. "Another way tae throw people off maybe."

"Clarissa shouldnae have said such things to Liam," Rosie said.

"Probably not," Inspector Winters said. "Especially if she knew he wasn't mentally well."

"Was it really just a coincidence that both Billy and Liam were reenactors?" I asked.

"We think so, though we're still working on timing."

"Did he unravel from there? He killed Billy?" I asked.

"He admitted he killed Billy," Inspector Winters said. "He was methodical though. We have his notes. He got tae know Billy at Stirling, tried tae be friends, but Billy was complicated too and didn't allow many people into his life. Liam rode with Billy on a caravan out tae Castle Doune, convinced him to stay with him and wait for another one. His original plan was tae throw Billy off the castle, but he hit him in the head with a rock instead, not the bat he had in the basement." He sighed. "This is what we understand so far—Gordon realized they were at Stirling together, and he told Liam he'd been uni-

versity friends with his mother. He asked Liam to be-
friend his son and lay the groundwork for Gordon to
contact Billy. Shortly after that contact had been made,
Gordon told Liam more about the past connections. Liam
found the items and confronted his mother. A confluence
of events.

"It's difficult tae understand because we don't know
Gordon's side yet, but I think that Liam wormed his way
so deeply into Gordon's and Billy's lives that he convinced Gordon to make contact with Edwin, try tae heal
past wounds. We don't even think Gordon knew that
Liam had a dirk, but—follow me here—we think Liam
told Billy tae give the dirk tae Edwin. I think Liam knew
enough then about the past tae know the dirk might stir
up some trouble. At least bring back old memories. I
think there's more tae learn about the dirk than anyone,
Edwin included, is telling us."

None of the rest of us acknowledged his observation.

I could see how the confusion regarding the meaning
behind the dirk had occurred. If only Edwin and Gordon
had talked to each other about it. But by that point, I
didn't think either of them trusted anyone from that time
long ago.

"Did you find something different that told you a dirk
did kill Moray Persley?" I asked.

"We're looking more closely at it."

"What about Leith Stanton? Did Liam kill him?"

"No, but he was planning on killing Edwin, after he
took care of Billy and Gordon and Clarissa."

"Did Liam try to break into Edwin's house?" I asked.

Everyone looked at me. I continued, "Edwin thought
someone tried to break in."

"I don't know. I'll try tae find out," Inspector Winters
said.

I nodded.

"Comic books led tae him feeling betrayed?" Hamlet said.

"In a way," Inspector Winters said. "They were something he thought he shared exclusively with his mother. When he found out that her very checkered past included them, he wanted tae better understand. But then he was shocked tae learn his mother had had another child, then devastated when tae him it seemed she cared more for that child than for him. Perhaps even a mentally stable person would have felt betrayed, though I doubt murderous."

"How's Grizel?" I asked.

"Ms. Sheehy is fine. You saved her life too. When she asked him about the tattoo, Liam thought Billy had told her something that might give away Liam's manipulations. I'm sure he intended tae kill her."

I shivered. "That's horrifying."

"But all's weel with her, lass," Elias said.

"What did Billy do for a living?" Rosie asked. "Did he have a job?"

"Nothing full time. His mother gave him most of his money. He was a handyman of sorts. He had troubles, mental health issues too. It was a difficult road for both of the Williams, but one became worse than the other."

"Billy and Liam," I said. "William Wallace. I should have figured that out. *Oor Wullie*. The name William was important to them all."

The front door burst open.

"Delaney!" Tom said. "What happened?"

"I might have called him," Rosie said.

"I'm glad you did," I said as I looked at his concerned cobalt eyes and Hector barked a greeting in his direction.

I was *very* glad Rosie had called him.

THIRTY-ONE

"SURPRISE!" we all exclaimed as they came through the door.

"Oh!" Aggie's eyes opened wide and her hand went up to her mouth. "Oh my!"

"Aye," Elias said. "Happy birthday, mo gradh."

I didn't need Hamlet to translate that one. I'd heard Elias say it many times by now. *My love.*

"Oh, Elias!" She searched the crowd. "Delaney, were you in on this too?"

"Elias planned it all. The rest of us just showed up," I said.

"This is unbelievable."

"Come in and let us sing tae you. Elias got a cake from next door and he says it's your favorite," Edwin said.

It was Edwin's bookshop, but tonight it was open in Aggie's honor, to celebrate her birthday. We hadn't locked the doors. Customers were welcome inside, and to have a piece of the other cake, the enormous one that Edwin had ordered just in case we didn't have enough of the first one. He had called Elias that morning and said he hoped to host the party that had almost been forgotten.

It had come together nicely and Aggie was totally surprised.

Regg poured and distributed cups of punch as we sang. Rosie and Hector sat next to Hamlet, who had been the one to see to the details like plates, forks, and napkins.

Aggie blew out candles and Edwin, seemingly happier than I'd seen him in a long time, distributed pieces of cake all around.

We were still missing pieces to the mystery, but only Edwin and Gordon could supply the answers to most of them. I wasn't sure if Edwin would ever tell the whole truth about what happened many years ago, and we still didn't know if Gordon would wake up. None of us knew how much Billy had truly known about his parentage. I thought that someday Edwin would have a good long talk with Fiona about many things, but maybe not. I didn't know how Fiona had reacted to all the news she'd received over the last few days, but I knew Edwin would take care of her, whatever that turned out to mean.

Tom thought that if perhaps Gordon hadn't faked his death, none of the subsequent tragedies would have occurred.

He'd said: *If Clarissa hadn't thought both Leith and Gordon, the man she'd given her son to, had died, maybe those things that reminded her of long-ago times might never have caused her such pain, and she might not have said the things she said to Liam.*

I wasn't sure I agreed, because I'd seen firsthand how disturbed Liam was. Something was probably going to break him at some point. However, it was impossible to know for sure.

Physically, I knew I would rebound. The swelling was gone from around my still-black eye. My arm hurt so much that it was almost unusable, but I tried to pretend it didn't hurt. I'd been sore before. Now, my sore was sore.

Clarissa and Liza Marie would both be fine, at least

physically. Who knew what turmoil and emotional torture was ahead for Clarissa. I hoped she'd seek some
help. It was going to be rough.

After greeting Aggie, I took a seat at the back table. I
needed a small break from pretending I wasn't in pain.
It was a good vantage point to observe my friends and
Scottish family.

But the person who had been on my mind the most
ever since that horrible few but impossibly long minutes
in Clarissa's basement was Edwin. Before we knew who
the killer was and in the middle of the panic, concern,
and horror, I hadn't seen how some things still didn't add
up. As life had calmed and some answers had become
clear, other things seemed to me to still be unanswered,
or maybe just a wee bit murky.

After he was certain everyone had cake, Edwin must
have felt me watching him. He looked at me and smiled
a little sadly. Then he joined me at the table.

"Delaney, how are you?" he said.

"Fine. You mad at me for . . . everything?"

Edwin laughed. "Not at all. You might get a raise. You
probably saved Clarissa."

"Is there a future for the two of you?"

"Oh, no, not at all. But there was a past that gives me
good memories. I'm grateful that she's going tae be okay.
A long time ago she was . . ."

The party was going well. Rosie and Regg were now
dancing as Hector sat on the desk and watched them.
Hamlet and Aggie were deep in conversation, and Elias
and Tom were looking at some books on a shelf.

"She was what?" I said.

"She was important tae me," Edwin said.

"Edwin, do you have a SPEC tattoo?"

"No, lass, I never did get one. Not my thing, I suppose."

"Tell me what happened on the boat," I said quietly.

Hector, having gotten a lift off the desk from Rosie, trotted toward the back table. I thought he might be coming to see me. He'd been giving me extra attention, probably because of my injuries, but he stopped at Edwin's feet and looked up at him expectantly. Edwin gathered him and put him on his lap.

"Aye," Edwin said as he scratched Hector's neck. "I know you've been trying tae understand, lass. I'll tell you. I feel like I owe you."

"You don't owe me, but I'd like to know."

"Aye." He paused. "It was planned, lass. It was a plan."

"Okay."

"We went out that night with one plan, tae kill the lad, Moray Persley."

"Oh. Maybe you shouldn't tell me," I said.

"No," he lifted one hand from Hector and put it over mine on the table, "I want tae tell you. You deserve tae know the truth."

I nodded once.

"We loved her, we all loved her," he said as he went back to petting Hector. "She was not only beautiful, but she was clever and kind. So talented. She told us she loved us all, but it's not what I led you tae believe, Delaney, or what she led you tae believe in the hospital. This was part of the pact we made all those years ago, that no matter who, no matter what, we would stick tae our story, Clarissa would gladly sacrifice her reputation. We would not tell anyone what really happened. It was just Leith, Gordon, Clarissa, and me in on it, but we fooled the other lads. We fooled everyone, for a long time." He smiled at me. "I slipped once with Rosie, but I caught myself before I told her everything. Still, I told her too much. But you weren't fooled, were you. You know, don't you?"

"I don't know anything except some things just . . .

don't fit. You weren't Billy's biological father? That was just part of the story, the pact?"

"Aye, correct, but have you figured out the rest?"

"I'm not sure. Moray Persley was Billy's biological father?"

Edwin smiled again. "That's right."

"And that made the rest of you angry, jealous? You, Leith, and Gordon?"

"No, that's the part you don't know. We were angry, but not why you think." He paused again, and I saw pain at the corner of his eyes. Decades old pain, still fresh and deep. "Moray Persley raped Clarissa. She hadn't had any sort of relationship with any of us that could have made one of us the boy's father. Moray Persley raped our girl, and we couldn't stand by and let him go on without being punished. We thought we were special enough to make those sorts of determinations."

"Oh, Edwin. I'm so sorry." In fact, that scenario hadn't even occurred to me.

"I am too."

We sat in silence a moment, the jovial party all around us. It was impossible not to feel sorrow for what Clarissa, and the men to some extent, had gone through. It was a different time, and the world had reacted differently to those sorts of horrors. The group of friends had done what they thought they needed to do, though it sounded like some of their choices had been misguided.

"I have more questions," I said.

"I'm listening."

"You could have said it was an accidental stabbing, but it ended up in the police report as only a drowning. Why wasn't the dirk in the police report, because there was a dirk, a stabbing, right?"

Edwin looked at me. Hector looked at me too and whined.

"Your family paid off the police, didn't they?"

"Aye. We all thought it a worthwhile blackmail though. Even the police, after my father told them the whole story."

"I see. Who killed Moray? Who stabbed him?"

"It could have been any of the four of us, Delaney, but that's the part I won't tell you because I think the answer would be a burden for you. I will not confirm which one of us it was. I've come tae know something about you. You have an intuition that sometimes tells you things, am I right?"

"Yes."

"Listen tae it, tae those voices, and I bet you'll figure it out."

I thought long and hard, listened for someone from any book to tell me something, but I heard nothing. "I have no idea who the killer was, Edwin."

"Of course you do," he said. "Or you will soon enough."

"Why did you all fake a passport with Moray's name on it?"

"How did you come to see that?"

"Artair found some things. He'll be here later. I'm sure he'll show them to you if you want."

"Interesting. The passport." He smiled sadly at Hector, who smiled supportively up at him. "Let's just say that Gordon's faked death wasn't the first time some of us in the group had considered doing such a thing, perhaps running away because the circumstances of a single pregnant woman were even more frightening than a rape had been. Besides, using Moray's name would have been a good cover and would have kept the police guessing—just in case, you know, something eventually happened to him. Fortunately, the police were . . . cooperative, and no one had to leave, except for Clarissa, but that was her choice. I'd like to see that passport."

"Your *Oor Millie* is with it too."

"I think Clarissa would like to see that. Well, maybe not, but we'll ask her."

"There's a handwritten note on the cover of the book. It's about naming the baby."

"Aye? I truly have no memory of that, Delaney. I'd like to look at it."

"You don't know who wrote the note? The signature on the passport and the note seem to be the same hand-writing."

"Interesting. Maybe that should tell us something. I'm not sure."

"Did you go to Glasgow to look for Liam?" I asked when he didn't say more.

"No, lass, I didn't think of Clarissa's other son that day. I went for work, something tae do tae keep my mind off of what was happening. It really was for work."

I took a deep breath and let it out slowly. "Your clothes. They were dry after the incident on the boat."

"Aye."

"That means that either you weren't there for whatever happened on the boat or you didn't try to save the man who went over the side." I paused again. "But Leith and Gordon, and all the others did."

Edwin looked at me as I stopped speculating aloud. He remained silent as he probably saw that my mind and my intuition, without the bookish voices, were working through the rest of it.

Or his dry clothes meant something else. Two things suddenly stood out in my mind; Edwin's continued re-fusal to talk to the police after Billy's murder, and Rosie's continued insistence that the police needed to be told about Gordon being alive.

If Edwin had killed Moray, he would not have cared about protecting himself if justice would be served if the truth came out. Rosie knew about the dirk and, possibly, the whole story. If Edwin had been the killer, she never would have kept insisting that someone needed to tell the police about Gordon, giving the police a chance to dredge up the past and jeopardize Edwin's freedom. She would have protected Edwin, no matter what.

And Edwin would have protected the woman he loved. No matter what.

Clarissa had been the killer. In fact, I thought maybe no one else on the boat had known her plan, or maybe Edwin had. When she'd stabbed Moray and he'd gone over, they'd—even Clarissa—had all gone over the side to try to save him. All but Edwin. He'd kept his focus on saving Clarissa.

"Clarissa was devastated she was pregnant?" I asked.

"She was hurt deeply from being violated, and devastated about being pregnant."

"Perhaps suicidal?"

He didn't say anything, but I could guess. Clarissa had planned on killing herself too. While everyone else was trying to save Moray, Edwin's only focus was Clarissa. She probably did go into the water when they were close to shore, but until then I imagined that Edwin kept her close to him.

"The pact came later? It was to keep secrets?"

"Aye. Blood oaths and all," he said sadly. "We were young, Delaney, young and scared. I was lucky because I had access tae money. Can you understand?"

I nodded. "I think so."

"That's good tae hear."

"Who did you think killed Billy?" I said.

"I hoped it wasn't Gordon, but that's what I thought at first. I thought that perhaps because he was ill and had been living a lie for a couple of years that he couldn't bear for Billy tae know the truth, and all the lies, and somehow everything was coming tae light."

"Were you going to kill Gordon yourself?"

"No. I wasn't sure what I was going to do, but as you were doing, I was seeking the truth too. You were just better at it than I was."

"The dirk made each of you think each other was the killer."

"I thought—I imagine Gordon did too—that the dirk was gone. We didn't know that it wasn't in the sea. We made assumptions when you showed it tae us, but clearly they weren't correct."

"Do you think someone really tried to break into your house?"

"I found the cigarettes. Now, I assume they were Liam's, but I'm not sure we'll ever know."

My boss had many secrets. I liked that he was letting me in on them, little by little, even the horrible ones. I wasn't sure he could trust me to keep all his secrets, and this unspoken one was brutal, but time would tell, I supposed.

At least things made more sense now, and maybe that's all I needed, to have *some* mysteries solved.

"Oh, look," Edwin said as he pointed to the front where Elias was giving Aggie her birthday gift.

Aggie tore open the wrapping paper Elias had so carefully folded and taped. She cradled the unwrapped book over one arm and then traced an outline around the edge of it with her finger. Finally, she lifted the cover and looked inside.

"Oh, Elias, it's wonderful. Perfect," Aggie said.

Elias looked back at me and winked.

"You were right, Delaney, that was wonderful tae see," Edwin said.

"It was, wasn't it?" I said.

"Books, they're most definitely the stuff of magic, don't you think?" Edwin said.

"Yes, Edwin, I do. I definitely do."

Edwin smiled and then deposited Hector on my lap. He stood and went to hug Aggie. I didn't think I'd ever seen her so happy before.

And despite everything—the pain in my arm, the recent terror, the revelations, and the almost revelations—I let my eyes lock on to some cobalt blue ones, and realized I knew exactly how she felt.

Read on for an excerpt of the next Scottish
Bookshop Mystery

Coming in April 2018
in hardcover from Minotaur Books!

LOST BOOKS
AND OLD BONES

ONE

The cold liquid splashed the back of my neck before it rolled down and underneath my shirt. I gasped and reflexively turned to see who had sloshed their drink my direction.

"Delaney! I'm so sorry. Oh dear. Here let's go tae the toilet. I'll get you cleaned up and you can have my shirt," Sophie said loudly with a drunken slur as she grabbed my arm and started to pull me through the crowd.

"But then what will you wear?" I asked, trying to raise my voice.

She didn't hear me above the crowd and band noise. I barely heard myself.

Though loud, the performers weren't, in fact, a band; they were a duo. Mad Ferret was made up of one Irish and one Scottish gentleman. Together they performed up-beat folk songs that brought out the jig in pretty much everybody.

I'd first seen them with Tom, my boyfriend, after the two Mad Ferret members had stopped by his pub one evening and invited him to a show. Tom had taken me to see them in a very dark pub that hadn't seemed quite big enough for the jubilant crowd inside. The setting was much the same tonight, though Tom wasn't with me and my new friends, Sophie and Rena, and my newest friend Mallory, whom I'd just met this evening. All the women were medical students at the University of Edinburgh.

A few crowd dodges later, Sophie and I made our way toward the small back ladies' room, a place where everyone wrote their name on the walls and the liquid soap smelled like the lavender hips scent my mom used in her kitchen back home in Kansas.

The three green-doored stalls inside were empty and the music fell into a muffled tinny bass beat when the bathroom door closed behind us.

"Your shirt is soaked through. I'm so, so sorry. I was careless. I'll have it cleaned," Sophie said as she turned me around so she could inspect my back. Then she turned me again to face her. "Here, take mine."

I stopped her just as she made it to the second button of her blouse.

"It's not a problem. I've been spilled on before," I said. "Don't worry about it."

She blinked her heavily mascaraed brown eyes my direction. Until tonight I'd only seen her and her roommate Rena with light to no makeup and hastily brushed or pulled back hair. They were usually dressed in scrubs or jeans. Their skirts and makeup as well as their posttest Friday desire to blow off some steam had surprised me tonight, though I remembered that feeling from when I was back at the University of Kansas.

I'd lost track of how many gin and tonics they'd downed, though it seemed that Sophie was moving double-time compared with the rest of us. Now, some of her latest drink was beginning to make my back sticky. I was going to smell like a pine tree, but I didn't really mind.

Reluctantly she said, "All right. At least let me buy you a drink tae make up for it."

I laughed. "I'm good, but I'm glad you're having fun."

"I'm going to have a wicked hangover tomorrow, but it's worth it. It's good tae let loose a little."

I smiled and redid the one button on her shirt. She didn't seem to notice as she leaned against the sink.

"It's a lucky twist of fate that we met you," she said.

"I feel the same about you guys. Come on, let's head back out and listen to some more music," I said, sensing an alcohol-induced love fest coming on if I didn't distract her.

A couple of months earlier, Sophie and Rena had come into The Cracked Spine, the rare book and manuscript shop that I'd traveled halfway around the world to work at. They'd brought in some old medical books that had been in Rena's family for decades. Rena's father had given her the books with the hope she could sell them and use the money to help with her own medical school tuition.

An Atlas of Illustrations of Clinical Medicine, Surgery and Pathology was made of up twenty-five books, all of them filled with colorful, gruesome pictures that depicted the many things that could go wrong on and in the human body. The books had been printed in the early 1900s by the New Sydal Society, with hand-drawn illustrations. My boss Edwin's eyes had filled with tears when he'd seen them; he'd swooned.

"Lass," he'd said. "These were from the time of the Industrial Revolution, when we didn't even know how much we were learning until later when we could look back and be utterly amazed at ourselves. These are the most beautiful things I've seen in a long, long while."

He'd pored over the books for days, dreamily. I'd thought that perhaps he'd had more than a few moments over the years when he wished he'd turned his biology degree into something medical, instead of founding and cultivating the most amazing rare and used book and manuscript shop in Scotland.

Edwin had given Rena slightly more than the books were worth. He couldn't decide what to do with them. He wouldn't resell them, but would either keep them for himself or donate them to a library, or perhaps to the University of Edinburgh Medical School. Edwin liked those sorts of happy endings. Someday, Rena might walk past a display case and look upon the books that had helped her and so many others before her learn the most respected of professions.

I found the medical books interesting, particularly when I could manage to look past the stomach-curdling images and let myself be amazed by the knowledge, work, and sheer will of patience that had gone into creating them. I knew that some of Edwin's most beloved treasures weren't the most expensive ones. I suspected he'd keep the books for himself.

Sophie bounced herself away from the sink but then leaned, in a weird slow-motion movement, back into it again.

"I need tae tell you something," she said as she grabbed my arm.

"Okay."

She glanced toward the door and then at the empty stalls. "You can't tell Rena."

"Um, okay," I said.

"I think I'm in trouble. I'm not having a good semester. And that test today; I'm sure I failed," she said.

"Oh, Sophie, I'm sure you're going to be fine. You've been brilliant so far. You're just . . . Well, you'll feel better tomorrow. Maybe not in the morning, but by the afternoon." I gave her a smile, but I didn't think she saw it.

She and Rena *had* been brilliant, attaining notoriety at the University of Edinburgh Medical School as two of its top students. They'd both come from Glasgow, started college twice, once when they were both eighteen and then again at twenty-five. Their first time, they'd flunked out. After a successful second run at undergrad, they'd begun medical school when they were thirty. Friends since they were younger, Sophie and Rena had made a pact to go through life together. They were an unbeatable team.

"No, no." She waved off my words. "Medical school is really, really hard, Delaney."

"I know, but I'm sure . . . Hey, let's not worry about that tonight. When will you know the grade on this test you took today?"

"Should be posted by Sunday."

"All right. I'll come over and we'll look at it together if that would help. Or you can come over to my house. Whatever is easier. I'm sure it will be fine, Sophie. You've had a fair amount to drink, and maybe that's causing some undue emotions."

She looked at me with glassy eyes, blinking heavily again. "I hope you're right."

"I know I am. Come on."

But before I could get her away from the sink again, the bathroom door opened, bringing Rena and Mallory into the already cramped space.

"There you are!" Rena said as she glanced back and forth between Sophie and me. "Everything okay?"

"Yep. We were just heading back out," I said.

Inside the small room, Sophie and Rena's similarities seemed even more obvious. Both were tall and thin with brown eyes and long brown hair. Sophie's hair had a wave to it while Rena's was stick-straight. When you looked closely, you could spot other differences too: Sophie's face was pleasantly round, Rena's was made with slightly sharper angles and she had a stronger chin. They didn't look like sisters, but could pass for cousins. In contrast, Mallory was shorter, curvier, and platinum blond. Her dark roots currently showed and she'd mentioned to everyone earlier that she needed to do something about them, but that there would be no time until the short summer break that began in a couple of months.

"Oh. Let's wait a bit," Rena said.

"Why?" I asked.

Rena and Mallory looked at each other.

"Dr. Eban is out there," Mallory said.

Sophie put her hand to her mouth. "He's here?"

"Aye," Rena said. "And he's taking note of the students he sees, I'm certain. He's rather evil that way."

"He's probably come tae ruin everyone's night," Sophie said. "Fail us all for having a wee bit of fun when we should all be home, crying about the grades he'll be doling out on the exam."

Rena's eyebrows came together as she looked at Sophie and then at me. "None of us want tae make an ill impression."

"He's a tough one," Mallory said to me with a small smile. "He's also a wee bit odd."

"Odd how?" I asked, noting that Mallory seemed more amused than horrified, as Sophie seemed to be. I chalked up the different reactions to the probable levels of alcohol each had consumed.

As I asked the question, a thought took shape in the back of my mind. None of these women, though Mallory was only twenty-seven to Sophie and Rena's thirty-two, was young or foolish. They were grown, long of legal drinking age. It didn't seem to me that they should feel the need to hide their behavior from anyone, including a professor.

Mallory seemed to consider the best way to further explain Dr. Eban, but Rena jumped in. "He begins every semester with a story about William Burke and William Hare. Those names familiar?"

"Of course," I said. "The men who killed for corpses." I cleared my throat. "That's a bit to the point, but . . ."

"Right," Rena said. "Back in the early 1800s they killed and sold the corpses of their victims tae Dr. Robert Knox, who used them for dissection in his anatomy classes at the University of Edinburgh. Anyway, Dr. Eban tells the story, and his rendition is filled with enough drama for a vampire story. He finishes off the lecture by saying that Burke and Hare probably saved more people than they murdered, considering what their contributions did tae assist medical students. He has a point, but it was still murder, and the way he tells the story . . . he's plain creepy. It's a tone he sets for himself early, and it's something he sticks with. That, along with his always-tough attitude, makes him the most talked about, and probably most feared, professor at the medical school."

Mallory added, "Either it's just the way he is, or the impression he wants tae give. And he conducts his classes in a theater that's set up the exact same way Dr. Knox's was, on purpose. There's a plaque about Dr. Knox on the wall outside the door and everything."

"In his office, he's a totally different man, when no one else is looking," Sophie said.

We looked at her as she leaned against the sink. I thought she might say more, but it seemed like she lost her train of thought.

"I could use a cup of coffee," she said a moment later.

"I think that's the best idea of the night," Rena said. "Come on, I saw a table in the back. It's small, but we'll see if we can grab it."

"I'll go order the coffee," Mallory said.

The musicians told the crowd they were taking a break just as we exited the restroom. I followed behind the other three and kept on the lookout for someone creepy as we weaved our way thought the mostly student crowd in the small pub.

I'd met a few students over the past couple of months. Rena and Sophie shared a flat close to the university. Most of the building's residents were medical school students, but not all. It was immediately obvious who the undergrads were. Other than the fact that they looked the youngest, they also usually seemed to be having the most fun.

As we made our way through the crowd I spotted a familiar woman leaning against the bar next to another woman I didn't recognize. The one I recognized lived on the bottom floor of Sophie and Rena's building, and had opened the building's front door for me a few times. She could spot visitors approaching though her window and seemed to feel compelled to let people in.

Though I'd never met Mallory before tonight, she lived in Rena and Sophie's building too, in a flat all her own. She'd already mentioned that she spent most of her time holed up there, studying, and studying some more. In the brief time I'd known her I'd already noticed that she had a quiet calm about her that Sophie and Rena didn't possesses. Maybe Mallory just worked harder to hide her stress.

I waved at the woman from the first floor, someone I'd pegged as an undgrad. I thought she was looking my direction, but she didn't wave back. I followed her line of vision and spotted who she must have been watching instead. A handsome man, probably about sixty, stood not far from the edge of the small dance floor. He wore dark pants and a dark peacoat over his tall, thin frame. His short dark hair was slicked back from his high forehead, and though I thought his nose should be hooked to match the rest of him, it wasn't. It was straight and almost regal. He was lazily holding a tumbler half full of liquid.

He didn't see me looking, and neither he nor the young woman noticed that I saw what happened next. Both the man by the dance floor and the woman sent a quick, furtive glance toward a third person, a man who seemed to be in a hurried exit out of the pub. The only features I caught of the third person were a head full of bushy gray hair and the back of a tall body that moved in defiance of the gray hair; strong and sure.

It could have been my imagination or the happenstance of my timing regarding their expressions, but in those brief beats of time, I thought both the man by the dance floor and the woman were concerned about the leaving man, or at least concerned about something. But the moment was over quickly, and I immediately doubted what I thought I'd seen.

As we approached the table Rena had spied, three men were also about to sit there. They sent us smiles of surrender and let us have the chairs.

After we sat, Mallory approached with a tray of four cups of coffee. "Freshly brewed," she said as she placed the cups in front of us one at a time and then leaned the tray against the wall. She angled herself into the tight space that held the last of the four chairs.

"Did you see him?" Sophie asked Rena.

"Yeah, just standing there being creepy," Rena said.

"The tall man in the dark clothes next to the dance floor?" I asked.

"That's him. That's Dr. Eban," Rena said.

"Did you guys see the gray-haired man leaving?" I said.

They all looked toward the door and said they hadn't.

"He must have left," I said, not sure why those brief seconds had made such an impression on me.

Mallory twisted around in her chair so she could see the man by the stage. "That's Dr. Eban, though. He'll probably just stand there all night and ooze horror, just tae set us all off balance. Take away our fun." Her words were ominous, but her tone was somewhat playful.

I looked at Rena.

She shrugged and said, "Believe it or not, that's probably exactly what he's doing. It's a power thing, I think. He likes bothering us."

"He teaches anatomy, huh?" I said.

"Aye," three voices said together.

"Here's the other part," Sophie said. "He's also one of the best teachers on campus. Really good. He's just . . . difficult."

"Unrealistic expectations," I said before I sipped the coffee.

It wasn't a question, but the three women looked at each other as if searching for the right answer.

"Yes," Sophie said.

"Sort of," Mallory said.

"I'm not sure they're unrealistic, but they are high. We should have high expectations, though. We're going tae be doctors," Rena said.

I watched for Sophie's reaction to Rena's words, but didn't see disagreement.

My back was to the wall. Since I was sitting in the corner seat, I had the best view of the rest of the pub, and I saw Dr. Eban moving in our direction. His eyes caught mine for an instant, and I knew our table was his destination.

"It looks as if he's headed our direction," I said without moving my lips or remaking eye contact with him.

Despite the instantaneous terror that blanched my tablemates' faces, there was no escape now.

TWO

"Ladies," Dr. Eban said as he stepped just a bit too close to the table, causing Mallory and Rena to have to lean sideways. "How are we this evening?"

"Hey, Dr. Eban," Mallory said. "Fancy meeting you here."

"I'm a big fan of the lads' music," Dr. Eban said easily.

"They're very good," Sophie said, working too hard to keep her words from slurring.

"Aye," Rena said.

For a moment I was perplexed by the dynamics. No one was doing anything wrong. But I had no way of knowing what their outside-school lives meant to their in-school lives. I was about to jump in and introduce myself to get us all past the awkward silence that seemed to fall over the table, but Dr. Eban jumped in.

"Will you all be attending the service this Tuesday?" he asked us all.

Briefly, they seemed as perplexed by the question as I was, but Mallory caught on first.

"Oh! For the corpses?" she asked.

"Aye," Dr. Eban said.

"Definitely," Rena said. "I think it's important."

"Services for the corpses?" I asked.

"Aye," Rena said. "Every year there's a service for the corpses that we are privileged tae . . . work with. We're required tae attend during our first year, but most of us attend after that anyway. These are people who donated their bodies tae the medical school, and we honor them every year with a church service. Sometimes their families show up and we get tae thank them in person. Many medical schools have such an event."

"That's really lovely," I said.

"Aye," Mallory said. "The public is invited if you're interested. It's Tuesday at Greyfriars Kirk."

"I think I would enjoy that," I said. I was curiously intrigued. The church was an architectural masterpiece, and I'd visited the neighboring graveyard a few times.

"Please join us," Rena said. It seemed she was about to introduce me to Dr. Eban, but he interjected another question before she could.

"Are you all pleased with your exam?" he asked, a happy uptick to his tone. Pointedly, he looked at Mallory first.

"I hope so," Mallory said with a smile.

"We'll see," Rena said. "But I feel good about everything."

Then everyone's attention turned to Sophie. Prompted by Rena's firm gaze in her direction, Sophie kept her back too straight as she said, "I hope so." But then, as if someone had unplugged her, she slumped. "But I don't hold out a lot of hope."

Rena closed her eyes and shook her head ever so slightly.

"Aye?" Dr. Eban said.

Without asking anyone, he reached around to an empty chair at an otherwise populated table and moved it into the small space between Rena and Mallory, causing all spaces to close up even more. We scooted and gave him room, but all of our knees were touching by the time he sat and leaned forward on his elbows, his concentration hard on Sophie.

I wanted so much for this moment not to happen. If Dr. Eban hadn't yet picked up on Sophie's state, I hoped he wouldn't hold anything she said against her.

"What has you concerned?" Dr. Eban asked.

"Everything," Sophie said with an all-encompassing hand gesture. "Every-damn-thing. I wasn't prepared for the test, Dr. Eban. Your exams are—"

"Dr. Eban," Rena interjected. "We're just blowing off a wee bit of steam tonight. Forgive us if we're emotional. You know how it is?"

"I do," Dr. Eban said. He turned back to Sophie. "You're a good student, lass. I'm sure you did fine."

I put my hand on Sophie's knee and squeezed. We weren't good enough friends for me to intervene in such a way, but I liked her enough as a person to jump in and at least try to keep her from continuing. Besides, her knee was practically fused to my own.

She looked at me, sending me another heavy blink. But then she returned my knowing smile.

"Thank you, Dr. Eban," she said as she looked at him again. "I'm sure I'll feel better about things tomorrow."

"Aye! Now, I know all the students at the medical school, and I'm sure you aren't one," Dr. Eban said to me. He extended a hand over the table. "Bryon Eban."

"Delaney Nichols," I said. "No, I'm not a student."

"An American? Visiting Scotland?"

"Yes. I'm living here and working at a bookshop in Grassmarket. I've been here almost a full year now."

"Delightful! Which bookshop?"

"The Cracked Spine."

"Aye?" Dr. Eban sat back, and his eyes got big. Everything he did and said seemed oversized, but not

in an off-putting way. Was this why he was considered
odd?

"You've been there?" I said. I spent most of my time
working in the warehouse but I racked my brain wondering if I'd seen him before. He wasn't one to blend
into the background, but I was sure he wasn't familiar.

"A few times." He looked around the pub. The musicians appeared to be readying their instruments for another set. Dr. Eban leaned farther over the table. Tell me
about Edwin MacAlister."

I smiled. I'd had this question a time or two. "He's a
great boss and an interesting man."

Dr. Eban nodded. "Right. Tell me about his secret
room, the place where he keeps all his treasures."

"That's just a myth," I lied easily. I'd had that question before too.

Dr. Eban inspected me. In fact, everyone did. Even
Sophie's wobbly attention was fixed on me.

"Come on, lass, you can tell us," Dr. Eban said. "You
know, I've heard he has a scalpel from Dr. Robert Knox.
He was the doctor who paid Williams Burke and Hare
for the bodies they acquired by murder."

"I did know about Burke, Hare, and Knox, but no,
there's no secret room. No old scalpels," I said, though I
wondered if there were. Were there old scalpels in the
warehouse, a place that most definitely did exist? I hadn't
seen any. Yet.

"Really?" Dr. Eban said.

"Really," I said.

He watched me a long moment, but I kept my expression firmly neutral, as I'd done with many people over
the last year. The secret of the secret room hadn't become
a burden; it had become part of my own secrets, and it
was one that I protected fiercely.

"Interesting. I'd love tae meet Mr. MacAlister. Any chance you'd introduce us?"

"It would be a pleasure," I said. "Give me a call at the shop, and we'll coordinate a time. I'm sure he'd love to meet you too."

"Aye?" Dr. Eban said.

"I'm sure."

Mad Ferret strummed a few chords and then began their set with a tune lively enough that I began to tap my toes even as they were crowded together.

"That would be wonderful. Ta," Dr. Eban said over the music and crowd noise.

I hadn't heard much of an accent in his voice, but his informal Scottish "Thank you" suddenly, and admittedly strangely, made me like him. I smiled.

"You're welcome. I look forward to your visit," I said.

Dr. Eban scooted the chair back from the table, releasing all the knees underneath.

"I'll ring you next week. A good evening, ladies. And, Sophie: I'm sure your exam will be fine."

I looked at Sophie, thinking she would just smile and maybe say thank you, but I was surprised to see something else entirely.

The smile, though still somewhat booze-infused, was not just a friendly smile. I swung my attention back to Dr. Eban. He had the same sort of look on his face, something that rang of that sort of affection that's supposed to be a secret but isn't. I zipped my eyes to Rena, who, with big eyes and a frown in my direction, seemed to confirm what I thought I'd seen.

It appeared that maybe Sophie and Dr. Eban were much more than student and teacher.

That couldn't be good.